The Mage's Sea

Book Three in the Mages of Martir

by Timothy L. Cerepaka

An Annulus Publishing Book

Annulus Publishing, Cherokee, Texas, 2015

Published by Annulus Publishing

Author: Timothy L. Cerepaka

Formatting by Timothy L. Cerepaka

Contact: timothy@timothylcerepaka.com

Cover design by Elaina Lee of For the Muse Design
(http://www.forthemusedesign.com/)

ISBN-13: 978-0692456972

ISBN-10: 069245697X

Acknowledgments

I would like to thank my uncle, James Wilhite, for helping me get this manuscript into publishable shape. I'd also like to thank the rest of my family for supporting me while I wrote this novel. You guys rock.

Chapter One

"What shall we do about Uron?" said Skimif, the God of Martir, to all of the hundreds of gods gathered in the Temple of the Gods. Ordinarily, he would have performed a roll call to make sure that every god was present, but as this was one of the most important meetings the gods had had in a while, he didn't bother. Besides, a quick scan of the area with his godly presence told him that every single god in both the Northern and Southern Pantheons was present anyway, making a head count redundant.

Except, of course, for the Mysterious One, Skimif thought, reclining on his massive marble-and-crystal throne, putting the tips of his fingers together as he looked at all of the gods. *We'll just have to make do without him, as always.*

That single question he had asked had made all of the gods silent, even though mere moments ago the gods had been trading news and making lots of noise. He saw the Historical God, the God of History, who resembled a green octopus with the head of a human, on the other side of the wide-open Temple look away nervously, while Tinkar, the

God of Fate and Time, leaned against his staff as if all of his thousands of years weighed heavily on his shoulders. Of the goddesses, Kano, the Goddess of the Sea, was muttering something to the Mechanical Goddess, Goddess of Machines, who was currently occupying the body of one of her automatons, the one called Calir, if Skimif recalled correctly.

Skimif wasn't shocked by their silence. After all, Uron was no ordinary criminal. Last year, he killed the Avian Goddess, and last month had led an army of half-gods to destroy World's End, where the Temple of the Gods was located. Uron had even proven to be a match for Skimif himself, which was why he had given the gods so much trouble recently.

Indeed, the only reason Uron was currently not a threat to Martir in general and the gods in particular was because of the brave actions of the minor spirit known as Durima. Skimif remembered well how shocked Uron had looked when Durima tackled him into the ethereal, that second plane upon which only the gods and katabans could travel. It had been quite satisfying.

Next to Skimif, Nimiko, the God of Light, shifted in his seat uncomfortably. "Well ... what is there to do about Uron, Lord Skimif? He's trapped in the ethereal. There's no way he can get out, and with no one in there, he can't hurt anyone, either. Maybe he'll starve to death, since there's no food in the ethereal."

"Starve to death?" barked the Loner God, the God of Solitude, Jungle, and Animals, from his seat on the other side of the huge chamber. "Oldest brother, I know how slow you are, but I didn't know you were that stupid. Uron is basically a god, as far as I am concerned, and gods don't die of starvation."

"The Loner God is correct," said Skimif, nodding. "While Uron technically isn't a god, I doubt he'll starve to death in there. He managed to survive as a bodiless spirit for thousands of years until just recently. If we leave him alone, he'll just become angrier and more hateful than ever."

Grinf, the God of Fire, Metal, and Justice, leaned forward on his metallic throne and raised his gavel. "I propose that we execute Uron in the style that my followers execute their criminals. It is only just."

Kano rolled her eyes. "You think we *haven't* been trying to kill him, brother? Have your flames burned your ears? Or are you just deaf?"

"Justice is not deaf," said Grinf. "Besides, sister, I don't see you coming up with any useful suggestions. Like the sea, you only wash away things, never build anything of use."

"Enough snipping," said Skimif, holding up a hand wearily. "Sometimes you gods are like children."

"Says the godling," said the Loner God under his breath.

Skimif glared at him, but shook his head. "I know we are all afraid of Uron, but we can't let our fear divide us or cloud our reasoning."

"Tell that to the Fear Goddess," said Nimiko, gesturing at a woman several rows down who appeared to be covered in blood and had a wide, disturbing smile on her skull-like face. "She's the one who controls fear around here, not us."

The Fear Goddess simply nodded to acknowledge that Nimiko had spoken to her. Out of all of the gods, only she seemed to be keeping her cool, though Skimif didn't find that very odd or strange, seeing as she was always one of the least jumpy goddesses, even with the knowledge of Uron running around trying to kill everybody.

"That's not what I mean," said Skimif. "I mean that as the gods of Martir, it is our sworn duty to deal with threats like Uron permanently. As long as Uron remains alive in the ethereal, his escape is always a very real possibility."

"Why don't we banish him into the Void?" suggested the Loner God. "Worked for Hollech, didn't it?"

The mention of Hollech—who had, according to Durima, been killed by Uron in cold blood in the Void—caused several of the gods to cough and shift uncomfortably in their seats. Skimif himself felt his neck growing hot from embarrassment, as the only reason that Hollech had been in the Void in the first place was because Skimif had banished him there thirty years ago as punishment for conspiring against him. It had seemed like a good idea at the time; after all, how else was Skimif supposed to know that Uron would kill Hollech three decades later?

Still, Skimif's popularity with the gods—already fragile and shaky in the best of times—had plummeted when the news of Hollech's death became common knowledge among the rest of the gods. He didn't want the gods to focus on his shortcomings at the moment, however, because they needed to be united as one, not divided as many.

So Skimif, in an attempt to change the subject, said,

"Because Uron has already proven that he can travel to and from the Void without trouble. Throwing him into the Void would be like exiling a murderer to a remote island with a fully-equipped sailing boat; it just doesn't make sense."

"Then I'm out of ideas," said the Lone God, shrugging and kicking back in his seat, resting his short, stubby legs on the throne in front of and below him, upon which the Chaotic Goddess, Goddess of Chaos, sat. "Anyone else?"

"Mechanical Goddess," said Skimif, his eyes flicking in her direction. "What do you think?"

The Mechanical Goddess made a series of clicking and beeping sounds, followed by a loud whistle of steam that made several nearby gods cringe. She then followed it up with a snap of her fingers.

Unlike the other gods, Skimif had always had a hard time understanding the Mechanical Goddess due to her complete refusal to speak in anything resembling a normal language. Even after thirty years, Skimif still didn't quite always catch everything she said, though he had improved enough that he could usually catch the gist of whatever she was trying to say.

And what the Mechanical Goddess said now made Skimif shake his head. "I doubt we could build a machine capable of draining Uron's life force. It would require a lot of knowledge we just don't have, and it might not even work anyway."

"Why not summon the Powers?" said Tinkar, looking up from his throne a few rows from Skimif. "Uron may be strong enough to challenge you in a fight, Lord Skimif, but he might not be strong enough to defeat the Powers. If we tell the Powers about the seriousness of this situation, then they might just kill him for us."

Skimif rested his chin on his hand. "The only question is, how do we contact the Powers? Last time I saw them, they said they were going to be working on a new world somewhere beyond the Void. And honestly, I don't want to risk the Powers changing their mind and deciding to destroy Martir again after they learn about Uron."

"This is getting boring," said the Loner God with a yawn. "I want to go back to my island. I think there might be some dumb humans who have crossed the Dividing Line and are going to land on the shores of my island under the mistaken belief that it is safe. In other words, I'm going to miss my free lunch if I stay here any longer."

Skimif held up a hand. "No. We all stay here until we come up with a plan to get rid of Uron once and for all, however long that might take."

The Loner God groaned, while several of the other gods and goddesses also made noises of impatience. Not that Skimif paid them much attention. As much as he understood their desire to leave, he didn't want a single god or goddess absent from what he considered to be the most important meeting the gods had ever—or would ever—have.

Uron is the worst threat Martir has faced in some time, Skimif thought. *As a matter of fact, he's the only major threat that our world has faced, at least that I know of. Maybe that's why we've had such a hard time figuring out how to deal with him.*

6

"What we need to do, in my opinion, is take away from the God-killer from him," said Kano. She looked around at her fellow deities. "Without the God-killer, do you think Uron would be as big of a threat as he is now? Of course he wouldn't. Therefore, if we are going to come up with a plan to destroy him, we first need to disarm him."

"Go right ahead, sister," said the Loner God, gesturing toward the air like a gentleman allowing his lady friend to enter the ballroom first. "You can be the one to do it. Of course, if you touch the God-killer, you'll die instantly, but I'm sure you're willing to make that sacrifice for the greater good, aren't you?"

"The point our loner brother is trying to make is that we don't have any real way of disarming him at this time," said Tinkar, shaking his head. "If any of us gods try, Uron will kill us; if we try to send any of our servants to do it, he will kill them even more easily than us."

Skimif nodded. "Tinkar and the Loner God are correct. While disarming Uron is a good idea, it's just not practical. We'll just have to figure out a different way to kill him without disarming him."

"Maybe the Ghostly God knows how to defeat him," said the Loner God with a yawn. "After all, he was the one whose dumb plan allowed Uron to become a threat in the first place, wasn't he?"

About three rows down from Skimif's left, the Ghostly God, the God of Mist and Ghosts, folded his arms across his chest as he snapped, "He manipulated me, you introverted idiot. How many times do I have to explain that I knew nothing about Uron until he revealed himself? I have done nothing wrong."

"Nothing except be the biggest fuck-up in the entire history of Martir," the Loner God remarked. "I just noticed that you've been awfully quiet during this whole discussion, brother. Don't you have any ideas? Maybe summon an army of ghosts to haunt Uron's dreams or tear Uron's soul from his body or something like that?"

The Ghostly God scowled. "Clearly, you don't actually understand my powers. Not that that is much of a surprise. Shut-ins like yourself rarely have much *practical* knowledge about the outside world, just your own vague ideas about how things *should* work."

"Shut-in?" said the Loner God, raising his voice slightly. "That's rich, coming from the god who shuns outside contact just as much as me, if not more so."

"What did I say about not snipping at each other?" said Skimif, before the Ghostly God could respond. "If all you're going to do is agitate each other, then we might as well free Uron and let him do as he pleases. It will accomplish the same effect as our current efforts."

The Loner God shrugged. "I thought getting my brother angry would liven things up a bit around here."

Skimif rubbed his forehead. He was now starting, as he had many times over the years, to wonder how the gods had managed to get anything done before he came to power. It seemed like all of the gods were constantly fighting with each other, as though the concept of 'teamwork' was as foreign to them as human culture was to the average aquarian.

And I am the idiot who is trying to bring them all together, Skimif thought. *Sometimes, I wonder what the Powers were thinking when they decided to make me the God of Martir.*

Then Skimif felt a slight tremor in his throne. It was so subtle that he almost missed it, but being the God of Martir, his senses were more sensitive than most, so he caught it. He glanced at his throne, puzzled about what it might have been, but it did not repeat.

While Skimif wondered what that tremor might have meant, Xocion, the God of Ice and Mountains, said, "I say we freeze Uron in an iceberg and banish him as deeply into the Void as we can. If Lord Skimif and I work together, we could do it."

"Doubt it will work," said Nimiko. "Even if you succeed in freezing Uron, he will probably break out at some point and make his way through the Void back to Martir. That is yet another temporary solution, which is the opposite of what we need."

Skimif opened his mouth to offer his opinion on Xocion's plan, but then he felt another tremor, this one slightly larger than the last.

The other gods must have felt it, too, because Tinkar looked to the dark-skinned, bald woman to his right and said, "Mica, are you trying to shake the foundations of our Temple or are you bored like our dear loner brother?"

Mica, the Goddess of Earth and Ink, shook her head. "This isn't my doing. Someone—or something—else is behind it."

"What is it, then?" said the Loner God, who was now sitting upright in his chair again, looking around the chamber for the tremor's source. "I have forgotten, but do earthquakes occur naturally on World's End or not?"

"They don't," Mica confirmed. "The land around here is too stable for that."

"I don't like this," said Kano. She stood up from her throne. "I say we should leave before—"

Through the thick glass dome above, the bright blue sky suddenly turned blacker than midnight. The entire Temple of the Gods was cast into blackness, causing the gods to cry out in surprise before Nimiko snapped his fingers and a massive light ball appeared in the center of the chamber, several feet above the sandpit in the center. Even then, Nimiko's light barely penetrated the darkness, as if the shadows were a massive tidal wave trying to put out a tiny candle.

"What in the name of the Powers is going on here?" said Tinkar, gripping his clock-topped staff tightly. "What is this darkness? Ooka, is this your doing?"

The God of Shadows and Knives, Ooka, who sat a couple of rows down from Skimif's right, shook his shaggy head of hair vigorously. "No, brother, I don't know what this darkness is or where it came from."

"No one panic," said Skimif, sensing fear creeping up in the chamber. "Whatever is happening, I am sure we gods can deal with it. We just need to remain calm and rational."

Calm and rational? came a light, feminine voice that

Skimif had never heard in his life. **No one can remain calm and rational in the face of the unknown, no one except a fool. And I trust that you tiny gods are no fools.**

Skimif shivered when he heard that voice, while Grinf barked, "Who are you? Where are you? Show yourself, whatever you are. Or are you too afraid of the collective might of the gods of Martir to do even that much?"

The feminine voice laughed as politely as an aristocratic woman at a joke that only the upper class could find entertaining. **Fear is an unknown concept to me, God of Justice. Besides, you already see me everywhere around you. I am not hiding from anyone, because I am nothing, and nothing is incapable of hiding.**

"Are you the darkness itself?" said Nimiko, looking around wildly. "I don't understand. Darkness cannot talk."

Darkness is only the form that your minds can comprehend, said the feminine voice. **I am surprised that you have not recognized me. After all, you see me every day and you banished one of your own to me when he acted out. I relished eating away at his sanity; I only wish he had lived a little longer, as I do not think I succeeded in destroying his sanity as completely as I would have liked.**

Skimif didn't want to say it, but he did it anyway: "Are you ... the Void?"

Bingo, said the feminine voice with another laugh, this one harsher than the last. **And no one, not even you gods, can ever completely escape the Void forever.**

So I hope you did not leave any important tasks incomplete or unattended to, because it will be a very, very long time before any of you will see the light of the sun again.

Chapter Two

As soon as the *Soaring Sea II* took off, Darek Takren decided that he did not like flying in airships.

Yes, he knew that they were supposed to be—in the words of the famous Itrijan philosopher and airship mechanic Donnya Xecon—a 'testament to the power and audacity of human creativity in a world ruled by gods and mages.' And yes, he knew that they were useful for non-magic humans, who often used them to transport cargo and passengers all over the Northern Isles far more quickly and efficiently than normal sea ships could.

Yet Darek did not like the loudness of the engines, which was like a bomb exploding in his ears every few seconds. He didn't like the fragile, lightweight feeling of the airship, knowing that the only thing keeping him from falling to his death to the ground below was the thin metal floor and walls of the airship. And he definitely didn't like the seats; they were hard and uncomfortable, and the belts tied around his waist and body were too tight and he had no way of adjusting them to fit his torso more comfortably.

Furthermore, this particular airship smelled like dried seaweed and old fish. Of course, the *Soaring Sea II* belonged to the Undersea Institute, the finest and best aquarian school for mages in the world, and probably spent most of its time underwater, which explained the smell. Still, Darek didn't like it, especially when he picked up the stink of oil and smoke mixed among the scents of seaweed and old fish.

Yet even that might have been tolerable if his stomach was not constantly rolling with every slight wind turbulence. Prior to boarding the ship, the pilot had cast a stomach-soothing spell on Darek to keep him from getting 'movement illness,' which was apparently a common affliction among people who weren't used to riding in airships. Darek suspected that the spell didn't work, though, because he kept his mouth firmly shut in order to avoid throwing up his earlier lunch of cooked baba raga ribs and iced silver stem juice.

Nor did it help that the pilot—an angler fish-looking aquarian mage who introduced herself as Itaka—had paid Darek little attention since casting that useless spell on him. She kept her strange, beady blue eyes focused entirely on the sky ahead of them, occasionally flipping switches or glancing down at monitors that made as much sense to Darek as the scribblings of a mad man.

Darek was under the distinct impression that Itaka was not used to interacting with humans. Her grasp of Divina was adequate yet poor, as if she had learned only enough to ensure she could be understood and no more. She avoided eye contact with him most of the time and had not asked him a single question about his life or anything. She hadn't even tried to break the ice with something as simple as 'Nice weather today, isn't it?' or 'How was your week?'

Maybe she's just shy, Darek thought, hugging his arms around his stomach to keep it from lurching. *Or maybe she's stuck up. Hard to tell with aquarians sometimes.*

Then again, maybe Itaka sensed that Darek was a Limitless. That wouldn't surprise Darek. Ever since becoming a Limitless, Darek had been treated differently by other mages. Most avoided eye contact with him and some, if they saw him walking toward him, would either turn around and go back the way they had come or cross the street to avoid him. When Darek had visited the island of Carnag a week back, one mage had even gotten into an extensive theological argument with a random stranger about Carnag's claim to be protected by Grinf for no reason other than he had apparently wanted to avoid talking to Darek.

Even though Darek understood why this was—most mages believed that Limitlessness was either evil or simply impossible, a thought not helped by the fact that an army of Limitless mages had recently tried to destroy North Academy, the most respected magical school in the entire Northern Isles—it was still one of the harder aspects of Limitlessness to adjust to. Darek didn't think of himself as intimidating or threatening, but sometimes it seemed like he could evacuate a whole city just by walking into a room.

I guess having Limitless power doesn't automatically grant you limitless respect, Darek thought.

The only mages who didn't treat him that way were the

students and teachers of North Academy and the Xocionian Monks. He was on good terms with most of the students and teachers of North Academy due to having grown up and studied there, while the Xocionian Monks were far less prejudiced against Limitless mages, though he suspected that it was because most of the Monks did not believe he was actually Limitless.

Still better than being treated as an outcast, I guess, Darek thought. *As long as I don't cause a lot of trouble for them, they will probably tolerate almost anything I do.*

Now, though, Darek wasn't sure if he found the rejection from most of the magical world better or worse than flying in an airship. Being treated like a walking corpse was not as sickening as feeling the bumps of an airship in flight; on the other hand, at least up here he didn't feel like he had to be ashamed of his Limitlessness.

Both are equally bad, Darek decided. *Though I will admit, one thing flying in an airship does have over social rejection is the amazing view of the ground below.*

That was true. When Darek peeked out the windshield, he saw clouds, ocean waves, and islands pass below them like items on a conveyor belt. Sometimes he would even catch glimpses of sea creatures, such as great gray sharks, hopping out of the water to catch the gulls soaring through the air, or massive trading ships from various Northern Isles nations heading to and from other lands. Once he thought he even saw a pirate ship raiding a trading vessel, but they flew by too quickly for him to be sure.

Yet even the beautiful view became tiring after a while,

because they had been flying for hours and hours without stopping. Itaka gave no sign as to when they would land or, for that matter, *where* they would land. She had said, at the start of the flight, that it would take them a few hours to reach the Undersea Institute, but it sure seemed like more than a few hours had passed to Darek and they didn't seem any closer to the Institute than they had when they had lifted off from the Great Berg.

Making sure that he wasn't going to throw up, Darek looked at Itaka and asked, "Uh, how much longer until we get to the Undersea Institute?"

Itaka didn't seem to hear him. She just turned a dial, then glanced at one of the monitors before returning her gaze to the sky before them.

Darek didn't want to raise his voice because he feared that he would hurl all over her if he did; nonetheless, he wanted answers anyway.

So, raising his voice as much as he could without upsetting his stomach further, Darek said, "Excuse me, but how much longer until we get to the Undersea Institute?"

That seemed to get her attention, because Itaka glanced at him briefly before looking back at the sky. Then she said, in hesitant Divina, mixed with that same gargled accent that all aquarians seemed to have, "Very soon."

Very specific, Darek thought. He didn't say that aloud because his stomach lurched then and he didn't trust himself not to throw up if he spoke.

So he sat back in his seat, trying to avoid thinking about his stomach. Instead, he thought about why he had accepted the invitation to come to the Undersea Institute in the first place.

A week ago, Darek had received a gray ghost from Archmage Yorak, the headmistress of the Undersea Institute, personally inviting him to visit the school. She had explained that she had heard all about his infiltration of the Limitless Army and how he had helped save North Academy from the Army and that she needed his help. The gray ghost she had sent hadn't said what she needed help for, but Darek had accepted the invitation anyway.

He had a pretty simple reason for doing so: He was paying her back. It had been only last year, after all, that Yorak, piloting one of the Undersea Institute's airships, had defended North Academy from Uron. He had never gotten a chance to thank her properly for it, nor had he ever found the opportunity to repay her in some way.

So when Yorak's gray ghost appeared and invited him to visit, Darek had accepted gladly. Besides, Darek had always been interested in learning more about aquarian magic. He had never even visited the Undersea Institute before, so he didn't quite know what to expect from it. All he knew for sure was that the school was underwater deep beneath the Crystal Sea, though its exact location had always been a mystery to him.

As he excited as he was about visiting it, he was also puzzled. He had not asked what kind of problem the Institute was facing that would require his help. Yorak, after all, was a mage on the same level as the late Magical Superior of North Academy. If the problem was too big for her to deal with, then how would Darek handle it?

Granted, I am a Limitless and she is not, but she has decades of experience on me, Darek thought. *Guess I'll just have to wait and see. I'm sure I'll be able to handle it, whatever it is.*

Another problem that occurred to Darek, as more turbulence made his stomach flip-flop, was how he would breathe underwater once they descended beneath the waves. Sure, the *Soaring Sea II* seemed airtight, so he doubted it would fill with water once they went under, but if Darek was going to be walking around the school, he would have to find a way to avoid drowning to death or being crushed by the pressure of the ocean depths.

That was another question he probably should have asked Itaka before they took off. He noticed a glowing red stone on her left arm—magic stones being how aquarian mages channeled their magic, in contrast to the wooden wands used by most human mages—but whether she would cast some kind of spell on him to help him breathe or do something else, he didn't know.

She probably knows we humans can't breathe underwater like them, Darek thought. *Right? I mean, the only reason she hasn't said anything about it yet is because there's no need, correct?*

Problem was, Darek didn't know for sure how knowledgeable Itaka was about human biology. She might have understood that humans couldn't breathe underwater like aquarians; at the same time, she might have forgotten.

And if she took the *Soaring Sea II* under the Crystal Sea

without first giving Darek some kind of ability to breathe underwater ...

The thought made Darek shudder. After making sure his stomach wasn't going to revolt, Darek said, raising his voice above the roar of the engine, "Itaka?"

The pilot glanced at him. "Yes?"

"When we go underwater, how will I breathe there?" said Darek, gesturing at his lungs to indicate what he was talking about. "Humans can't breathe underwater. We're not amphibious like you guys."

Incredulously enough, Itaka actually smiled and said, "Yes, breathe underwater you will. No worry there."

Darek frowned. Itaka had clearly not understood what he had said, but he didn't see any reason to correct her. She seemed to have some sort of plan to make sure Darek wouldn't drown. What that was, he didn't know, but he was reassured at least that she was not going to let him sink or swim.

Then Itaka yelled, "Going under. Hold on!"

He had no idea what that meant until the *Soaring Sea II* dipped forward. He likely would have gone flying out of his seat if the belt—which until just this moment he had considered a useless nuisance—hadn't caught him. Of course, it had caught him directly in the gut, which did not help his movement illness at all, but better that than being flung out of the ship at a hundred miles an hour, at least.

Even though Darek was pretty sure that he was safe, he grabbed onto the edges of his seat with both hands, praying to the gods for protection. The sea was getting closer and closer now, a swirling mass of blueness and white foam that no doubt would have been quite loud if the roaring of the wind and engine in Darek's ears had not been there.

Then they crashed into the sea with a loud splash. The windshield suddenly became obscured by bubbles, making Darek think that there could be anything on the other side of those bubbles, maybe a giant sea monster, and that they might just end up flying straight into its open mouth.

But that was only for a moment, because soon the bubbles went away, showing Darek nothing but the blackness of the Undersea as the roar of the engine suddenly became muted. The *Soaring Sea II* shook and groaned and he heard what sounded like dozens of mechanical parts moving all at once, making him wonder if the entire ship was falling apart.

A quick glance at Itaka, however, showed that the pilot was quite content with their situation. She didn't seem concerned at a loud mechanical groaning noise just behind Darek's right. She did, however, flip a switch and suddenly multiple bright lights shone outside, allowing Darek to see schools of fish swim out of their way as the *Soaring Sea II* dove deeper and deeper into the Crystal Sea.

Soon, Darek forgot all about his worries about the *Soaring Sea II*'s durability. His eyes were focused on the water outside, which looked grayish in the head lights of the *Soaring Sea II*. This was the first time he had ever been underwater, so everything was all so new to him.

The deeper they descended, the stranger things Darek saw. He saw a glowing crowd of jellyfish, much larger than any he had ever seen, followed by luminescent weeds shaped like claws. A great gray shark swam by, the light reflecting off its blood red eyes, and then he caught a glimpse of the tentacles of what might have been a kraken slipping away into the shadows of a cave they zoomed past.

A couple of aquarians, carrying what appeared to be tridents, crouched low over a nearby ridge. The aquarians looked up at the *Soaring Sea II* as it passed, but he did not get a good look at them because they went by too fast. He guessed they were hunters, based on their equipment, but what they were hunting, he didn't know.

Perhaps the strangest thing he saw on their way down was what appeared to be a long length of red ribbon, twice as long as he was tall, stretching over the entrance of another cave they passed. Unless his eyes were mistaken, he thought that the ribbon itself had eyes that followed them as they passed, but as with the hunters before, they went by it too quickly for Darek to tell for sure.

"You like?" said Itaka, causing Darek to tear his eyes away from the windshield to look at her.

Darek nodded. "Yes. I do. I mean, I've read about the Undersea before, of course, and I've heard much about it, but actually seeing it in person is amazing."

Itaka chuckled. "Good. Very different from Surface, yes?"

"Excuse me?" said Darek. "What did you say?"

"Surface," said Itaka. She gestured toward the ceiling of the *Soaring Sea II*. "Above. Where you live."

"Oh," said Darek, nodding again. "The Surface. That's

what you aquarians call the part of the world we humans live in?"

"Yes," said Itaka. "Believe that that is what it translates to in human tongue. Surface."

"As good a name as any, I suppose," said Darek. "How much father until we reach the Institute?"

"Half hour, maybe," said Itaka. "Not much longer now. Going as fast as can. Archmage said to get there fast as possible."

Since that answered his question well enough, Darek looked out the windshield again at everything they passed. The sea became darker the further down they went, but he didn't feel quite so nervous or scared as he thought he would. Actually, he found that he liked traveling inside the *Soaring Sea II* underwater rather than above water. It was smoother; indeed, it was almost like he wasn't inside an airship at all.

No, not an airship, Darek thought. *This is more than an airship. Airships don't work underwater. I believe the aquarians called it a 'submarine,' if I remember correctly. They're even smarter than I thought.*

The *Soaring Sea II* shook slightly. Itaka frowned before flipping a switch and glancing around nervously. Then Darek heard something that sounded like metal clanging against the side of the ship, as though someone had thrown a pipe at it.

"What was that?" said Darek, glancing at Itaka, who looked even more nervous than before.

"Problem," said Itaka. She said the word like it was some

kind of curse. "But maybe not. Maybe not. Maybe just noises made outside. Strange sounds underwater, yes? Always strange. Never know what it be."

Itaka's rambling made her Divina harder to understand than ever. Considering they were an unknown amount of feet underwater, inside a tiny metal ship, Darek did not like not knowing what was attacking them or why Itaka was so nervous.

Then, again without warning, the *Soaring Sea II* lurched to the left. Darek grabbed the edges of his seat again as Itaka grabbed the steering wheel and pulled it to the right, but it didn't seem to be working because the ship kept moving to the left. It was like something was pushing the ship, but Darek couldn't see it through the windshield, whatever it was.

"What's going on out there?" Darek asked, looking at Itaka, who now looked as frightened as a kitten. "What's attacking the ship? You know what it is, don't you?"

"I do," said Itaka, her words barely understandable above her gargled accent, made even less intelligible thanks to the obvious fear in her voice. "We ... it ... erm ..."

She was clearly struggling to find the right words in Divina to express her thought. Darek thought about reading her mind to get past the awkwardness, but realized that would be equally as useless as having her speak, because if Itaka couldn't speak Divina well, she probably didn't even think in it at all.

So as the *Soaring Sea II* lurched to the left, Darek asked, "Is it related to the problem you guys wanted me to help with?"

Itaka nodded. "Yes, but no time to explain. Must get rid of it."

"But how do we get rid of it?" said Darek, wincing at the sound of something metal tearing off the outside of the ship's hull. "Does the ship have some kind of exterior weapons?"

"Some," said Itaka as she reached for a small gray button that looked entirely unremarkable. "But only temporary."

Darek had no idea what that meant, but before he could ask for an elaboration, Itaka pressed the gray button.

As soon as she did, a loud *boom* echoed from the outside, followed by what sounded like a monster's roar and something huge swimming away. The *Soaring Sea II* stopped lurching, righting itself as Itaka pulled a lever and flipped another switch.

The ship picked up speed, zooming through the water so fast that Darek actually feared for his life. He kept expecting them to smash into something, but Itaka must have known the route they were taking, because they did not crash into anything. The water seemed open and free in front of them, though they did scare a handful of tiny fish out of their way.

Just as Darek was starting to think that they were home free, what appeared to be a thick, large net appeared in front of the *Soaring Sea II*, directly in its path. The net appeared metallic and thick in the lights of the ship and they were going too fast to stop or change course.

The *Soaring Sea II* crashed directly into the netting, making loud metallic scraping noises against it upon impact. The sudden impact threw Darek against his belt, making him gasp in pain, while Itaka's head snapped forward and then bounced backward against the back of her seat.

The ship swam into the netting, but it wasn't making any progress. The netting, whatever it was, held them tight, which made Darek wonder just what kind of material it was made out of.

"What is that?" Darek asked, looking at Itaka. "Itaka?"

Itaka's head was bowed on her chest. Her hands limply held the controls and she was as still as a rock.

Oh my gods, Darek thought, his eyes widening in horror. *She was knocked unconscious when we crashed.*

He reached over to grab her shoulder and shake her awake, but then he heard something huge moving through the water and looked out through the netting and windshield instinctively.

His heart failed him at the sight. Two massive eyes— round and yellow, almost like a lighthouse beacon—were staring at him from the other side of the netting. Thick green fangs stuck out of its mouth, while its slimy black skin glistened in the headlights of the *Soaring Sea II*.

Unless Darek's eyes were playing tricks on him, he was currently looking at the face of the largest eel he had ever seen in his life.

And he had no way to fight it off.

Chapter Three

When Durima—a katabans, also known as a minor spirit and servant of the gods—woke up this morning in her apartment in World's End, went to the wash room to clean out her fur and get ready for the day, and looked out the window and saw the huge black dome covering the Temple of the Gods, she knew beyond a shadow of a doubt where that dome had come from, and why.

Nonetheless, Durima wished she didn't. She saw dozens of her fellow katabans, many of whom resembled humans with oddly-colored hair or animalistic features, gathering around the dome, pointing at it and trying to figure out where it had come from. The Soldier of the Gods, instantly identifiable thanks to their crystal armor, were urging citizens away from the black dome. For good reason: Durima saw one katabans get past the Soldiers and touch the dome, only to be sucked into it without another word.

Durima wanted to go down there and tell everyone what that dome was, but then a slimy, serpentine hand fell on her shoulder, causing her to look over her shoulder at its owner.

A tall, muscular, naked being with purplish-black skin

stood behind her, his yellow eyes fixed with some satisfaction on the dome covering the Temple. His touch was revolting, like someone had poured a bucket of slime on her body, but she didn't shrug it off because she wasn't even sure he was real half the time, despite having seen him every day for the past month or so.

"There we go," said Uron, his mouth twisting into the most disgusting smile Durima had ever seen. "With the gods out of the way, I would say this is the perfect opportunity to put the rest of my plan into action."

"How did you do that?" said Durima, gesturing at the dome. "How did you get the Void to do that? I didn't even know the Void could be reasoned with."

Uron's smile never wavered. "What do you think I was doing for that full year in which I did not set even one foot in Martir? It wasn't gathering that army of half-gods, a feat I accomplished in about two months. It was studying the Void to learn how to communicate with her."

Durima wrinkled her snout. "Her?"

"The Void is technically genderless, but I have always referred to her with feminine pronouns because she reminds me of a female I once knew in my past life," said Uron. "Anyway, the point is, the Void is a force of nature that desires to consume everything in its path. She has always wanted to consume Martir, so I offered her a chance to do so in exchange for letting me use the Void as a base of operations for a while."

"How come she has never done this before?" said Durima, looking back at the dome that seemed to grow darker around the Temple of the Gods with every passing minute.

"The Powers, of course," said Uron. "When they first created Martir, they set firm limits on the Void, preventing it from coming any farther into Martir than it was allowed to. I discovered and weakened those limits, which is why she has only managed to cover the Temple so far, though I imagine she's making progress to cover the rest of Martir even as we speak."

"Don't you think this could backfire?" said Durima. "Maybe the Void will want to destroy you, too?"

"I've considered it," said Uron, "and decided that I could deal with her as necessary. I know how to strengthen those limits again if I need to. She is not as powerful as she likes to think she is."

"What if the gods break free?" said Durima. "Ever consider that?"

"They can't and won't," said Uron. "The Void is much stronger than they are. So long as she wills it, the gods are trapped like rats. Even Skimif will not be able to escape. The gods will stay there until I am free from the ethereal; afterward, I will enter the Temple and slaughter the whole lot of them, as they deserve."

Durima looked at Uron again. "I still don't understand how you can be right here *and* in the ethereal. It makes no sense."

"In simplest terms, what I did was transfer a bit of my spirit into your body," said Uron. "Not enough that Skimif or any of the gods would notice, but enough so I could appear to you. The problem is, of course, that only you can see me and only you can interact with me, which is why I need you to help me get out of the ethereal."

"What if I decide to ignore you?" said Durima. "Or maybe tell everyone that you are in my head?"

Uron leaned down close to her ear, his breath as disgusting as a corpse as he said, "If you really wanted to do that, you would have done it by now. The simple fact is, Durima, that you cannot prove I am in your mind, and even if you could, you wouldn't. You are the hero of Martir, remember? Pardoned by Skimif himself, even. You wouldn't sacrifice that title for the world, now would you?"

Durima growled at Uron, mostly because what he said was true. Ever since she had succeeded in banishing him to the ethereal, Durima had been treated with far more respect than she could ever remember being treated with before. Random strangers on the street of World's End would shake her hand and tell her how much they appreciated her help. The Soldiers of the Gods saluted her whenever she walked by them, and even the gods themselves would nod at her if she happened to pass one of them.

And she did like it. Durima had had a hard time adjusting, at first, due to the fact that she had been Martir's most wanted criminal for a while there. Going from wanted criminal to beloved hero in a single day was not an easy transition to make; nonetheless, she had made it.

She glanced out the door of her wash room at the rest of her apartment. On her small wooden desk, a large pile of letters—largely thank-you letters from various katabans she didn't even know—stood there, as messy and unorganized as ever. Durima had opened and read each letter, even replied to most of them despite not being a very good writer, and she still received new ones every day.

"I know what you will and won't sacrifice, Durima," said Uron, patting her on the shoulder like an old friend. "You don't want people to think of you as the one who serves Uron. You want to be remembered as the hero who stopped him, the hero who saved the world when even Skimif could not."

Durima looked down at the tiled, water-stained floor, and said, "What do we do now?"

Uron pulled away from her ear and said, "Next, we find a way to unlock the ethereal. If we can do that, then I can escape quite easily."

Durima turned to face him. "Skimif locked it. When Skimif does something, no one else can undo it without his permission."

"I am aware of that," said Uron. "But you are assuming I want you to get Skimif to do it. I know he won't. He'd rather die than free me again."

"Well, then you are going to have to get used to being in the ethereal, because if we can't get Skimif to do it, then there's nothing either of us can do about it," said Durima with a shrug. "Maybe you should tell the Void to let the gods go."

"Are you really that naïve?" said Uron. "There is another way to open the ethereal, a way to bypass Skimif's lock. It will be dangerous to get to, but if you simply follow my instructions, you should get there no problem."

Durima raised an eyebrow. "What if I decide to go back to my bed and call it a day? If no one else can see or hear you, then you can't tell other people about yourself and ruin my reputation."

Uron shook his head. "So simple, Durima. I forgot that you lower lifeforms tend to assume that we higher ones do not think through our plans very well. Observe."

Uron raised his right arm. At the same time, Durima's right arm jerked upward before she could do anything about it. She struggled to put it back down, but it wouldn't budge an inch.

"Being inside your body gives me a little bit more control over you than you think," said Uron, lowering his right arm as he spoke. "So yes, you could try to go to bed, but then I'd just force you right back out of it. I suggest voluntarily following my orders, unless you have always wanted to know what being a puppet feels like."

Durima punched Uron with her free hand. Unfortunately, her left fist went straight through Uron's stomach and smashed into the wall of her washroom behind him. She pulled her arm back, shaking it as plaster fell from the wall, while Uron chuckled.

"Watch that temper of yours, Durima," said Uron. "Do you want to wreck your apartment? This is your only home, after all, so I suggest not wrecking it."

Durima lowered her fist, but she didn't look at Uron. "All right. What must I do to undo Skimif's lock on the ethereal?"

"Have you heard of a place known among the gods as the Old Ruins?" Uron asked.

Durima shook her head. "No. I haven't. What is it?"

"The remnants of my world," said Uron. "When the Powers created Martir, they did not use every last thing from the ruins of my world. They left behind scraps, bits and pieces here and there that they could not use. These bits and pieces can only be found deep beneath Martir's surface, where no mortal or katabans can normally reach them."

"Then why even mention it to me?" said Durima. She turned and walked out of the washroom, even though she had not actually washed her fur. "If I can't get there, then you might as well not have told me about it at all."

She heard Uron following her as he said, "Weren't you listening to what I said? It's a place where no mortal or katabans can *normally* reach them. But if you had help, help from me, then yes, you could reach the Old Ruins, and with it, the secret to unlocking the ethereal."

Durima stopped and turned around to face Uron again. "How far are the Old Ruins from here?"

"Very far," said Uron. "You won't be able to walk down the street to them, which of course is why you will need my help to get there."

"I don't see how we could possibly get to it," said Durima. "I can't teleport—never bothered to learn it—and the ethereal is locked from the outside. Unless you suggest I find a katabans who can teleport, though there aren't too many of them around and even fewer of them would be willing to help me without knowing why."

Uron shook his head. He was so tall that his head almost scraped against the ceiling of Durima's apartment, though of course he couldn't, seeing as he couldn't interact with the rest of the world.

"This is not something I want you involving any other katabans with," said Uron. He gestured toward the only other window in Durima's apartment, which was above her desk. "Any katabans who knew what you are about to do would do everything in their power to stop you. I intend to make this journey as quick and easy as possible."

Durima frowned. "And how, pray tell, do you intend to do that? Am I going to have to take a boat or a ship or are you going to have me use one of those annoying airships that the humans use?"

"Neither," said Uron. "I know of someone who may be willing to help. I've never actually spoken with her myself, but I believe that, with a little convincing, she could be easily made to agree to take you to the Old Ruins."

"And who might that be?" said Durima. "Is it someone I know?"

"Of course," said Uron. "I'm sure you remember the name Aorja Kitano, don't you?"

Durima searched her memory for the name. It sounded familiar, but it had been so long since she last heard it that she barely recalled who it had belonged to.

Then it came back to her. Durima snapped her fingers and said, "I remember. Aorja Kitano was a human servant of the Ghostly God, just like I ... and ... and Gujak were."

Uron nodded, but then frowned. "Are you still broken up

over Gujak's death? I thought you had gotten over it by now."

Durima looked away because she could feel tears forming in her eyes and she didn't want Uron to see them. She involuntarily flashed back to Gujak's death, seeing Erich killing him in her mind's eye, before forcing herself back to the present. She wanted to sneer at Uron, tell him it wasn't any of his business, but her throat seemed to have constricted and she couldn't talk.

Uron sighed. "Never mind. Gujak is irrelevant to our current discussion. What is relevant is that I think that Aorja Kitano could help you get to the Old Ruins."

Durima wiped the tears from her eyes as discreetly as she could, and then looked up. Uron's face held no sympathy for her, but she wasn't looking for any of it. More than anything, she wanted to tear his smug, serpentine head directly off his body, even though she knew it was impossible.

"Where is she?" said Durima, sniffling involuntarily. "Is she on World's End?"

"Of course not," said Uron. "Most mortals do not live on World's End. She is somewhere in the Northern Isles, on the run from the authorities, probably because she recently broke out of Rock Isle. She is alone, paranoid, and vengeful, which makes her the perfect candidate for the job of escorting you to the Old Ruins, don't you think?"

Durima rolled her eyes. "Oh, she certainly sounds like a mortal with an absolutely winning personality."

"Indeed," said Uron, though Durima had a hard time

telling if he was agreeing with her or being sarcastic himself. "Even better, she is a Limitless, which is the reason I want her. She should be able to help you get past whatever obstacles may lay between you and the Old Ruins, assuming she decides to help us, of course."

"If we don't know where she is, how can we ask her to help?" said Durima. "'Somewhere in the Northern Isles' is pretty vague, as the Northern Isles is extremely large, too large for one katabans to search on her own."

"That is simple," said Uron. He tapped the side of his head. "I may not be fully present in Martir, but I still have access to most of my powers. I mentally summon her through your mind and she will be here before you know it."

At that, Durima scratched the back of her neck uncertainly. "Why would she ever listen to you? You want to destroy Martir. I can't see her agreeing with that."

"When did I say I would tell her what I actually want?" said Uron. "Remember, Aorja desires revenge above all else. I will tell her that in order to get that revenge, I need her to take you to the Old Ruins."

Durima shook her head. "If you can't interact with the rest of the world, then how can you mentally summon her?"

"I can augment your own mental abilities a hundredfold," said Uron. He reached for her forehead. "Don't worry about how long it will take for me to locate her; as she is a Limitless, finding her should be easy."

Uron wrapped the slimy fingers of his bare hand on Durima's head. Before Durima could react, he tightened his grip on her skull so hard that for a moment Durima though her head would collapse under the pressure.

Thankfully, it did not. Instead, a surge of energy, much like a blast of fire, poured into her body; no, into her mind. She struggled against Uron's hand, but it was impossible to break free of his iron grip. Uron's voice passed through her head—*Come to World's End, where you will find the revenge you desire*—though she barely paid attention to it due to the pressure on her skull.

Without warning, Uron let go of her face. Durima staggered backward, wiping the slime off her forehead as furiously as she could, even though she knew it was only in her head. It was sticky and smelled like a corpse mixed with a snake, making her wonder if she would be stuck with that stink for the rest of her life.

"Message sent," said Uron, folding his arms. "Now all we have to do is wait, though if Aorja is anything like most mortals, we probably won't have to wait very long for a response."

Chapter Four

Darek breathed hard as he looked at the massive eel floating in the water before him. He tried to level his breathing, as he knew that breathing hard would only make him more nervous, but it was hard to calm down knowing that he was hundreds of feet underwater, trapped in a relatively small airship, staring at the biggest eel he had ever seen, with the pilot of said airship currently out for the count.

Not to mention it feels like our air supply is rapidly dwindling, Darek thought. *Or maybe I'm just getting light-headed from the fear. I don't like either option, to be honest.*

So far, the gigantic eel had not done anything except stare at Darek. That was the good news. The bad news was that Darek didn't know when or if the eel would attack. He just kept looking at those massive green fangs, which looked more than capable of ripping apart the *Soaring Sea II*, and with it, him and Itaka.

Darek had drawn his wand, but he wasn't sure how effective his magic would be down here. He may have been a Limitless, but that eel was still much bigger than he and could easily kill him if it felt threatened by him. Of course, it might not even see him at all; after all, he was very small and currently inside the submarine. If he was smart, he might be able to get a spell or two in before it realized he was there.

On the other hand, what if the eel reacted violently after being attacked? Causing it even the slightest bit of pain might make it to think that the ship itself had attacked it. Darek was no expert on the behavior of giant eels, but there was one universal fact about animal life that he was absolutely sure of: If they were in pain, and the thing causing their pain was not as big or as strong as them, they would attack it until it was dead and no longer causing them any pain.

Thus, Darek shook Itaka as much as he could, trying to get her to wake up, but she must have hit her head pretty hard because she didn't even stir. He thought about yelling, but when he realized that that would just waste precious air, he decided to remain as silent as possible.

Wake up, damn it, Darek thought, glancing up at the giant eel visible through the metal netting that lay over the windshield of the *Soaring Sea II. This is not a time to be napping, even if you're technically unconscious.*

Frustrated, Darek gave up and looked out the windshield again, through the strange metal netting covering it. It was unnerving how the eel still had not moved. Even though he could see its eyes, he had no idea what it was thinking or if it was thinking at all. It might have been waiting for something ... perhaps waiting for the perfect moment to strike.

But this is *the perfect moment to strike,* Darek thought. *Pilot's out cold, ship is immobile, I'm basically useless.*

He decided not to focus on that thought. Right now, the most important thing to do was get the giant eel out of the way of the *Soaring Sea II*. He needed to distract it or scare it off, but he had no idea how to do that.

Thinking fast, Darek looked toward the back of the *Soaring Sea II*. He saw nothing except about a dozen seats on both walls for passengers, several unopened parachutes underneath the seats, and a crate full of old books.

His eyes narrowed on the crate. When he first boarded the ship earlier today, he remembered asking Itaka about the books. She had said, in broken Divina, that it was a delivery she was making to the Undersea Institute, because Archmage Yorak had also asked her to pick up some rare books from a bookseller to add to the Institute's library on her way to pick up Darek.

Darek had accepted the explanation earlier, but now he was wondering if the books might hold clues as to how to defeat the eel. He had given the crate only the most cursory of glances upon boarding the ship and hadn't thought about it at all since the *Soaring Sea II* took off, but now he was desperate enough to try any idea that seemed even remotely likely to work.

So Darek dashed toward the crate. Its lid was partially open, perhaps from Itaka looking in it earlier to confirm it had all of the correct books. He was glad that it wasn't shut tight, because this gave him the opportunity to open it easily.

Darek flipped the lid off the crate and stared inside eagerly. His face fell, however, when he saw that these 'books' didn't look much like books.

He lifted one of them out and stared at it in dismay. It was round, like a wheel, and was made out of some rubbery type material that felt strange in his hands. Written on the cover was a bunch of strange squiggles and swirls that he recognized as the written form of Aqua, the primary language spoken among aquarians.

He flipped the 'pages' open and saw more of that same unreadable text. The ink looked faded and impossible to read to him, and not just because it was in a language he didn't understand, either. There weren't even any illustrations to help him understand what he was reading.

Frustrated, Darek tossed the old book to the floor and, bending over to extend his reach, dug through the crate for more books. Yet the more he dug, the more he found that all of the books looked just like the first one: Wheel-like, written entirely in Aqua, and more than a little rubbery. They didn't even have much variety in color; they came in sea-blue and sea-green, which made the black text written on them look quite strange.

Useless, Darek thought, standing upright and scowling at the crate. *Completely useless.*

He looked over his shoulder just to make sure the eel was still there.

It wasn't.

Darek ran back up to the cockpit of the *Soaring Sea II*.

He leaned over his seat, peering as deeply into the ocean outside as he could, but even with the headlights on at full brightness, the gigantic eel was nowhere to be seen.

Don't panic, Darek, Darek told himself as he stood up, though his heart beat a little faster anyway. *Don't. Panic. Panicking is the least helpful thing you could do in this situation. This could be a good thing, after all. Maybe the eel got bored and went looking for tastier prey. Maybe it saw something shinier and went after that. Yeah, that's probably it.*

He still didn't like the utter silence that permeated the ocean around the submarine like a toxic fume. Even the *Soaring Sea II*'s engine was as quiet as could be. The only sounds he heard was his own bated breath and the occasional scratching of metal against glass as the netting outside moved with the sea currents.

Just as Darek began to believe that they were going to be safe, the *Soaring Sea II* shook as violently as if it had been struck by an earthquake. Because he had been standing, Darek was thrown off his feet and onto the hard metal floor as the *Soaring Sea II* groaned loudly. A red emergency light began flashing, along with a loud, clanging alarm that almost completely deafened him.

Shaking his head, Darek sat up as the ceiling above buckled. Water began trickling in, splashing all over his hair and clothes, causing him to roll to the side as more cracks began appearing in the ceiling. Then the floor began cracking as well, sending the smelly, gelid seawater gushing forth like a fountain.

Wondering what the hell was going on, Darek stood up and waved his wand at the cracks in the ceiling and floor. Thick ice blocks covered the cracks, but it was useless because the *Soaring Sea II* was still creaking and groaning. More cracks burst from the back, splashing all over the books, though that was the least of Darek's troubles now.

Sheer panic gripped his heart, panic unlike anything he had felt before in his life. He pushed it down, however, and made his way toward the cockpit, where Itaka was still uselessly unconscious. As he made his way there, another crack sent a column of salty, disgusting water splashing in his face, knocking him flat off his feet.

The water continued to gush over him, but Darek didn't let it keep him down. He rolled along the ankle-deep water and made a mad dash for the control panel.

Pushing Itaka out of the way, Darek quickly scanned the controls before him. All of the levers, switches, buttons, and monitors looked exactly the same to him. He felt as useless as he had a year ago, during Skimif's fight with Uron, only now it was compounded by his sheer ignorance of airship controls.

Still, Darek didn't have time to panic. He recalled Itaka pressing some button to get rid of another sea monster that had attacked them, but with the constantly flashing red lights, the creaking and groaning of the *Soaring Sea II* as it rapidly crunched, and the loud sound of water filling the ship, he had a hard time remembering which button he was supposed to press.

Then he remembered. The gray button, near the steering

wheel, which was small and not too noticeable; nonetheless, Darek reached for it as soon as he identified it.

Then he heard a loud crack.

Pausing with his hand hovering over the button, Darek looked up and saw that a thick crack had appeared in the windshield. It looked like someone had taken a metal pipe and smashed it against the windshield, yet there wasn't any water spilling through it yet.

The next moment, the windshield exploded, sending the water of the sea flooding into the entire airship. The water slammed into Darek with the force of a rampaging baba raga, knocking him down and sending him stumbling backwards with the surging waves.

Panicking, Darek lashed out with his arms and legs, but it was no use. The water was in his mouth and lungs and his air was rapidly depleting. His wand was ripped out of his hand, becoming lost in the murky green water that filled every nook and cranny of the *Soaring Sea II*.

Water went up his nose, too, as Darek hurtled crazily through the wave. He couldn't breathe. He couldn't see. He couldn't do anything, and when his head slammed against the crate of aquarian books, he could do nothing ever again. The last sound he heard as he fell into unconsciousness was what might have been a monster's roar, though the water muted it too much for him to tell.

Chapter Five

Durima walked down the beach of World's End, squinting at the beautiful blazing sun above. She thought the sun was too bright for this early in the morning, especially when it reflected off the crystal clear ocean water that surrounded World's End on every side. It hurt her eyes and made her a little cranky.

Uron walked beside her ... sort of. While she could see his legs moving, when she looked down at the pure white sand at their feet, she only saw her own footprints. This made sense, seeing as Uron technically only existed in her mind, but it was still unnerving to see his feet walk upon the sand yet leave no clue that they had been there.

Today, this beach—known as the Last Beach by the katabans of World's End, due to its position facing the Void —was empty. There were no katabans fisherman out, taking their boats out to get an early catch; no children playing games like stick toss or magic bright; not even any singing leapers or other wildlife. The reason for that was obvious: When Durima had left her apartment this morning, she had seen almost every remaining inhabitant of World's End gathered around the Void that shrouded the Temple of the

Gods. Everyone had been so busy trying to find out what happened that they hadn't even noticed Durima, which Uron had thought a good thing because it meant that no one would delay them.

Wish someone would *delay me,* Durima thought as she knocked a seashell out of her path. *I do not want to meet up with a crazy female mortal who wants revenge.*

As it turned out, the female mage known as Aorja Kitano had indeed answered Uron's call via gray ghost. She had said it would take her a few hours to reach World's End, largely due to the immense distance, but that she would definitely get there in time to meet them. It boggled Durima's mind that a mortal could possibly teleport from the Northern Isles all the way to World's End by herself, but if Aorja was indeed a Limitless, then maybe it wasn't as crazy as it first appeared.

That was why Durima and Uron were walking along this beach. Uron, through Durima, had told Aorja to land on Last Beach, as it was the place most likely to be abandoned at this time of day. Aorja had given them no specific time for when she would arrive. She had simply said that they should wait for her there.

"Ah, the Beach," said Uron, snapping Durima out of her thoughts. "It has been ages since I last walked on one like this, so carefree and without worry or fear. I forgot how ... pleasant it could be."

Durima looked at him. Uron was looking out at the Beach and the ocean water glistening in the sun, as if he was remembering the good old days.

"You had beaches in your world?" said Durima.

Uron glanced at her before returning his gaze to the sand. "Many. All of them superior to this one, but I admit that the Powers did make Last Beach a little better than the other beaches I've seen on Martir. Still, like everything else in this world, it, too, will have to end."

Durima huffed. "You, end the world all by yourself. Sure."

Uron raised the God-killer, its silver surface shining in the light of the sun. "Of course I can. With the God-killer by my side, I can do anything. You haven't even seen its full power yet."

Durima raised an eyebrow. "Its full power? I thought it was already acting at its fullest possible power. If it can kill a god just by touching one, then I don't understand how it could be any more powerful than it already is."

Uron lowered the God-killer, his hands swaying by his side as he walked. "During that year in the Void, I did more than merely gather up those freakish half-gods and try to convince the Void itself to help me. I studied the writing on the God-killer in an attempt to translate it."

Durima's eyes darted toward the God-killer. Written on its knuckles was indeed many words too faded and old to read, not to mention written in a language Durima did not know. She had always assumed that they said the same thing as the one word she could read—*God-killer*—but hearing Uron talk about translating them made her rethink that theory.

"I didn't think that writing was anything special," said

Durima as a warm breeze blew in from the west, blowing through her fur. "I thought it was the word *God-killer* repeated in multiple languages."

"Of course not," said Uron, shaking his head. "What a silly thought. For what reason would the Powers write the same word over and over in many different languages on the God-killer? It makes no sense. No, the words written here have some … interesting things to say about the God-killer, to say the least."

"Like what?" said Durima. She was starting to get annoyed by the wet sand clinging to the bottom of her feet, but she ignored it for now.

Uron chuckled and patted Durima on the head like she was a small child asking questions too big for her to understand. "Oh, Durima, I *would* tell you, but you know, I think you should find out for yourself. And you will, soon, once I display the full power of the God-killer after I am freed from the ethereal."

"Why didn't you display its 'full power' back when you weren't in the ethereal?" Durima asked. "It's not like there was anything stopping you."

"I did not fully understand it at that point," said Uron. "I was hesitant to use it, because I did not want it to backfire. It's dangerous even for someone of my power to tap, but now that I have thus far failed twice to kill Skimif, it appears I will need to adopt drastic measures in order to succeed."

Durima would have asked what those 'drastic measures' were, but Uron did not seem inclined to talk about them with her. Besides, she doubted there was anything she could do to stop them even if she knew exactly what he was planning. All she knew was that it probably included tapping the 'full power' of the God-killer, whatever that meant.

Aorja still had not arrived, so Durima decided to change the subject. She asked Uron, "Back in the Void ... Gujak, Hollech, and I saw the half-gods dancing."

Uron didn't look down at her, though he did nod. "Yes."

"They were dancing around a fire," said Durima. "A strange fire that changed colors every now and then. Sometimes it showed images; crystalline buildings, faces I'd never seen before. What was it?"

Uron didn't answer at first. No doubt he was thinking of how to answer Durima's question without giving away important or secret information he would rather keep to himself.

Finally, Uron said, "It was a Vision Flame. The images you saw were images from Martir. It was how I kept tabs on everything that occurred here while I remained in the Void."

"I've never heard of a Vision Flame," said Durima in a skeptical voice. "I didn't even know that was possible."

"It's old magic," said Uron, gesturing toward himself. "The kind that was common on my world. I didn't know if it would work, seeing as Martir operates by different rules from the ones my world does, but apparently it does. Of course, it makes sense. Martir was built from the remains of my world; no doubt that means that some of my magic can still work, however incompletely or inefficiently."

"Why were the half-gods dancing around it, then?" said

Durima. "They looked like they were being forced to."

"Vision Flames have the unfortunate—or fortunate, depending on your needs—side effect of inflicting insanity on people who stare at it for too long," said Uron. "I am largely immune to it, having trained myself to avoid that effect long ago, but the half-gods weren't. I allowed what little sanity they had left to evaporate because it made them easier to manipulate."

Not knowing anything about Vision Flames, Durima had no idea if Uron was telling the truth. Still, it did seem to fit with what she knew of the half-gods. They had certainly seemed as mad as wandmakers to her, if not madder, though she suspected that there was more to the Vision Flame than Uron revealed.

Then Uron held up a hand, causing Durima to stop.

"She's coming," said Uron. "Right now."

Before Durima could ask who 'she' was, at the other end of the Beach, a female mortal appeared out of thin air. She staggered along the Beach and fell to her hands and knees, looking as tired as a sprinter after a long run. Durima paused, watching as the female mortal stood up and brushed the sand off her clothes.

"There she is," said Uron, pointing at the female mortal. "Aorja Kitano. Go and meet her right away."

Durima stayed where she was, however, and said, "I just realized, how am I going to talk to her? I can't speak the mortals' bastardization of Divina. And I doubt she can speak Godly Divina, considering that those humans don't seem to teach it at their schools."

"Good question," said Uron. "But ultimately an irrelevant one. Since I am in your head and I can speak and understand Divina, I can provide you with the ability to speak and understand the language."

"Really."

"It's true," said Uron. "Trust me."

"That's like a snake saying 'Pet me,'" Durima said. "Fitting, considering how you used to be a snake."

Uron scowled. "Just go and talk to her. Leave the understanding to me."

Rolling her eyes, Durima continued walking, but not because Uron had ordered her to. She walked at a slow and steady pace, however, because she did not want to start Aorja. Even from a distance, Durima could sense Aorja's power; not as strong as a god's, true, but far more powerful than Durima's own.

The closer she drew to Aorja, the more she saw of the woman. She had short blonde hair, beautifully blonde, reflecting the rays of the sun, although the edges of the hair were frayed and ugly. She wore a black prisoner's outfit, but it was dirty, and torn around the shoulder areas, as if she had not taken good care of it.

As Durima approached, Aorja looked up suddenly, as if noticing Durima for the first time. Her eyes were as violet as flowers, but there was a deep insanity in them that Durima had not seen in the eyes of another being since the Katabans War. It was the kind of insanity that you were born with, the kind Durima had seen in the eyes of some of her fellow soldiers, the ones who fought not because they wanted to protect their people or fight for their ideals, but because they liked killing and wanted to do as much of it as possible while it was socially acceptable for them to do so.

In other words, Durima was looking into the eyes of a killer. And this killer had Limitless magical energy.

"Are you the one who summoned me?" Aorja questioned. Her voice was shrill, hardly threatening, but Durima kept her guard up anyway.

Durima was surprised she understood what Aorja said, but she didn't show her surprise. Instead, she said, "My name is Durima. Is that familiar to you?"

Aorja shook her head. "No. Why?"

"We both worked for the Ghostly God at one point," Durima explained. "Remember? Back at North Academy, you distracted the mages and allowed me and my partner to enter the school unseen."

Aorja let out a sound like the growl of a tiger about to jump on its prey. "Don't mention that Ghostly God idiot to my face. He abandoned me as soon as I was tossed in Rock Isle. I don't want anything to do with that bastard anymore."

Durima nodded in understanding. "And he abandoned me after I and my partner were wanted for accidentally killing a goddess. I've come to learn that the Ghostly God is not very reliable or loyal to anyone except for himself."

"Isn't that the truth?" said Aorja with a harsh laugh. "You know, I'm starting to think all men are like that. Darek, Jakuuth, the Ghostly God ... not a single one of them gives a damn about females like you or me. Bastards, every last one of them."

Durima opened her mouth to disagree (she didn't think it was a 'male' thing so much as it was a problem with people in general), but then Uron, who stood by her side silently, shook his head. He clearly didn't want Durima getting into an argument with Aorja about the occasional unsavory behavior of men.

So Durima said, "As fun as it is to talk about the stupidity of men, that's not why I summoned you. I need your help."

Aorja folded her arms. "For what?"

"Getting somewhere," said Durima. "It's a hard-to-access place, very difficult for mortals and katabans, but if we work together, I think we can do it."

"Why should I?" said Aorja. "What do I have to gain from it? Are you going to pay me millions of coins?"

Durima bit her lower lip. She had a hard time thinking about what to offer Aorja. Yes, Uron had made it seem like Aorja would jump at the chance to get revenge against the gods, but it was now clear to her that Aorja was less bitter towards the gods in general and more bitter towards men. That offer didn't seem like it would work with her.

Then Uron whispered, "Tell her she can get revenge against Darek, Jakuuth, and the Ghostly God if she helps you. Tell her she will have a chance to teach them all a lesson for hurting her."

Durima did not nod to indicate she had heard, mostly because she didn't want Aorja to get suspicious.

So she said to Aorja, "If you help me, you will get the

power to get back at all of the men in your life who have hurt you. You won't be manipulated or betrayed by any male idiots again."

Aorja seemed to consider the offer for a minute. She looked out toward the sea, toward the Void, and then glanced at the back walls of the Throne of the Gods.

Finally, Aorja said, "How do I know you can guarantee me that?"

"Because I am a katabans of my word," said Durima. "That's why."

"What if the gods try to stop us?" said Aorja. She glanced at the Throne of the Gods again, taking a step away from it as she did so. "Coming to World's End was risky for me, far too risky, and if they find me—"

"They won't," Durima promised. "The gods—*all* of the gods—are currently indisposed. They couldn't even swat a fly buzzing in their ears if they wanted to. This is the best time for us to act."

Aorja frowned. "Well, that does make the offer a bit more tempting, I admit. I was planning to get revenge by myself soon, but if helping you will make that easier, then I guess I could help."

Beside Durima, Uron smiled as triumphantly as ever. His expression clearly said, *See, Durima? This all worked out just as I said. Why would you ever doubt my genius?*

Durima wanted to punch him in the face, but knowing how odd that would look to Aorja, she merely nodded and said, "Wise choice, Aorja. You and I will make a great team, I think."

"Yeah, sure, whatever," said Aorja. "I'm only helping you because I've been on the run for a month now and am sick of it. And if this will let me get back at Darek and those other idiots, then I'm ready to do whatever you want."

"Then what are we waiting for?" said Durima. "I will tell you where we need to go. Then we can simply teleport there and everything should work out just fine."

Aorja's shoulders slumped. "Not right away. Teleporting all the way from Ruwa to World's End ... that's not easy, even for a Limitless. I need to rest for about an hour or so, then we can leave."

Uron's hands balled into fists, as though he was angry at the delay, but Durima—who was in no mood to make sure Uron's plans were completed in a timely manner—said, "That's fine. I'm in no hurry. I have all day to do this."

"Also, we will need to stop by Ruwa on our way there," said Aorja. "I have a friend I made while on the run from the law, a friend I would like to bring with us. You don't mind that, do you?"

Durima looked at Uron. The otherworlder frowned disapprovingly for a moment before he nodded.

Then Durima looked at Aorja again and said, "As long as your 'friend' doesn't get in the way, I guess they could tag along if they wanted to."

Aorja smiled, though it was the smile of a maniac rather than the smile of a happy person. "Great. After I'm all rested up and ready to go, we can head north. In the meantime, why don't you tell me about our destination? I can't teleport to somewhere when I don't know its location, after all."

"Sure thing," said Durima, doing her best not to show her own reluctance toward explaining the subject to her. "Let's start with the fact that it is under the sea."

Chapter Six

Was Darek dead or simply unconscious? He had no idea what the answer to that question might be, as he had never died before and so couldn't be sure what death actually felt like.

He recalled getting knocked over by a powerful surge of water and even remembered hitting his head into something (though what it had been, he couldn't remember, which meant he must have hit his head pretty hard).

He probably should have died; after all, he had been hundreds of feet underwater, trapped in what amounted to little more than a glorified metal can, with a rapidly dwindling air supply and no way to give himself the ability to breathe underwater. Getting knocked out ought to have guaranteed his death.

But then he felt a coldness in his body that couldn't have been death. Yet as cold as he was, he also felt his body warming at a slow, yet steady pace. His Xocionian Monk robes felt heavy with wetness, which meant that he was most definitely alive; after all, he couldn't have felt his clothes if he was dead.

Somehow, then, he had survived. How he could have

possibly survived, he didn't know, but he was thankful for it anyway. He wondered if Xocion or one of the other gods had saved him; whether or not they did, he prayed a quick prayer of thanksgiving to them anyway, just to be safe.

The only question now was, where was he? His eyes were still closed and he felt nothing except for a flat, rock surface under his body, a soft, spongy pillow was under his head (though it didn't feel like any pillow he had ever slept on before), and his own wet and heavy robes.

Better get up, Darek thought. *If I'm in some kind of dangerous situation, then I can't just sleep here like a sitting duck.*

His eyelids felt heavy as a winter coat; nonetheless, he managed to pry them open, allowing him to see exactly where he was.

He was in a small rock cave, with luminescent flowers— like the kind he had seen on his way down into the sea earlier—acting as the only source of illumination. There wasn't much in the room except for the rock tablet he lay on and the oddly spongy pillow under his head, though he was too tired to lift his head to look at the pillow better.

Opposite him was a cavern entrance that seemed to open up to the outside, although that didn't tell him where he was. He tried to look out the exit as best as he could and was surprised when he saw a fish swim by, though it swam too quickly for him to identify its species.

A fish? Darek thought. *Am I still underwater?*

Then Darek looked around again. He did see water now. He hadn't noticed it before, but water was everywhere, just like air on the surface. It was even in his mouth, although he barely tasted it.

He sat up, but sluggishly, as his robes weighed him down heavily. Panicking, he closed his mouth to conserve what little air he could before he realized that there was no air to conserve. He was clearly, unambiguously underwater, maybe even on the bottom of the ocean floor for all he knew.

Why am I not drowning? Darek thought in panic. *Or being crushed to death by the sheer pressure of the water? I should be dead.*

He felt his neck and winced at the gills that were present. Then he looked down at his feet and started. There was webbing between his toes, just like the kind he had seen on the feet of the aquarian students from the Undersea Institute a while ago. Not only that, but his fingers also had webbing in between them, slightly transparent in the glow of the luminescent flowers above.

By the gods, Darek thought. *Am I ... I can't be ... am I part-aquarian now? What the heck is going on here?*

Just then, Darek heard—no, more like felt the vibrations in the water, though he thought of it as 'hearing' nonetheless—someone swimming outside the cave. He had no idea who or what it was, so he reached for his wand only to find it no longer attached to his belt. He almost panicked before remembering that he had lost his wand when the water broke through the windshield of the *Soaring Sea II*.

Will just have to use my hands to channel my magic, then, Darek thought as the sounds of the person swimming drew closer and closer to the exit. *Just have to hope I won't die before I can do it.*

Just as Darek began to think about what the best spells to use underwater would be, a familiar manta ray-like face—with goggles strapped over the eyes—peered into the cave. Darek almost froze the newcomer before he recognized that face and relaxed.

"Kuroshio?" said Darek in surprise, lowering his hands onto his lap. "Is that you?"

Darek's voice sounded strange underwater, just as gargled as aquarians speaking Divina. He barely understood his own words, making him worry that Kuroshio might not have, either.

Thankfully, Kuroshio simply smiled and said, in Divina that sounded quite clear in the water, "Yes, Darek, me. Long time, no see, yes?"

When Kuroshio entered the cavern, he looked just like how Darek remembered him: Stout and wide, with the usual black-and-green jumpsuit uniform that all Institute students wore. His magic stone was still attached to the armband around his right arm, glowing green and bright as always.

Darek could not help but smile in return, briefly forgetting his panic and confusion at his current situation. "Yes, it has been a while since we last saw each other. How are you?"

"Good, good," said Kuroshio, nodding as enthusiastically as ever. "Going to graduate this year. Will go to East Yudra to work under famous botamancer Eerk Dah."

Darek had no idea who 'Eerk Dah' was or even what East Yudra was, but he said in a polite voice, "Sounds great. I just graduated from North Academy last year. Good to hear you're also about to graduate."

Kuroshio smiled sheepishly. "Thank. I am happy. Yorak work us hard, but good headmistress and teacher."

"I bet she is," said Darek. Then he rubbed the back of his head, which still hurt from where he had knocked it against the ... whatever it was he had knocked it against earlier. "By the way, where am I? Why do I have gills and webbed feet and hands? Is the *Soaring Sea II* all right? What happened to Itaka?"

Kuroshio held up his hands as if trying to calm Darek down. "Too many questions. Will take you to Archmage. Told me to tell her if Darek awoke. Come with?"

Darek looked down at his wet robes, which felt like weights on his body now. "I'd like to, but I don't think I can swim like this."

"No problem," said Kuroshio. He pulled out a folded green-and-silver Institute uniform from nowhere. "Here go. Put on. Easier to swim."

Kuroshio threw the Institute uniform to Darek. It floated through the water into Darek's hands. It felt like sponge and rubber, but also quite smooth. He liked it.

"I go outside and wait," Kuroshio said, gesturing toward the cavern exit. "Give privacy. Once dressed, come out and we go to Institute main building."

Before Darek could respond, Kuroshio was gone, leaving him alone in the cave once again. Darek wished Kuroshio had answered his questions right away, but maybe that was for the best. Kuroshio didn't speak Divina very well, so even if he tried to answer Darek's questions, he would probably just confuse Darek more.

Stripping out of his monk robes underwater was difficult, to put it lightly. First, he had to get off the stone slab he had rested on, which due to his wet, heavy robes was far harder to do than it should have been. After that, he had to actually remove the robes, which was tricky at first due to the way they stuck to his body and tangled his legs. Eventually he came up with the idea of tucking in both arms to his sides and ducking out of the robes, though tucking in his arms required a little work because his sleeves clung to them almost like a second skin.

Leaving his robes to slowly sink to the floor of the cave, Darek now had to remove his undergarments. Unfortunately, these were cotton thermal undergarments, pretty standard for Xocionian Monks due to the sheer coldness of the Great Berg, but like a second skin underwater. Peeling them off was hard, so he was forced to pick up a sharp rock he found on the ground and cut through them, even though he didn't want to.

Now that Darek was completely naked—which felt strange underwater, though not uncomfortable—he picked up the Institute uniform that Kuroshio had given him and unfolded it as best as he could in the water. Kuroshio had at least gotten the size right; it looked like it would fit him perfectly.

Actually putting it on was another matter entirely,

however. He had to unzip its back, which he could not help but find odd because the Academy mage uniform had not had any zippers on it. Then he jammed his legs into the leggings, but with the leggings floating freely in the water, he ended up jamming his feet into the knees instead. So he had to meticulously, slowly put one leg in after another, a task made no easier by his webbed feet, which he still found strange and unnatural.

He had not been given any shoes to put on his feet, but he figured they were not necessary because of his webbed feet. It was just like swimming, which meant of course that shoes were unnecessary, though he still wondered what happened to his old shoes and whether Kuroshio might know where they were.

After getting both of his legs into the spongy jumpsuit, sticking his arms into the sleeves was easy. Granted, his webbed fingers did make it slightly more difficult to fit his arms through, but it wasn't as difficult as fitting his legs in the leggings.

Once that task was accomplished, he reached for the zipper behind him—awkwardly, of course. The zipper was low behind his back, almost too low for him to reach, very close to his behind. He moved strangely in the water as he tried to grab his zipper, grateful that no one could see him because he knew how embarrassing it must have looked.

Still, he managed to grab the zipper and pull it all the way up. Once he did, the jumpsuit fit him surprisingly well. Of course Darek had thought it would fit, but now that it was actually on him, it was like a second skin, though in a better way than the thermal underwear had been. It wasn't quite as warm or comfortable as his robes, which lay on the ground a wet and muddled mess, but as he could move more naturally in the water with this uniform than with his robes, he thought it was a fair tradeoff.

So Darek turned in the water with less effort than before and began swimming toward the exit. Despite his new uniform making his underwater movements easier to do, Darek had never been the best swimmer, as he had not been given many swimming lessons at North Academy growing up.

Still, Darek succeeded in reaching the exit, where he found Kuroshio floating with his back to the exit.

"Hey," Darek called. His voice still sounded weird to him, but no longer quite as incomprehensible. "Kuroshio, I'm ready to go."

Kuroshio turned as Darek approached. "Like uniform?"

"It's pretty nice," said Darek, nodding as he came to a stop before Kuroshio. He landed on the lip of the exit and stretched his arms. "I see why you Institute students like to wear it. It was tricky to put on, though."

"Designed for underwater movements," Kuroshio said, waving his arms as if to show by example. "Usually designed for aquarians, but have human designs on hand, too, for visitors."

"How many human visitors do you get usually?" said Darek.

"Very few," said Kuroshio. "Tell more later. Right now, us go to Archmage's office. Sent gray clone to Institute main building letting her know."

Darek tilted his head to the left. "Gray clone? What's that?"

Kuroshio scratched the side of his head, as if thinking hard about the right words to use. "Think you call it ... gray ghost, correct?"

"I didn't know you aquarians had a different name for it," said Darek. "That's confusing."

Kuroshio shrugged and turned around. "Follow me. Stay close. Archmage waiting."

With that, Kuroshio began swimming forward. Darek pushed himself off the lip of the cave mouth to begin swimming, but as soon as he crossed the threshold and looked down, he was taken aback by what he saw.

His tiny little cave room was actually located near the top of a tall undersea cliff. If they had not been underwater, he would have plummeted to his death, most likely. It looked like the cliff side was dotted with other cavern entrances just like his; he even saw some aquarians near the bottom swimming in and out of the holes.

"What is this place?" Darek asked, gesturing at the cliff as he struggled to keep afloat in the water.

Kuroshio stopped and looked over his shoulder. "Oh ... um, called Cliff Comb. Like honey comb, yes?"

"What is it used for?" Darek asked. "Does it belong to the Institute?"

"Place where injured students rest," said Kuroshio. "Sometimes, visitors stay here, too. Property of Institute, yes."

"Why couldn't you build a medical wing in the Institute?" Darek said. "Wouldn't that be more convenient than using this place?"

"Not my decision," said Kuroshio with a shrug. "But hurry. Archmage impatient."

Kuroshio took off again. Darek glanced at the Cliff Comb one more time before following after Kuroshio, though he had to swim slowly due to his inexperience in swimming. He did, however, find that his webbed hands and feet helped propel him through the water quite a bit, which made them feel more natural now.

Thankfully, Kuroshio must have noticed Darek's slow swimming pace, because he was clearly swimming at a slower pace than he normally did. It made Darek feel a little embarrassed, but thankful, as he didn't want to get lost in the sea by himself.

As they swam, Darek peered in the direction in which they swam. He had never seen the Undersea Institute campus itself before; indeed, he had never even seen a picture of it, nor had he ever asked Kuroshio or anyone else who had been to it to describe it.

The campus that stretched out before them looked almost nothing like the Arcanium or any other part of North Academy. It had been built on flat lands, from the look of it, with no walls or anything else to protect it or separate it from the rest of the Undersea. There were perhaps two dozen buildings, all made of stone or coral (it was hard to tell from a distance), with a large stone tower—though by no means as big as the Arcanium—dominating the center.

None of the buildings, as far as he could see, had doors or windows. Instead, they had openings on the roofs and on the sides, wide enough for most aquarians to swim through. Indeed, as Darek watched, he saw Institute students—all wearing the same green-and-silver uniform that he himself wore—constantly entering or exiting buildings, sometimes carrying stacks of those strange aquarian books, other times clearly in conversation with each other.

The entire Undersea Institute campus seemed to be laid out like a square, with half of the buildings on one side and the other half opposite them. A few miles to the west lay what appeared to be an enormous open, yet quite dark, trench, while to the east, he saw purple and yellow lights on the 'horizon,' if you could call it that, which could have been some light fish or maybe a nearby town or city. He thought about asking Kuroshio what they were, but then decided against it, as they didn't seem very important or urgent.

As they drew closer to the school itself, Darek saw more details. Near the edge of the campus was what looked like a greenhouse. He assumed that because he saw plants—most unfamiliar to him, as he hadn't studied Undersea flora very much in his school days—of a variety of colors and shapes growing in there. Kuroshio, too, glanced at it with a concerned look on his face; considering Kuroshio was a botamancer, it made sense he would be worried about it, though as far as Darek could tell, there was nothing wrong with the greenhouse.

Another thing Darek noticed as they swam toward the Institute was how chaotically everyone moved. Students swam over, around, or under each other, through the opening of one building only to emerge on the other side, and generally took any route they pleased to get to their destination. No one walked in the streets between the buildings; no surprise, since walking underwater was a chore.

As they swam through the campus grounds, Darek stayed as close as he could to Kuroshio to avoid getting separated. Not that it would be difficult to get reunited, seeing as the campus didn't seem very big or confusing, but Darek had become aware that many students looked at him as they passed. It was hard to read their expressions due to their fish-like faces, but if Darek had to guess, most of them were either curious or hostile.

No one stopped to talk to Darek or Kuroshio, however. It seemed like everyone was in a hurry to go somewhere, maybe to their classes. Darek was grateful for that. He didn't hate talking to aquarians, but he was so curious to find out what had happened while he had been out that he didn't want to stand around and talk to anyone right now.

Despite that, Darek couldn't help but stare at the students as they passed. No two students looked even remotely alike. Some resembled humanoid whales, similar to Yorak, except much thicker, while some looked like craw fish or shrimp. Darek had always known that the aquarian species was as varied as the rest of the Undersea creatures, but seeing it in person like this, in their natural environment, was something else.

"Darek?" Kuroshio called, snapping Darek out of his

thoughts.

Darek looked and saw that Kuroshio was quite far ahead of him. The Institute student was swimming in place in the water, frowning at Darek. A shrimp-like student swam over Kuroshio's head, but he didn't even flinch, as if she hadn't swam over him at all.

"What standing for?" said Kuroshio. He gestured toward the stone tower in the center. "Archmage awaits."

"Sorry," said Darek as he swam toward Kuroshio. He ducked to avoid a crustacean who soared by so fast that he appeared to be propelled by a motor. "I was just ... distracted by all of the students."

Kuroshio tilted his head to the side. "Never seen much aquarians?"

"The most I ever saw in one place was when you and your fellow students came for a visit last year," said Darek, shaking his head. "North Academy didn't have any aquarian students, mostly because the Great Berg is even more hostile to aquarian life than it is to human life. And the Xocionian Monks are entirely human as well. Seeing so many aquarians all in one place is pretty shocking to me."

"Understand," said Kuroshio. "Felt same way when visiting North Academy last year."

"Just how many students attend here anyway?" said Darek, glancing at all of the students hurrying to and fro.

Kuroshio bit his lower lip, like he was thinking about how to express that number in Divina. "Two one hundreds."

"Two hundred?" said Darek in surprise. "That's more students than North Academy had when I was attending it."

"Yes, quite a bit," said Kuroshio. "Two tens of teachers, plus Archmage Yorak."

"Hmm, that's more teachers than North Academy," said Darek. "I always thought Undersea Institute was smaller than North Academy for some reason."

"Campus smaller," said Kuroshio. He turned back to the tower and gestured for Darek to follow. "Come. No time to waste."

As they approached the stone tower that was apparently Yorak's office, Darek took this opportunity to look at it. It was tall; again, not as tall as the Arcanium, but taller than the rest of the buildings, which all appeared strangely small to Darek. The top of the tower was shaped like a dome, with openings on every side at regular intervals.

Kuroshio swam up towards one of those openings, so Darek followed him. While most of his energy was taken up by his swimming, Darek nonetheless found the plainness of the Undersea Institute strange. His memories from before the crashing of the *Soaring Sea II* were still jumbled and confused, a veritable mess, but he did recall how amazing and wonderful the Undersea had looked when he first entered it.

There aren't even any statues of the gods down here, Darek thought, glancing to the left and right. *Granted, North Academy doesn't have a whole lot of statues, either, but we do have a few here and there. If I hadn't seen the magic stones strapped to the students' bodies, I wouldn't have thought that this was a mage school.*

He didn't ask Kuroshio if there might be any statues of

the gods nearby, however, partly because he didn't want to waste time talking, partly because he was putting so much effort into swimming that he couldn't gather enough strength to speak. He supposed that the aquarians had different ways of honoring the gods than humans did.

Soon they passed through the front opening of the tower and ended up inside a very wide-open room. It was so wide-open that for a moment Darek almost forgot that they were inside a building, rather than outside in the open sea.

Even more so than the sheer size of the room was the interior itself. The floor and ceiling were covered with the largest murals Darek had ever seen in his life. The mural painted on the floor below appeared to be a map of the entire Undersea, because he saw names written and borders drawn everywhere. It was a highly detailed map, too; every single town—from the smallest villages, such as one that appeared to be only four huts in all, to the biggest cities— was accounted for. Not only that, but each country had its own color; red for one, blue for another, yellow for a third, and so on, making the map look like a great big splash of paint. He didn't really know what any of the colors meant, but they certainly looked pretty.

As impressive as that map was, the mural above was even more so. It featured what appeared to be hundreds of aquarians, showing even more variety than the Institute students, and it took Darek a moment to realize that he was looking at a mural of every single god in the Northern Pantheon. He only recognized it for what it was because he recognized Kano, Goddess of the Sea, Sand, and Poetry, because she still resembled a woman made of water, albeit an aquarian woman made of water. He thus had to assume that the rest of the aquarians around her were the other gods, even though he could not identify any of them aside from her.

The mural appeared to show the gods preparing for war, because all of them carried a weapon of some kind, in addition to wearing coral battle armor. Who they were going to war against, Darek didn't know, as the mural only showed the gods. It was impressive nonetheless, whatever its purpose, making Darek feel like he had entered a place that was truly devoted to the gods.

Then a familiar aged, feminine voice said, "Darek Takren. I'm glad to see you again."

Darek looked in the direction of the voice. An elderly-looking female aquarian with a whale-like face was seated on a coral throne that rose from the floor. By her side, a younger female aquarian with a goldfish-like head floated, waving at Darek when he noticed her. The older one wore a soldier green uniform, which also hung more loosely around her frame than her younger counterpart, who wore a traditional green-and-silver uniform.

"Archmage Yorak," said Darek as he and Kuroshio approached the throned aquarian. "I'm pleased to be here. More importantly, I'm pleased to still be alive."

Yorak nodded as she closed the book on her lap that she had apparently been reading. "As am I. We almost thought our healing magic wouldn't work, but I'm glad to see that it did."

Darek stopped several feet from Yorak and then looked at the aquarian floating next to her. "Hey, Auratus. Long time, no see."

Yorak's pupil did not verbally respond, but she nodded nonetheless to show that she understood. Darek didn't expect her to say anything, seeing as he knew that Auratus was mute, though he still didn't know why she was mute or why the Institute mages had not yet healed her vocal chords with their magic.

I'll worry about that later, Darek thought. *I have much more urgent things to worry about at the moment than that little mystery. Maybe it's just an aquarian custom I don't understand or something.*

"How do you feel?" Yorak asked. Her Divina was as fluent as any human's, though the water distorted it somewhat. "Did you swim all the way here from the Cliff Comb yourself?"

"Yes," said Darek. He rolled his shoulders. "I feel pretty good, but the gills and webbed hands and feet are hard to get used to."

"It always is for visiting humans," said Yorak. "Normally, I do not cast the Amphibious Spell on unconscious humans, but considering how critical your health was earlier, I had no choice."

"So you did cast a spell to give me this stuff," said Darek, gesturing at the gills on his neck. "I was wondering how I was going to breathe underwater earlier. By the way, what kind of spell is it?"

"A shape-shifting spell," said Yorak. "And a much more

thorough one than you might think. The gills and webbed hands and feet are only the most obvious manifestations of the spell's effects. Your whole body was changed, even though it looks essentially the same, to operate underwater more efficiently."

Darek touched his chest. "Do you mean you replaced my organs with fish organs or something?"

"Not exactly," said Yorak, shaking her head. "I simply modified them to handle the pressure of the sea depths better and to allow you to breathe without difficulty. Don't worry; it's not permanent. Once you help us here and want to return to the surface, I can reverse the effects of the spell, though you might find yourself craving seaweed for a few weeks afterward."

That thought made Darek feel sick, as he had always found seaweed disgusting. He was glad to hear Yorak could reverse the spell's effects, at least.

Then Yorak closed her book and handed it to Auratus, who took it without question and held it under her right arm like a package she was going to deliver.

Putting her hands together, Yorak said, "Darek, I first want to say that I am sorry to hear about the Magical Superior's passing. The last time I saw him was well over a year ago, when I visited your old school, and we didn't part on the best terms."

A thick sadness rose in Darek's chest, which he tried to ignore. He didn't want to break down and cry in front of Yorak, Kuroshio, or Auratus, mostly because he didn't think it would be appropriate in this situation. Though he did briefly wonder what crying underwater would be like or if he even could do it at all.

Keeping as level a tone as he could, Darek said, "It's fine. In his last moments, the Superior didn't hold any grievances against anybody. He gave his life to save the school and everyone in it. You don't have to regret anything."

"But I still should have contacted him at some point before then," said Yorak with a regretful sigh. "At the very least, I should have led my students to help fight off Jakuuth's Army. We only learned about the attack after it was finished."

"There was nothing you guys could have done against the Limitless Army," said Darek, shaking his head. "They were too powerful, and would have won if it had not been for ... well, the point is, what's past is past. We should focus on why you summoned me here, which is the more pressing question."

Yorak seemed not to hear Darek for a moment, because her small eyes looked distant and misty, as if she was reliving all of her memories with the Magical Superior right there. All Darek knew about Yorak and the Magical Superior was that they had been close friends for many, many years, since their youth; beyond that, he didn't know the full extent of their relationship, though considering how pained she looked, it must have been close.

"You are right," said Yorak, refocusing her eyes on Darek and nodding. "Chen is dead and nothing I say or regret will change that. I wish I could have visited the funeral, but we were held up down here by a certain issue that we could not ignore."

"You mean the reason I'm here?" said Darek. "You're finally going to tell me about it?"

"Yes," said Yorak. "But first, do you know if Lord Skimif has appointed a new Magical Superior of North Academy yet?"

Darek shook his head. "No. Right now, my mom, Jenur Takren, is temporary Magical Superior. Last I heard, she had almost finished her list of potential candidates and is going to present it to Skimif sometime this week for his approval."

"I hope she has better luck in contacting the gods than I have," said Yorak, sounding a little disgruntled. "I have been trying to contact them for the past day or so, but no one has answered. Not even the God of Messages has responded. It is complete silence from the gods."

Darek frowned, mostly due to the effort he had to exert in remaining afloat in the same position. "Maybe the gods are busy with something else at the moment. It's probably not worth worrying about."

"Of course it's worth worrying about," said Yorak, throwing her hands up. "While my office has never been as well-respected by the gods as the Magical Superior of North Academy, I usually don't have trouble contacting them."

"Monsters, too, attack," Kuroshio added. He gestured toward the eastern wall of Yorak's office. "Gods not dealt with them. Must be from somewhere else."

"What?" said Darek, looking at Kuroshio in confusion. "I don't understand. What monsters?"

"I guess we had better return to the real topic," said Yorak, "that topic being, of course, the whole reason you are here."

Yorak gripped the arms of her coral throne and pushed herself up. She swam up above Darek's head, causing him to crane his neck to follow her progress.

"Come with me outside," said Yorak, gesturing at Darek to follow her as she swam toward one of the exits. "I think you need to see in order to understand what it is we're facing."

Darek groaned internally, as he did not want to do more swimming. Nonetheless, he swam after Yorak without complaint, with Kuroshio and Auratus following closely but silently behind.

Out on the roof of the stone tower, Yorak landed on it and gestured toward the south. "Do you see that, Darek Takren?"

Resting his feet on the stone underneath him, Darek peered in the direction that Yorak was pointing in. He saw the massive trenches he had noticed earlier, so dark that it was impossible to tell for sure what lay within. All he knew was that he felt repulsed by the shadows of the trenches, though why, he wasn't sure.

"Yeah, I see that," said Darek. He looked at Yorak as Kuroshio and Auratus landed nearby. "Does it have anything to do with that giant eel from earlier? The one that attacked the *Soaring Sea II*? By the way, what happened to the *Soaring Sea II*? Was it destroyed? And where is Itaka?"

He asked those questions one after another, similar to how he had asked them of Kuroshio earlier, not to be rude, but because he had been wondering about them for so long now that he couldn't keep them inside anymore.

Yorak rubbed the side of her head and sighed. "Perhaps I should tell you about Itaka first: She's dead. Killed by the eel. And you would have died, too, if we hadn't saved you."

Darek scratched the back of his head, which felt weird underwater, as his hair was floating above him. "Oh ... I'm sorry."

"Itaka knew something like that could happen," said Yorak, looking out toward the trenches in the south. "I told her to teleport you here, but she said that your body would have an easier time adapting to the Undersea if it came in the *Soaring Sea II* first. If I had not relented ... she might still be with us today."

Kuroshio and Auratus both looked sad as well, which to Darek meant that Itaka must have been much-loved by the general student body of the Institute. It made Darek wish that he had tried to talk to her more while she lived, learned more about her. But, he supposed, what passed was past and there was no point in dwelling on her death any further, at least for him anyway.

So Darek said, "If Itaka died, how did I survive?"

"Luck, and perhaps the favor of the gods," said Yorak with a shrug. "You should have drowned or been crushed by the pressure of the sea, but instead you were unconscious long enough for us to rescue you. Quite the miracle, if I do say so myself."

"How did you guys know that the ship was under attack?" said Darek. "I didn't think we were that close to the school."

"You weren't," said Yorak. "The original plan was that Itaka would pilot the *Soaring Sea II* to the halfway point between the Surface and the Institute, after which a group of students and teachers, led by me, would escort the ship the rest of the way."

"So you were waiting there for us?" said Darek.

"Yes," said Yorak. "But you didn't quite make it to the halfway point and we didn't realize what was going on until we heard the crunching of metal in the water."

"Fought off the eel," Kuroshio said, sounding proud of himself. "Used magic to scare it off, but *Soaring Sea II* ..."

"Completely destroyed," said Yorak. "Even the crate of rare books was destroyed, which is a shame, because it took me years to track down all of those books in one place like that, and some were the only known copies of those books in the whole world."

Darek's head throbbed when Yorak mentioned the crate, but he didn't know why. He rubbed it, trying to remember why his head hurt, but unfortunately his memory was still foggy and unclear, so he decided to forget about it for now in order to devote his full attention to their current situation.

"The eel is gone," Yorak continued. "Where, we don't know, but it will probably return again, except with friends. That was the first time I had ever seen it alone."

Despite his fuzzy memory, Darek had no trouble

remembering the giant eel, especially its yellow eyes and thick green fangs. "You've fought that thing before? And it has friends?"

"A few times," said Yorak. She gestured toward the trenches. "It usually comes from the Trenches and tries to attack the school. So far, we've kept it at bay with our magic, but in the last attack it killed half a dozen students and injured twice that many."

Darek looked out over the campus grounds all around him. Students and teachers were still swimming all over the place in that same chaotic mess from before. None of them seemed injured or afraid to him. It looked like a normal day at school to him, though that didn't mean much, seeing as Darek didn't know what the aquarians defined as a 'normal' day at school down here.

"Shouldn't you evacuate the students, then, if this giant monster keeps attacking and killing people?" said Darek. "This school doesn't seem very safe."

Kuroshio gasped, while Auratus looked down at her feet in shame. Darek had no idea what they were so shocked about until he noticed how Yorak glared at him with the kind of glare only an elderly person tired of youthful foolishness could muster.

Yorak poked Darek in the chest with one of her large fingers and said, "I thought you most of all would understand that, Darek Takren, seeing as you were a student at North Academy. Learning about and studying the gods is paramount; besides, I don't recall the Magical Superior evacuating the students at North Academy when

Uron rose."

Actually, we did *plan to evacuate everyone initially,* Darek wanted to say, but seeing how offended Yorak was at the suggestion that they evacuate the Institute students to somewhere safer, he decided to keep that thought to himself.

Instead, he said, "So you don't think your students are in any real danger? Then why did you invite me to help? Sounds to me like you have the situation under control."

"Because the problem might be bigger—*much* bigger— than this giant eel and its friends," said Yorak. "And I would rather be safe than sorry. If we can destroy the problem before it gets too big, we might just survive."

"How much bigger?" said Darek. He looked out over at the dark trenches in the distance. "As big as Uron?"

"Thank the gods, no," said Yorak with a shudder. "But big enough to make me worry. Trust me, it takes a lot to make me worry."

"Start at the beginning, then," said Darek, crossing his arms over his chest. "What is the problem?"

Yorak rubbed the magic stone strapped to her left wrist, the one that glowed a variety of different colors. She seemed to be trying to think about where to start, which told Darek that he was in for a long story.

Finally, Yorak said, "It was last month, around the same time that Jakuuth's Army attacked North Academy, that the first students began vanishing."

"One a day," said Kuroshio, rubbing his hands together anxiously. "One by one. Like picking out seaweed stalks."

Auratus was nodding as if Kuroshio had used the most perfect analogy to describe what had happened to the students.

"Disappeared?" said Darek. He glanced at the Trenches, still feeling repulsed by the shadows he saw. "Why?"

"Monsters," said Yorak. Then she frowned. "At least, we think so."

"Think so?" said Darek, tilting his head to the side. "How can you not know for sure?"

"The monsters appeared at the same time that students began disappearing," said Yorak, gesturing towards the massive trench west of the school. "The Trenches lie in that direction. I'm sure you can see them."

"Biggest and deepest trenches in Undersea," said Kuroshio, offering an explanation, no doubt because he saw Darek's puzzled expression. "Home to lots of marine life. Dangerous."

"Ah," said Darek. "Are they always dangerous?"

"Normally, yes," said Yorak, nodding. "But they've always been manageable if you understood the risks. In the past month, however, they've become veritable death traps."

"Darkness," Kuroshio added. "Big darkness. Eats light."

"Big darkness eats light?" said Darek. He looked out toward the Trenches, though he was too far away to see them in any detail. "What does that mean?"

"Kuroshio means that a powerful darkness has recently taken over the Trenches," Yorak said. "We don't know where it came from or what caused it. Originally, I sent students there to investigate its origins, but when the fifth student didn't return, I stopped sending them entirely."

"Then the monsters attacked," Darek said. "Right?"

"Yes," said Yorak. "The eel, but many others, including strange grasshopper-like insectoids. We think they came with the darkness, maybe even came from it for all we know."

"How could they have come from it?" said Darek. "I mean, the darkness is probably some sort of natural Martirian phenomenon, yes? Maybe one of the gods created it. Maybe it was Ooka."

Kuroshio and Auratus exchanged puzzled looks before Kuroshio said, "Who?"

"Ooka," Darek repeated, looking at Kuroshio and Auratus. "The God of Shadows and Knives. You've heard of him, haven't you?"

"He's referring to Salor," Yorak explained.

The light of understanding shone in Kuroshio's eyes, while Auratus nodded to show that she understood now as well.

"Ah," said Kuroshio, doing a thumbs up. "Remember now. Learned that name in human studies class."

Unfortunately, Darek was now the confused one, forcing him to ask, "Salor? His name is Ooka, isn't it?"

"I see that Chen didn't teach you about the different names of the gods, then, while he still lived," said Yorak. "To put it simply, we aquarians use different names for the gods than you humans. We use the human names when interacting with humans in order to communicate more easily, but among us aquarians, we use our own names."

Darek tugged at the sleeve of his jumpsuit without thinking about it. "I wonder why no one ever taught me that."

"Probably because you humans can be very parochial, assuming that you are the center of the universe and everything," said Yorak with a contemptuous tone. "But this is not the time to discuss the differences between human and aquarian cultures. To answer your question, no, this darkness is clearly not a product of the gods or Martir in general."

'Parochial' was hardly the word Darek would use to describe humanity, but he agreed with Yorak that pushing the issue would be unwise. Best to remain on topic, especially when the subject threatened many innocent people, human or otherwise.

"How do you know it's not from Martir or the gods?" said Darek, putting his hands on his hips. "It doesn't look that out of the ordinary to me."

"I do not sense the power of the gods radiating from it," said Yorak, gesturing toward the Trenches. "I do not sense anything at all from it, actually. It feels like a void, as though emptiness itself had consumed a portion of the Undersea."

"You don't think it could be *from* the Void, do you?" Darek asked. "Like the half-gods that attacked World's End?"

"There's no way to know for sure," said Yorak. "All I know is that the monsters that have come with it are almost completely different from anything on Martir. Sometimes our magic seems useless against them; other times, it works the same as always. There is little consistency."

"So how am I supposed to help?" said Darek. He gestured at his waist, where his wand belt would normally be. "I don't have a wand anymore, after all. It's dangerous even for a Limitless like myself to use magic without some kind of conduit."

"We will get you a magic stone," said Yorak. "No worries; we have hundreds of extra magic stones in storage on the campus grounds. I will have Kuroshio fetch one for you later."

"Okay," said Darek, "but even so, I still don't see how I am supposed to help. It's hardly as if I know how to get rid of this darkness, after all."

"Then let me get straight to the point," said Yorak. She looked Darek straight in the eyes and said, "We want you to go into the darkness and destroy its source."

Darek's eyes widened as he glanced at the Trenches. "You mean the same darkness from which none of your students have ever returned?"

"Yes," said Yorak. "I know it is dangerous, but I think that as a Limitless you are better equipped to deal with whatever is lurking in there than any of us are. I would do it myself, but it is important that I, as the Archmage of the Undersea Institute, stay with my students so they do not lose morale or panic."

"Believe," said Kuroshio, putting a hand on his heart and then pushing out toward Darek. "Have faith you."

"Thanks for the support, Kuroshio, but I don't know if I

can do it," said Darek. "I mean, if that darkness really isn't from Martir, then even I might not be able to stop it. And besides, look at how awkwardly I swim. I'd probably get killed as soon as I entered."

"Kuroshio and Auratus will escort you into the darkness," said Yorak, nodding at her two students, though she didn't look happy about it. "They have volunteered to help you in whatever ways you need."

Darek looked at the two in surprise. "You mean you two are willing to risk your lives just to help me? But why?"

"To protect our school," said Kuroshio, saying each word carefully, as if he was trying to make sure he got them right. "Right, Auratus?"

The only response Auratus gave was a smile and a brief nod of her head. She then pointed at her magic stone on her ankle, which Darek noticed was a deep black.

"Auratus will be particularly useful to you, most likely, because she is a fuscimancer, and a very good one at that, too," said Yorak. "This darkness may not be from Martir, but Auratus's control darkness should prove helpful nonetheless."

Yorak did not sound at all thrilled at the idea of two of her students—one of them her pupil—going into the mysterious darkness, but based on her weary tone, Darek suspected that she must have already had had a long discussion (or argument) with Kuroshio and Auratus about this. Considering how Auratus was looking at her feet now and Kuroshio seemed to be distracted by a tiny fish that swam by, it was pretty obvious that neither of them wanted to start the argument all over again.

Darek folded his arms and looked up at the sky. Technically, of course, he was just looking at more water, as the Undersea didn't really have a sky; still, he looked up anyway, thinking about the offer.

"If you decide you want to go back home, that's your right," said Yorak. "But we already came to the aid of North Academy once. We think it only fair that you help us in our hour of need."

There was no arguing with that logic, so Darek said, "All right. I'll go into the Trenches and see what I can find. If there's anything there that shouldn't be, I'll get rid of it."

Yorak smiled. "Wonderful. All we need to do now is get you your own magic stone. Then you, Kuroshio, and Auratus can go into the darkness. May the gods protect you always."

Chapter Seven

Frankly, Durima didn't see any reason why someone would want to live on the island known as Ruwa, because as soon as she and Aorja teleported onto the island, Durima was assaulted by the humidity of the tall jungle in which they had appeared. It was in sharp contrast to the cool sea breeze that had blown through Durima's fur back on World's End; it was so humid that Durima felt like she could barely breathe.

Thankfully, they were just on the edge of the jungle, because Durima could see what appeared to be a tiny, rundown village just beyond the treeline before them. She caught pale-skinned, dark-haired humans passing between small, muddy-looking huts that comprised the village, humans that looked practically nothing like Aorja. She also smelled something like human waste and sewage somewhere, though it was hard to tell where that stink was coming from because it seemed to be everywhere at once.

"We're here," said Aorja, spreading her arms to indicate the trees all around them. Then she lowered her arms and frowned. "Well, okay, technically we're not actually in Deeproots yet, but I don't like teleporting directly into the village. I don't like surprising the villagers like that."

"Deeproots?" said Durima, covering her nose so she didn't have to smell the stink anymore. "What is Deeproots?"

"That village just beyond the treeline," said Aorja, gesturing at the huts that Durima had seen earlier. "The villagers call it that because they claim to be descendents of the original settlers of Ruwa. Still a stupid name, though."

Uron didn't seem bothered by the stink at all, though that was probably because he wasn't physically there like she was. He just stood there next to Durima, looking a bit off-put, probably because he thought this side trip was an unnecessary detour on their journey to the Old Ruins. Durima would have smirked at his annoyance, but she wanted to avoid arousing Aorja's suspicions, so she didn't.

"You live in the village?" said Durima to Aorja, nodding at the huts just beyond treeline.

"Of course," said Aorja. "I may be a wanted criminal hated by everyone, but there's no need for me to rough it in the wilderness. And anyway, I am on very good terms with the villagers. Let's go and say hi."

Aorja went walking through the mud, her boots squelching in the slop underneath. Durima did not hesitate to follow, as she thought that she might be able to escape the stink and humidity of the jungle by walking out into the open village.

Aorja must have defined 'good terms' differently than Durima, because almost the minute they walked into the village, every last villager who had been outside of their huts ran. The scrawny, pale-skinned, dark-haired humans took off toward the jungle just outside of the village, not even bothering to go for the safety of their homes.

Those few mortals who had not been outside when Aorja and Durima entered Deeproots slammed shut the chipped and broken shutters of their windows. Durima even heard noises from the doors that sounded like they were barricading them, though with what, she didn't know, as she doubted any of these poor, scrawny little things owned any truly heavy furniture.

In less than a minute, Deeproots went from being a small, though fairly lively, village, to a ghost town that might have been abandoned for decades for all the activity it showed.

"I thought you said you were on good terms with them," said Durima, looking at Aorja in surprise. "Why did they all run as if you were a southern goddess?"

Aorja smiled the smile of a madwoman. "Oh, that's just a game we play. When I enter the village, they all go and hide in the jungle or in their houses. If I can't find them all, they get to live another day; but if I can find them all, then I slaughter the whole lot of them. Sounds like fun, doesn't it?"

Psychotic, more like it, Durima thought.

"I think it sounds like fun," said Uron, who still stood by her side. "Though tiring. There must be at least fifty of them here, maybe more. It must take a long time to find them all."

Durima wanted to glare at Uron, but knowing how strange it would look to Aorja if she glared at empty air, she just satisfied herself with muttering, "Shut up, Uron."

"What was that?" said Aorja.

"Nothing," said Durima, shaking her head. "Now, where is your friend? The one you said we needed to pick up on our way to the Old Ruins?"

"In my hut," said Aorja. She pointed over the thatched roofs of the huts. "Mine's all the way on the other side of the village, so we'll have to walk to it. Shouldn't take long; Deeproots is a pretty small place, after all."

"And rundown," Durima observed, looking at one of the huts that had a hole in the roof that appeared to have been there for quite some time. "It looks like the gods themselves have condemned this place. What happened here?"

"Eh, Ruwa got ruined by some dumb king or something a long time ago," said Aorja, waving off the thought like it was irrelevant to their current discussion. "I don't know. All I know is that there is no law, no order, and no rules; therefore, I can do almost anything I want.."

Aorja looked at a nearby hut. While all of the huts in Deeproots were tiny, unimpressive, and decayed, this one in particular looked as if it had been abandoned for years. It had no door or windows, not even those terribly thin, cracked shutters used by some of the inhabitants of Deeproots.

Durima didn't know why Aorja was looking at it until she drew her wand out of her wand belt and pointed it directly at the hut.

Then, without so much as a hint as to what was going to happen, the entire hut blew up. Durima crouched low to the ground as the hut's roof soared through the air like a flying boulder. Huge tendrils of flame ate at the rest of it, whirling around in the air like octopus tentacles.

Though the hut was dozens of feet away, Durima could feel the heat as clearly as if she was standing right next to it. She took several steps back, while Uron simply watched the flame with interest. Only Aorja did not move a muscle, as if she saw this sort of thing every day.

Above the roar of the flames, people shouted and screamed in the other huts. Some of the flames fell on the roof of a nearby hut, causing it inhabitants—a father and his young daughter—to burst out the front door and head for the jungle so fast that they were gone before Durima even blinked.

A moment later, Aorja lowered her wand and the flames vanished. Only a darkened patch of earth remained where the hut had stood, as well as a thick pile of ash that produced an even thicker trail of smoke.

"What was that for?" said Durima, looking at Aorja in horror. "What did that hut do to you?"

"Nothing," said Aorja, sounding a little disappointed as she put her wand back into her belt. "I just thought that someone might be hiding in there. Looks like it was empty. How disappointing."

Then she began walking into the village, her shoulders slumped as if her day just could not get any worse. Durima got over her shock quickly and ran to join her, though she kept behind the mortal mage to avoid having to talk with her.

Uron, meanwhile, was stroking his chin, his tiny nostrils occasionally dilating as if he was taking in smell of the smoke. Walking alongside Durima, he looked down at her and said, "You know, I am starting to rethink killing this woman. She is so vicious, so powerful, so ready and willing to do anything that she needs to. Maybe I will spare her life and let her live in the old world, when I bring it back to its original glory."

Durima scowled, glancing over her shoulder at the blackened, burning remains of the abandoned hut. She then said to Uron, keeping her voice as low as possible so Aorja wouldn't hear, "I thought you wanted to destroy *everything*."

"You're right," said Uron, nodding. "What was I thinking? Aorja would be out of place in my world. She is a psychotic soul, an active volcano good for nothing more than laying waste to everything around her. She would be more trouble than she's worth, to be honest."

That Uron had apparently seriously considered sparing Aorja at all didn't surprise Durima all that much. Considering how mad he was, she could see the two of them being best friends if only Uron didn't want to destroy everything Aorja knew and loved.

Maybe they could even get married, Durima thought. *They'd probably kill each other on their wedding night, though.*

After only five minutes of walking—during which Aorja did not blow up more abandoned huts in an attempt to murder innocent villagers, though she fingered her wand anyway—they arrived at yet another hut, this one set apart from the rest. It looked a little nicer than the rest of the village; it had actual glass windows, for one, though they were cracked and broken in several areas and dirty in the places where they weren't; a wooden door, its red paint almost completely chipped off; and a roof that had no holes in it at all, mostly because it had been hastily patched in several places with boards of various lengths and widths.

There was even what appeared to be a tiny flower garden in front of the hut. It had little variety; mostly red-tipped flowers, with a handful of yellow ikadori flowers that seemed out of place in this bleak place.

"Here we are," said Aorja, spreading her arms as they approached the hut. "Home sweet home."

Then she stopped and put her hands together. Durima stopped just behind her, uncertain what she was going to do, while Uron folded his arms across his chest with a smirk on his face.

"Oh, Zeeree!" Aorja called. "Zeeree! I'm home!"

Durima had no idea who or what 'Zeeree' was until the front door of Aorja's hut burst open—almost flying off its squeaky hinges—and a disturbing being, bent over to avoid smashing his head against the door frame, dashed out.

The being looked like a monstrosity of nature, like something from the imagination of a mad, dying beast. Its legs were metallic, like the legs of an automaton, but rusty and loose, as if it had not been cleaned or repaired in years. From the waist up, however, it was like some kind of disgusting ogre, with a fat belly, green skin, and the most lopsided mouth Durima had seen on any living being. Its eyes were very simple and small.

The giant creature—whatever it was—stopped before it accidentally crushed the flowers in the garden. As though it had been trained to do this, the giant creature stepped around the garden. Then, slowly but surely, it resumed walking toward them, looking almost like a dog happy to see its owner again.

Durima walked up to Aorja's side and looked at her. "What in the name of every god on Martir is that?"

"A half-god," said Uron in a disbelieving voice, now standing right behind both Durima and Aorja.

"My pet," said Aorja in the voice of a proud pet owner. "And servant. He's ugly, but he's also very obedient and strong, right, Zeeree?"

The giant creature stopped when it heard its name. Then it nodded enthusiastically, like it had somehow understood what she had just said, though Zeeree could just as easily have been responding to Aorja's kind tone.

"It's a half-god," said Uron, looking directly at Durima now. "One of the few that managed to escape World's End after I was banished into the ethereal. I thought that the gods had destroyed them all already, but I can see that a few managed to escape alive."

"I found him about a week after I came here," Aorja continued. "He was wandering around, terrorizing nearby villages, killing innocents and stuff. Everyone wanted him dead and they even asked me to kill him, but I couldn't bring myself to do it. Look at how innocent he is."

Zeeree lifted up his left foot and looked under it. One of the yellow ikadori flowers from the garden was smashed under his foot and stuck to his heel, which he had no doubt stepped on accidentally in his answer to Aorja's calls.

He then peeled the flower off the bottom of his foot and stuffed it in his mouth like it was a delicious candy. He chomped on it hard, with a satisfied look on his face that told Durima that the failed creation of the Powers thought he had done a pretty good job at whatever he thought he was doing.

"How did you tame him?" said Durima, still staring at the strange half-god. "He's bigger than you. And stronger, too, by the looks of those muscles."

"True, but he's not very smart," said Aorja. "After I gave him a little display of my power, he very willingly chose to serve me, like the good pet he is. He's much happier obeying my orders than he was running around on his own, scaring and killing villagers for no reason."

"Taming a half-god," said Uron, shaking his head. "I never, ever expected to say this about any native Martirian, but I am impressed. Maybe I should seriously consider sparing her life, after all."

Durima did not look at Uron when he said that, again because she didn't want to arouse Aorja's suspicions. Nonetheless, Aorja impressing Uron, even if unintentionally, only supported her earlier theory that the two of them belonged together.

Aloud, however, she said to Aorja, "Do you want to bring Zeeree with us?"

"Yes," said Aorja, nodding. "I don't feel right leaving him alone in this village."

"Why?" said Durima. "Because you are afraid he will kill everyone?"

"Of course not," said Aorja. "I just don't want him to be alone, that's all. Besides, I think he will be very useful for our trip to the Old Ruins, since we have no idea what's down there. He's strong enough to beat anything."

Durima glanced at Uron, wondering if he would agree, seeing as he knew more about what awaited them in the Old Ruins than they did. He was still shaking his head in disbelief, muttering under his breath in a language that Durima did not understand or recognize.

How did I ever get in this situation? Durima thought. *Tinkar must hate me or something, though I don't know what I did to make him give me such an awful fate.*

"So is Zeeree the only 'friend' of yours that we need to bring with us?" said Durima, cocking her head at Aorja.

"Pretty much," said Aorja. She smiled at Zeeree again. "He's the only person I trust. Even then, he wasn't always this sweetheart you see before you. And sometimes he lapses back into his old ways, like the time he got a thorn stuck in his palm."

Durima looked at Zeeree, who was now distracted by a small buzzing silver beetle flying around his head. He swatted at it, but his movements were slow and clumsy, while the silver beetle darted around as quick as a sea darter around his head.

"You don't think he could be a liability, do you?" said

Durima.

"Zeeree? A liability? Of course not," said Aorja. She huffed and brushed her bangs out of her eyes. "He is the most helpful half-god I've ever met. Much better than Darek or Jakuuth or the Ghostly God, at any rate."

"Uh, sure," said Durima. "Well, now that we have Zeeree, don't you think we should continue our journey to the Old Ruins now?"

"All right," said Aorja. "Stop badgering me like that. I didn't forget about it, don't worry. Just let me run into my house real quick and grab a few things I had forgotten."

Durima didn't object, although she heard Uron groan impatiently beside her. She just watched as Aorja ran past Zeeree, brushing her hand against his belly lovingly as she ran, and into the interior of the hut.

The God-killer fell on Durima's shoulder, causing her to look up at Uron. A strange, urgent expression had crossed his face, like he had something important to tell Durima that he could not put off any longer.

"What?" said Durima, though she made a conscious effort to keep her voice low so that Aorja wouldn't hear her from inside her hut. "I can't talk to you. Zeeree is listening."

She pointed at the half-god, although he proved her claim false by continuing to attempt to swat at the silver beetle. When it flew in front of his face, Zeeree smashed his fist directly into his nose, sending him staggering backwards, though he managed to recover in time to catch himself before he fell onto Aorja's garden.

"He doesn't understand a word you're saying, most

likely," said Uron, his voice the same volume it always was. "The half-gods are barely rational creatures, more like beasts than mortals. We can talk freely until Aorja returns."

"What do you even want to talk about?" Durima demanded, glancing at the open door to Aorja's hut just to make sure that the psychotic mage wasn't standing there listening to her every word. "If you're going to ask me to ask Aorja to marry you, you've got another thing coming."

"Matrimony is the last thing on my mind at the moment," said Uron. He leaned toward her closer, as if he feared someone might eavesdrop on their conversation. "The Void is the more pressing issue."

"What about the Void?" said Durima. "Don't tell me you have a crush on 'her,' too."

"Crushes are trivial in the grand scheme of things," said Uron. He stopped, like he had heard something, and then continued. "You know how I and the Void are technically working together? It's hardly the strongest alliance, but it is so far working out for both of us."

"Yes, and?" said Durima, still glancing at Aorja's hut. "What of it?"

"She's gone and betrayed me," said Uron. "She has begun advancing on Martir despite previously agreeing only to do so *after* I escaped the ethereal. Even worse, I can sense that she's using her darkness to obscure the entrance to the Old Ruins in an obvious attempt to keep me from entering it. The witch."

Durima blinked skeptically. "How do I know you're telling the truth?"

Uron immediately grabbed her head before she could react. A second later, Durima saw a vision of the darkness of the Void creeping toward World's End from across the sea inch by inch.

Then the vision faded and Durima shook her head. She looked up at Uron again, her vision slightly disoriented from the mental image he had shown her.

Uron was scowling now. "She must be getting stronger ever since I weakened the bonds that the Powers used to keep her in check, so she probably doesn't think she needs me anymore. And of course, she also most likely doesn't want me to destroy Martir; after all, she has made it clear to me several times that she wants Martir more than anything."

"How will this affect our journey to the Old Ruins?" Durima asked.

"Depends on how actively she fights against us," said Uron. "But knowing how obstinate she can be, I have no doubt that she will be the most difficult obstacle standing between us and the Old Ruins by far."

"What do we do about it?" said Durima, scratching her arm. "Do we give up?"

"Of course not," said Uron, shaking his head. "We keep going. I will not spend the rest of my years in the ethereal, not when I am so close to freedom. We will do whatever we need to do in order to get to the Old Ruins, no matter who or what stands in our way."

"Is that why she's blocking the entrance to the Old Ruins?" said Durima. "Do you think she's afraid of you?"

"She certainly doesn't want me getting in her way," said Uron. "But whether she is afraid of me, I do not know. All I know is that she will learn that she has made a very, very bad mistake in double-crossing me, once I am free again."

He said that last sentence with a hungry sort of viciousness, as if he was thinking of exactly how he was going to punish the Void once he was out of the ethereal. His serpentine tongue shot in and out of his mouth as he said that, a disturbing sight to Durima.

Then Aorja appeared at the door to her hut with some kind of rucksack over her shoulder and waved at Durima as she said, "All right, Durima, let's go! The day isn't going to last forever, after all."

She sounded so cheery and upbeat, as if she could not wait to get started. Durima, on the other hand, wondered if she could possibly try running at this point, but then dismissed it as fruitless. There was no going back now at this point, no matter how much she might have wanted to. She would have to keep going, regardless of what lay ahead.

Chapter Eight

Darek readjusted the glowing white magic stone strapped to his chest every now and then as he swam. Despite having assured Kuroshio and Auratus that the strap they had given him fit his torso perfectly, he found swimming with it awkward. The magic stone itself was rather light; nonetheless, Darek was completely aware of its smooth surface tight against his chest at all times. He wondered how Kuroshio and Auratus swam so easily, seeing as their magic stones had to be strapped at least as tightly to their bodies as his was.

I guess they're just used to it, Darek thought as he shifted the strap again. *They probably grew up learning how to use it, after all. I wonder how they would handle using wands instead.*

Ahead of the trio was the beginning of the Trenches, a wide, pitch-black gaping canyon entrance that looked like the maw of a giant monster. Every bone in Darek's body was screaming at him to run away, to never look back, as if the darkness itself was trying to repeal him. And it wasn't just basic fear, either, but an instinctive fear he had no rational answer to except to keep swimming.

Even Kuroshio and Auratus seemed afraid, because he noticed that they didn't swim quite as quickly or gracefully as they usually did. He was just grateful that they were by his side; even his Limitlessness could not override his instinctive fear of the shadows entirely.

Just take it easy, Darek, Darek thought. *This darkness might not be from Martir, but you can still handle it. You've faced Uron, after all, and survived, so you can probably handle a little bit of shadow too.*

Of course, the last time Darek had fought Uron, he had lost miserably. It made him grateful that Uron was currently stuck in the ethereal, a threat to no one. If Uron was still running around free as well, then Darek would have probably lost all of his confidence completely.

In just a few minutes, Darek, Kuroshio, and Auratus arrived in front of the blackness of the Trenches. Darek tried to sense if there was anyone in the darkness, but he sensed absolutely nothing at all on the other side, which worried him.

"All right," said Darek as the three of them floated in front of the shadows. "Remember the plan. We go in, find whatever caused this darkness, deal with it, and then leave. If we're smart and quick, we should be able to get out of there before the sun sets."

Kuroshio frowned. "Trenches big. Takes days to travel. Sometimes weeks. Still not fully explored, too."

"Well, why don't we pray to Dranyx and ask for some of her luck?" said Darek.

Kuroshio's frown became confused, while Auratus

blinked those large eyes of hers as if she was not sure she had heard him correctly.

Darek sighed and said, "I forgot. You guys have different names for the gods than we do. By 'Dranyx,' I mean the Goddess of Luck."

"Oh," said Kuroshio, nodding in understanding. "Us call her Goda. Not sure if possible to get, though. Gods not answering."

Darek remembered what Yorak had said about not being able to contact the gods, and shrugged. "Eh, it doesn't matter. As long as we are careful, we should be in and out of the darkness in no time. We just need to be smart, that's all."

"Every student went there was smart," Kuroshio said. He nodded at the shadows as he said that. "Smart doesn't guarantee anything."

"Even so, we should keep our guard up at all times," said Darek, patting his magic stone as he spoke. "Be ready to use any spells on anything we might run into."

Both Kuroshio and Auratus nodded and checked their own magic stones to prepare for entering the darkness. Once they made sure their stones were securely strapped to their bodies, Kuroshio said, "We ready."

"Good," said Darek. "Then follow me."

Entering the darkness of the Trenches was unlike stepping into normal darkness. It was deeper than pitch-black, worse than the Black Nights that sometimes fell over the Great Berg during winter, and it was completely silent, aside from the sounds of Darek, Kuroshio, and Auratus swimming through the water. Even that seemed muted, however, as if the shadows were like a sound-dampening blanket.

Not only that, but Darek had the strangest feeling that they were being watched. He sensed a presence just outside of his reach watching their every movement. He even thought he felt it in his soul, as if it was slowly filling his body up with sand and mud. It made him shudder, but he said nothing because he didn't want to attract the attention of any monsters that might have been lurking within.

Auratus swam ahead of him; he couldn't see her, but he could hear her legs swishing through the water before him, felt the bubbles she kicked back across his face. He had no idea if Auratus could actually see in this darkness. He wished they had some way of communicating; he knew she could use telepathy, but considering how she had not shown even the slightest hint of being able to speak Divina, that was a fruitless thing to worry about.

Darek also heard Kuroshio behind him, swimming at a steady pace. This made him feel a little safer, as it lessened the possibility of something attacking from behind, but he now worried for Kuroshio's safety.

Anything could happen in here, Darek thought. *And if that giant eel is somewhere nearby, then I am not so sure even my power will be sufficient to keep us safe.*

So Darek prayed a brief prayer to Xocion, asking him to grant them safe passage through the darkness. He didn't sense Xocion respond, but that was okay because Xocion rarely responded to his prayers anyway.

Then behind him, he heard Kuroshio whisper, "Darek, stop."

Without waiting, Darek came to a stop, knowing that if Kuroshio was asking him to stop, then his friend most likely had a very good reason for it.

"What?" Darek whispered back. "Did you hear something?"

"Auratus tell that creature nearby," Kuroshio explained. "Must be still so won't see us."

Darek gulped. "What kind of creature?"

"Not clue," said Kuroshio. "Quiet."

Darek shut his mouth, but he didn't know how to swim quietly. He barely knew how to swim at all. He just hoped that the creature, whatever it was, would pass by without noticing them. He wished he could at least see it, though considering how frightening the giant eel had been, he wasn't so sure he wanted to see what else might have hid in this darkness.

Somewhere nearby, just to Darek's left, were vibrations in the water that he recognized as the sound of the creature's movement. It seemed to be moving slowly, whatever it was, but it was impossible to tell for sure just how close it was. He found it hard to judge distance in this place, mostly due to the shadows.

Then he smelled something like tar in the water, a stink that would have made him gag under normal circumstances, but Darek had to keep as quiet as possible in order not to attract attention. The smell was so overwhelming that all he wanted to do was swim as far away from the creature as possible.

He couldn't even hear Kuroshio and Auratus now. It was like they had been swallowed up by the darkness, even though he knew they they were probably still in front and behind him as before. Most likely they had simply learned how to swim silently, a skill Darek wished he had picked up at some point himself.

You just never know what you are going to need sometimes, Darek thought.

Then Darek felt something long and slimy rub against his thigh. The sudden slimy sensation surprised Darek so much that he kicked out instinctively, striking something soft and squishy, and causing the creature, whatever it was, to growl in pain.

As soon as Darek registered his mistake, a dozen tentacles latched onto his arms and legs, followed by that thick tar smell funneling up his nose. He yelled in surprise and kicked and beat against the creature, but he only succeeded in making it hold onto him ever more tightly. Its suction cups burned where they touched, like a stove top, draining him of the strength he needed to swim.

Around him, Darek heard Kuroshio and Auratus moving through the water, probably trying to figure out how to free him without hurting him, but it was no use because the monster was dragging him deeper and deeper into the darkness. Darek continued to struggle, but he made no progress until he remembered the magic stone strapped to his chest.

Then he closed his eyes and focused on it. Earlier,

Kuroshio had explained to Darek that the magic stone allowed a user to channel magical energy through it, if they wished. It also offered protection for a mage's hands if they decided to channel their energy through their hands, but as Darek's hands were currently stuck at his side, he would have to channel his magic directly through the stone itself.

Drawing as much magical energy as he could, Darek unleashed a beam of ice-cold energy directly at the beast. He heard the ice strike straight and true, heard the monster roar in agony, and then felt its tentacles' grip weaken around his body.

Ripping his arms and legs out of the monster's grasp, Darek swam backwards and fired another ice beam from his chest. He heard it strike the monster, heard the monster roar again, and then heard it swimming off, though it sounded slower now, as if half of its body was frozen solid.

Bet it is now, Darek thought as he rubbed the sores on his arms that had appeared after the monster's tentacles had let go. *Just as it deserved, too.*

A hand fell on his shoulder and Darek, whose nerves were already on edge from being attacked like that, whirled around to fire another ice beam before he heard Kuroshio say, "Darek! There you are. Thought might be hurt."

Darek relaxed when he heard Kuroshio's voice. He also felt someone swimming nearby, no doubt Auratus, as Kuroshio did not seem worried and it didn't sound like anything else.

"Okay?" said Kuroshio. "Feel fine?"

Darek almost nodded instead of speaking aloud before

remembering that Kuroshio was just as blind in here as he was.

So he said, "Sort of. I'm not dead, which is great and all, but I have these awful sores on my arms and legs. They might go away on their own, but I just don't know for sure."

"Need to heal," said Kuroshio. "Too dangerous to plow ahead wounded."

"It's fine," said Darek. He rubbed the sores on his arms, which still burned, though not as badly as before. "All perfectly fine. We just keep going forward. The sores aren't a big deal."

"If say so," said Kuroshio, although he sounded skeptical. "Bad idea use magic in dark, anyway. Not panamancer. Nor Auratus."

"Right," said Darek. "But will we still be safe? What if other creatures in the darkness heard my tussle with the monster?"

"Not idea," said Kuroshio. "Maybe come, maybe avoid. No way know sure, so why worry?"

"Because we can't see in the darkness," said Darek. "Except for Auratus, but she's mute, so communicating with her is a bit difficult, obviously."

"That be why we can't let guard down," said Kuroshio. "Why you be quiet. Silence is friend."

"Guess you're right," said Darek. He still rubbed the sores on his arms, though the ones on his legs hurt, too. "Maybe I should cast a quick pain-relief spell on my arms and legs. I'm no panamancer, but I know a few basic spells for just this sort of situation."

"Very well," said Kuroshio. "Be quick. No time to waste."

Darek nodded, but before he could cast the healing spell on his limbs, Kuroshio grabbed his arm. Feeling Kuroshio's powerful hand grab his forearm so suddenly like that made Darek pull back involuntarily.

Then Darek felt another hand grab his other arm: Auratus's hand, gripping his previously free arm as tightly as a claw. Then they both began pulling Darek away in some random direction, and fast, too, as if they were in a hurry.

"Hey," Darek protested as they dragged him through the water. "Where are you two taking me? What's going on?"

"Auratus saw other monster," said Kuroshio's voice from the darkness, hard to hear over the water rushing in Darek's ear. "*Big* monster. Maybe eel."

Horror rose in the pit of Darek's stomach as he remembered the giant eel's glowing green fangs and large yellow eyes. He ceased protesting immediately, because he was in no mood to see that creature again, not if he could avoid it.

"Where are we going?" Darek asked, straining his ears to hear the giant eel. "Are we going to hide somewhere?"

"Auratus saw cave," said Kuroshio. "Too small for monster to fit in. Hide in it. Should be safe."

"What if it's home to some other sea monster?" said Darek.

"Chance worth taking," said Kuroshio.

Darek opened his mouth to say that it actually might not be a chance worth taking when he saw two large, green curved swords glowing in the darkness behind them. Then two huge yellow orbs opened up just above the green swords, the malevolent eyes of the eel.

A low hissing sound emitted from the eel's throat before it opened its mouth and shot toward them like a raging baba raga. Darek jerked his arms out of Auratus and Kuroshio's hands and swam down as the eel barreled by overhead. He was afraid that it might have hit Kuroshio and Auratus as well, but then he heard a couple of beings swimming nearby and he knew that they were safe.

Darek whirled in the water, trying to spot the giant eel, but in the absolute blackness of the Trenches, it was impossible to see anything. He heard something huge moving through the water, but it wasn't until he spotted the eel's yellow eyes and green fangs again that he knew its exact position.

And unfortunately for him, it was coming right at him like it wanted to finish the job it started earlier today.

Darek didn't know if the eel recognized him or not, but he wasn't going to take any chances. He tapped his magic stone—a move that technically wasn't necessary but which he did anyway—and a burst of ice shot out of the stone, the force of the blast sending Darek spiraling backward in the water uncontrollably.

The ice chunk flew through the water toward the eel, but the eel twisted its body out of the way and the ice chunk flew past it out of sight.

Then the eel shot toward Darek again, opening its maw wide as it swam closer to him. At that moment, Darek unfortunately remembered what it had been like to be inside the *Soaring Sea II* when that eel had crushed it like a can and that thought paralyzed him where he floated.

But before the eel could swallow him, he heard Kuroshio yell to his right and then Darek felt his world shift around him. A moment later, he was back in the cold, black water of the Trenches, but he could no longer see the eel coming for him. He heard it barreling through the water nearby, but he no longer seemed to be in its path.

He wondered for a moment how that was until he felt Kuroshio's hand grab his arm and began pulling him through the water again, probably towards the cave that Auratus had noticed earlier. It was then that Darek realized that Kuroshio must have teleported him out of the eel's way, a feat his fearful mind somehow managed to be impressed by, as hands-off teleporting was a difficult magical feat to pull off.

"Help swim," said Kuroshio, his voice strained, as if he was putting all of his strength into dragging Darek along. "Kick! Going to cave. Auratus already there."

Darek didn't question that. He just kicked as hard as he could with his legs, but he was already worn out from all of the swimming he had done today, so he doubted his feeble kicks helped much. Still, he did it anyway because it made him feel less like deadweight.

From all of the thrashing about he heard in the shadows, Darek guessed that the giant eel was looking for them. He hoped it wouldn't find them; at least, he hoped that by the time it did, they would be deep inside that cave Auratus had found where it couldn't get them. Unless the cave mouth was big enough for the eel to enter, though he tried not to think about that.

Then Darek spotted a glow of yellow and green and he knew that the giant eel had found them. He kicked harder than ever, trying to speed up their progress even a little, but he had no idea how much he was actually helping or worse, if he was somehow getting in Kuroshio's way.

"Almost there," said Kuroshio, his voice so strained now that he was practically whispering. "Little closer ... closer ..."

A rumbling in the water told Darek that the eel was now coming at them at a frightening speed. He didn't need to feel that rumbling in order to know that, however, because he saw its eyes and fangs drawing closer and closer every second.

"I don't think we're going to make it!" Darek shouted at Kuroshio. "It's coming too fast and we're too slow!"

He felt Kuroshio's swimming slow down significantly. Alarmed, he shouted again, "Kuroshio, buddy, don't slow down, you idiot! Just because I said we're too slow *doesn't* mean—"

"Keep going!" Kuroshio shouted, cutting Darek off. "I hold back eel."

Before Darek could ask what that meant, he felt Kuroshio pull him ahead of the aquarian student so that Darek was now in front of him. Then Darek felt Kuroshio's hand on the small of his back, and felt a surge of magical energy hit that same spot. The next moment, Darek was hurtling through the water towards only Xocion knows what, unable to control his trajectory or speed.

Darek was hurtling too fast to speak, but he did manage to turn his head and see the eel's eyes and fangs in the shadows. Kuroshio's outline was visible in their glow for just a second before the eel clamped down on it like a piece of candy.

Then Darek, before he could really register what he saw, hit something thin and organic. He realized it must have been Auratus, because he felt her hands grabbing him and dragging him through the water, though he paid little attention to that. He was too busy staring at the glowing eyes and fangs of the eel as it chomped on Kuroshio.

"Kuroshio!" Darek cried out. "No!"

He tried to fight against Auratus's hands, but it was no use because she held him tight and he was too tired to break free. He wanted to avenge Kuroshio's death, even though he doubted that he could do much against the eel. That didn't matter, however, because his mind was aflame with rage at the thought of losing one of his friends.

A moment later, however, the eel made a strange, shuddering sound as if it was about to throw up. Then a second after that strange sound uttered from its mouth, the eel exploded into heat and flames, flames so bright that for a moment all of the darkness in the Trenches was dispelled and Darek was briefly blinded.

He could still hear the eel's screeches of pain, a sound so satisfying that it was almost enough to dispel the grief in his heart over the fact that Kuroshio had died killing the eel. Almost.

Thus, Darek allowed Auratus to drag him deeper into the

cave, knowing that there was nothing else they could do for Kuroshio now except make sure that the mission—and by extension, Kuroshio's sacrifice—did not end in vain.

Chapter Nine

Normally, Durima liked to swim. It was one of the few advantages that she felt physical bodies genuinely had over spiritual bodies. Yes, she had a heavy, hairy body—not normally the kind conducive for swimming even in shallow waters—but she still enjoyed the sensation of the water flowing against her muscles anyway.

But Durima had never gone underwater before, as in, to the part of the world that mortals called the Undersea. She had never been employed by sea goddesses like Kano or the Kraken Goddess, so she had never had any reason to go down there. Even if a god or goddess had hired Durima to do that, she likely would have hesitated to do so.

The Undersea was a scary place; at least, if all of the legends and stories Durima had heard about it were true. Not only had it once been home to the Sleeping Beast, a massive monster that had frightened even the gods before its death at the hands of the Powers, but other dangerous sea monsters were said to dwell down there, in addition to lethal natural phenomena like underwater volcanoes, plants capable of strangling prey, and the intense pressure of the water itself. Not to mention there was no air, which made it nigh impossible to go down there unless you were an aquarian or sea creature of some sort.

Thus, when Uron insisted that the entrance to the Old Ruins was located in the Undersea—more specifically, in a place known as the Trenches—Durima had hoped that he had been joking.

But no, he had not. After retrieving Zeeree, that bumbling oaf of a half-god, from Ruwa, Durima had given Aorja instructions on how to teleport them to the bottom of the ocean. Aorja had at first protested, saying that they couldn't breathe underwater and that even if they could, how would they navigate the darkest depths of the Crystal Sea without getting killed by all of the various dangers that lived down there?

For once, Durima agreed with Aorja. Indeed, Aorja's argument had been so well thought-out that Durima had thought that Uron might even agree with it and give up on this mad quest of his to escape the ethereal.

But Uron, of course, had already seen ahead and so knew exactly how to get around that little problem. He had given Durima information about how to cast a spell that, if done correctly, would give Durima and Aorja the ability to breathe and swim underwater as naturally as any fish.

That idea made Durima more than a little skeptical, to say the least, even though she had heard about such spells before. Nonetheless, she explained to Aorja how to do it and in a few minutes, the two were as amphibious as aquarians. Zeeree didn't need the spell, apparently because he could already breathe underwater for some reason.

When they teleported underwater, Durima almost panicked when she felt the water enter her mouth and soak her fur. Down here, the water was as cold as ice and so dark that she could barely see where she was, even after the transformation spell had increased her night vision to work in the darkest depths of the ocean.

Beside her, Aorja clung to Zeeree's back. Her eyes were wide with fear, her hair floating around her head as they floated above the grimy ocean floor, though since she obviously wasn't drowning, it was probably just her natural human instincts kicking in. That was also probably why she wasn't talking; she was too shocked by not drowning to utter so much as one word.

As for Zeeree, he didn't seem perturbed by the water, even though the Amphibious Spell had not been cast on him. That made Durima wonder if he had originally been intended to be some kind of sea god before the Powers abandoned him or if he was just too stupid to realize where he was.

And of course, Uron wasn't affected by the water at all. He simply looked around in interest, as if he had never been this deep underwater in his life, his yellow eyes following the progression of some kind of small green fish swimming by his head. What disturbed Durima most about his appearance was that he looked completely dry. Granted, it made sense, seeing as he technically wasn't here at all, but it looked strange to her nonetheless.

"I have always wanted to explore the deepest depths of the ocean," said Uron, looking down at Durima. "Too bad I won't be able to do that today. We must head for the Old Ruins immediately."

Durima raised an eyebrow, but she did not say the question she wanted to ask because she did not want Aorja or Zeeree to hear her speaking to Uron. Nor did she look directly at Uron, instead viewing him out of the corner of her eye.

"Why don't we just teleport there?" said Uron, in answer to Durima's nonverbal question. He gestured at Aorja. "As powerful as she may be, the Old Ruins are too far below Martir's surface for even the most powerful of mages to teleport into. A magical force field keeps out everyone who is not a god ... or me."

Then Durima cocked her head.

"It is still possible for us to enter via other means, even if teleportation is rendered useless by that force field I mentioned," said Uron. "There is a cavern entrance near here that should take us into a tunnel that will lead us down there. I will guide you and you in turn can guide Aorja and Zeeree."

How far is it? Durima thought.

"Not far from here," said Uron. He gestured ahead of them. "Keep swimming until you see the Trenches. They aren't hard to find."

Durima nodded and then turned to look at Aorja and Zeeree. "Come on. The Trenches aren't far now. We just need to keep going."

It felt strange speaking underwater. Her voice sounded distorted to her ears and air bubbles escaped from her mouth, so she didn't know how well Aorja understood her.

Thankfully, Aorja nodded and said, in a voice just as distorted by the water as Durima's, "Lead the way. Zeeree is a good swimmer. He'll follow."

So Durima began swimming in the direction where Uron had pointed. Uron swam by her side, even though she suspected that he didn't have to and that the only reason he did that was to avoid distracting Durima. In a few seconds, Zeeree swam by her other side, stroking his massive arms and kicking his thick metal legs as they headed further into the Undersea.

In just a few minutes, what appeared to be a massive sea trench appeared ahead, through the murky water. It was huge—she couldn't see the other side from their current position—and long, because it seemed to stretch on forever in each direction.

But what really caught her attention, more than anything else, was a familiar blackness in the trench that she had seen just earlier today. It looked blacker than midnight and reminded Durima far too much of that horrible day when Uron killed Hollech a month ago.

There was no doubt about it: That darkness inside the trench ahead of them was the darkness of the Void.

"See?" said Uron, smirking, probably in response to the realization dawning on Durima's face now. "I told you the Void was working against us now. I imagine she must have all kinds of terrifying little creatures lurking in her darkness. Maybe she even recruited a few of the remaining half-gods who were not slaughtered at World's End."

Durima glanced at Zeeree. The half-god did not seem to notice the Void yet, though that may have been because his tiny intellect only had so little energy to focus on anything except for his immediate actions. Aorja, still clinging to Zeeree's back, was squinting at the darkness, though she probably had no idea what its true nature was, seeing as she had never been inside the Void before.

"Thinking Zeeree will betray us?" said Uron. "That's a possibility, to be sure. The half-gods tend to follow whoever is the biggest and meanest leader around ... and the Void happens to be much bigger and meaner than Aorja, if you catch my drift."

Durima scowled, trying to ignore Uron, who she thought was just trying to shake her up for no reason.

"On the other hand, the Void may simply try to destroy him along with the rest of us," Uron continued. "The Void never struck me as the kind to let her enemies live, even if they once served her. I imagine she will see Zeeree the same as you and I and Aorja, but there is always that possibility that she may not."

Just tell me where the entrance to the Old Ruins is, Durima thought, directing her thoughts toward Uron.

"So you're going in there after all," said Uron. "I thought that after your previous failure in the Void, you would be too afraid to go back into it."

Not like I have much of a choice at this point, Durima thought.

"Quite true," said Uron. "Anyway, once we enter the darkness of the Void, keep swimming down until you reach the floor of the Trenches. Then head to the left and—you know what? I will simply tell you where to go once we get down there. How does that sound?"

Doesn't matter to me, Durima thought. *Just as long as we get there and don't get killed by whatever lurks in the shadows.*

"I doubt you will," said Uron, slapping her on the shoulder like an old friend. "You are Durima the Hero, after all, jailer of the evil Uron, savior of Martir and the gods. There's no problem too big for you to handle, especially with your trusty sidekicks Aorja the psychotic mage and Zeeree the dim-witted half-god."

Durima glanced at Uron with disbelief as they swam, but only for a moment, again to avoid arousing Aorja's suspicions. *For someone who wants to destroy Martir and everything on it, you are completely insane, you know that?*

Uron chuckled. "Just having a bit of fun is all, Durima. It was a reference to a favorite story of mine from my world. I should write it again once I destroy Martir, as I still remember it quite well. I am going to need some good entertainment to distract me from the blood of the gods that I will no doubt splatter all over my body."

Let me correct myself, Durima thought. *You're not insane. You're just morbid, like a serial killer.*

"All I want to do is bring back my home," said Uron. "What is so 'morbid' about that?"

Durima rolled her eyes, but said nothing in response. She just kept swimming, ignoring the deep, instinctual fear bubbling in the pit of her stomach as she swam nearer and nearer to the darkness of the Void that should not have been there but was anyway.

Although in truth, it wasn't so much an instinctual fear as it was a memory. Or maybe it was her memories of the place—memories of her time with Gujak—that supported her instincts. Either way, the feelings were almost too much, but Durima knew how to handle intense feelings, which meant ignoring them like ill-behaved children until it was safe to pay attention to them.

"Durima!" Aorja called, causing Durima to glance at her quickly. "Are we going into that darkness up ahead?"

Aorja's voice, Durima was pleased to note, was full of fear. No doubt Aorja, like every other creature in Martir, had a deep-seated fear of the Void. Had Aorja been swimming on her own, she likely would have turned and swam away by now.

Durima nodded. "Yes, we're going into that darkness. Be prepared; there could be anything in there."

"Zeeree isn't happy about it," said Aorja, patting her half-god pet on the back of his neck. "See?"

Aorja had a point. Zeeree's deformed face was twisted into a scared grimace, as if he also had bad memories of the Void. What those bad memories were, Durima didn't know. Maybe he remembered his friends being killed by their fellow half-gods prior to Uron uniting them or maybe, as a creation of the Powers, he also had an instinctive fear of the Void.

"It doesn't matter how Zeeree feels about this," said

Durima, shaking her head. "The only way we can reach the Old Ruins is by going directly into that darkness. Unless you want to abandon the power you need to get your vengeance on Darek, of course."

That worked like a charm. Aorja scowled angrily and returned her attention to the Trenches ahead, urging Zeeree to swim faster. Nonetheless, she looked less arrogant than she normally did, like she still wanted to run away and hide —an understandable feeling, though Durima did not feel any sympathy toward her for it.

Entering the Void a second time was as easily done as the first time. Durima did not feel anything stopping her; indeed, it briefly felt just like normal shadows, with no malevolent, ageless intelligence controlling it.

But then that coldness—the dead coldness of the Void— entered her bones and she found herself slowing down considerably. She could no longer see Uron by her side, nor Aorja and Zeeree, though she heard those two swimming nearby. She wanted to turn and flee, swim away until she was as far away from this darkness as possible, but she did not.

Uron's voice floated out of the darkness on her right. "I do not sense anything nearby. Though of course, the Void probably already knows we're here. She senses everyone who enters her. There is no such thing as 'sneaking into' the Void."

Uron's incessant talking made Durima nervous, but she followed his directions anyway. She said to Aorja and

Zeeree, "We're going to keep swimming downwards. Stay as close to me as you can so we don't get separated."

"Easy for you to say," said Aorja's voice from somewhere behind her. "This darkness is as thick as mud. Can't even see Zeeree's neck hair, for the gods' sake."

"Zeeree can see," said Durima. "Right, Zeeree?"

She didn't actually know if Zeeree could see or not. She suspected that his status as a half-god somehow granted him the ability to see in the Void's darkness, but she did not know for sure. At least he should have an easier time maneuvering through the shadows than Durima, anyway, unless he happened to be even dumber than he had initially seemed.

But then Durima heard a low rumbling sound in the water, followed by Aorja saying, "Zeeree can. That's his affirmative rumble."

"Good," said Durima. "We'll need as many eyes and ears open as we can while we're done here. No telling what might attack."

"I doubt anything will," Uron said. "Though if the Void decides to send her minions after us, there is very little we can do to stop them."

"Shut up," Durima snapped. "You're not helping."

"I didn't say anything," came Aorja's indignant voice from somewhere behind her, the words hard to understand in the water. "Maybe *you* should shut up."

Durima rolled her eyes. "I wasn't .... oh, never mind. We all need to be as quiet as mice if we are going to get to the Old Ruins. We should not attract any unnecessary—"

She was interrupted when she heard the sound of something swimming through the water toward her. It moved swiftly and without delay, almost like a missile. Not only that, but it was so loud that it sounded as if it was coming from all sides, making it impossible for Durima to figure out what direction she should defend from.

A moment later, the teeth of some kind of sea animal sunk into her right arm. The pain that jolted her brain made Durima cry out as she swung her other arm at the creature, but the impact of her blow was lessened by the water and her own inexperience in underwater combat.

In fact, her free fist didn't even hit anything at all. She felt the teeth let go of her and heard whatever it was that had attacked her retreat back into the darkness. Her fist ended up uselessly hitting the water as the scent of her own blood filled her nostrils. She slowly began to sink, as the pain in her arm had distracted her too much to swim.

"Durima, what was that?" Aorja asked. "Did something get you?"

"I don't know," Durima said, grabbing her bleeding arm, trying to stem the flow of blood. "Something with sharp teeth. Keep your ears open. It might come after you next."

"What did it look like?" Aorja said, her voice full of worry and panic. "Was it big and dangerous?"

"How am I supposed to know?" Durima said. "It's pitch-black in here, for the gods' sakes. It might have been as big as a mountain for all I know. Why don't you ask Zeeree? He probably saw it."

"I doubt it," said Uron. "It left too abruptly for Zeeree to see it. Even I didn't catch more than a glimpse of its appearance; a scaly hide, teeth sharp as knives, and fins like swords."

Durima tried to picture the animal Uron was describing, but she could not recall having seen anything like that before in her life. Not that it mattered much. The creature was still here somewhere, probably waiting for another opening so it could finish the job, which meant she had no time to visualize its appearance right now.

"Zeeree, if you see anything, kill it right away," said Aorja, the worry and panic in her voice replaced by anger. "Show these dumb fish why we humans rule the—"

Her sentence was interrupted by a blood-curdling, gargled and distorted screech that made Durima sink even further in surprise. The screech was followed by Zeeree roaring, the sound of something heavy flying through the water, and then the sound of something small and lightweight hurtling past Durima's right ear, so close she could practically taste it.

"Aorja, what happened?" Durima asked, looking over her shoulder in the general direction in which she had last heard Aorja and Zeeree. "Are you all right?"

"I'm ... fine," Aorja said, though her voice sounded weaker now. "Bastard tried to tear off a chunk of my shoulder. Think Zeeree got a good hit on him, which is why he ran away. Good Zeeree."

Zeeree made a happy sound, while Durima continued to hold her wounded arm and kick her legs in an effort to stay afloat. She tried using some panamancy on her arm, casting a basic healing spell, but it was too dark for her to see the full extent of her damages, so she could only do so much to stem the leaking blood from her arm.

A little help here? Durima thought, hoping Uron would hear her.

"Sorry," said Uron. "I'm not much of a healer, and even if I was, I couldn't heal you anyway. Don't forget that I'm not actually here, even though you may be able to see me."

How could I forget? Durima thought with an angry snort that sent bubbles out of her nose. *You're useless.*

Uron didn't respond to that, probably because Durima was right and he didn't want to admit it. She returned her attention to her wounded arm, which was bleeding less now that she was using magic to heal it, but she also remained aware of her surroundings in the event that the creature from before was still around.

Not like there's much I can do against it, if it is, Durima thought. *If it attacks now, I doubt I'll be able to defend myself.*

That was when Durima felt a slight disturbance in the water. It wasn't like someone was swimming nearby; no, it was like someone was speaking, as if words were vibrating along the water and into her ears. It was a voice she had heard only once before and had hoped to never hear again.

Halt, the voice said. **Do not go any further, intruders, or you will never leave my realm alive.**

"Durima?" said Aorja's confused voice. "Who is talking?"

I am talking, said the voice, sounding annoyed. **I, what you mortals refer to as the Void.**

"The Void?" said Aorja. "Impossible. The Void can't talk. You must be someone pretending to be the Void."

How dare you accuse me of lying, said the Void. **The Void does not lie. The Void speaks the truth always.**

"This is unexpected," sad Uron, sounding more intrigued than afraid. "I didn't think she would actually talk to us. I thought she would just send her minions after us instead."

That I will do, Uron, in good time, said the Void. **But first, I must warn you to leave my domain. I have claimed this part of the mortal world as my own. I have already disposed of many mortals who dared to intrude on my territory and you will go the same way if you do not leave immediately.**

"Uron's in the ethereal," Aorja said. "He's not here. And what do you mean, *your* territory? The Trenches belong to the aquarians, don't they?"

They belong to whoever is strong enough to lay claim to them and defend them from others who want them, the Void replied. **And I am the strongest being in all of Martir at the moment, even stronger than your pathetic, trivial gods. Go against my will, and suffer the consequences.**

"Oh yeah?" said Aorja, though her voice trembled just the same. "And what might these 'consequences' be, O fake Void? Are you just going to make it even darker? Or have your pets bite us a few more times?"

The Void's voice sounded like it was all around them now, though that was no surprise, since the Void was the darkness in which they swam. **Very well. I will grant you a glimpse of the consequences I inflict upon those who dare trespass my domain. Behold.**

Without warning, the darkness of the Void vanished beneath Durima, allowing her to see the bottom of the Trenches for the first time. She also noticed Aorja and Zeeree floating nearby, Aorja clutching her injured shoulder, though she barely paid them any attention.

Down below, lying in the mud of the bottom of the Trenches, were what initially appeared to be whitish gray sticks connected together in ways that made them appear humanoid. There were dozens, if not hundreds (though they were all too mixed together for her to tell for sure), of these whitish gray sticks, most of which looked like aquarians if their fish-shaped heads were any indication.

"I don't get it," said Aorja. "What are we looking at? What's so scary about a bunch of white sticks?"

Then Durima looked again and finally understood what she was looking at. She didn't want to—indeed, she hoped she was wrong—but the more she thought about it, the more she realized that that was the case.

"Those aren't white sticks in the mud, Aorja," said Durima with a shudder, the pain in her wounded arm flaring up suddenly. "Those are bones ... bones of all of the aquarians that the Void has killed."

Correct, said the Void, though it said that without any glee. **And soon, your bones will be the first human and katabans bones to join the rest of them, once my minions are done with you two—though I**

cannot guarantee that your bones will be as complete as these ones, of course.

Chapter Ten

Darek and Auratus swam through the strangely deep cave that they had hid in to escape the giant eel. Though the explosion was long over by now, whenever he blinked, Darek still thought he saw the eel exploding into flames upon swallowing Kuroshio. He wondered if Auratus was thinking the same thing, though due to the darkness obscuring her features and her own inability to speak, he doubted he would ever know for sure.

Neither of them had tried to communicate with the other since Kuroshio's death. Partly because they had no reliable way of doing so, partly because they were both still overcome with grief at Kuroshio's sudden passing. Granted, he had died a hero, maybe even taking the eel with him, but that didn't make his death any easier to take.

First the Magical Superior, now Kuroshio, Darek thought, his heart aching at the thought of those two recent deaths. *I guess both of them died doing the right thing, but to hell with that. I want them both back, I want them both alive and well. It's not fair that they had to die in order to save us.*

As angry and confused about Kuroshio's death as Darek

may have been, he knew better than to allow his emotions to cloud his thinking. He could not forget their mission, which was to find out what was going on here, and to correct it if possible. There would be time to mourn Kuroshio later, in a way that would be more appropriate than cursing the gods, as appealing as that seemed right now.

Besides, Auratus didn't seem to be letting Kuroshio's death stop her. In the darkness, Darek heard her swimming as normally as ever. He doubted she had already made her peace with his passing, but he still felt jealous of her apparent ability to keep going and not look back.

I should ask her how she does it, Darek thought. *Then again, will I be able to understand any answer she gives me?*

That was when he heard another voice in his head, a voice he had never heard before in his life. It was small and timid, speaking as haltingly as a child just learning how to speak for the first time.

It took him a second to realize that it was Auratus's voice, communicating with him telepathically. She was saying, *Rest?*

Even in his head, Auratus's voice had that distinctly aquarian accent to it, although it was much thicker than Kuroshio's, which made it harder to understand.

It took him a moment to understand what she meant by that one word, but once he did, he replied with a mental *Yes.*

The two landed onto the floor of the tunnel—which was

what Darek suspected this 'cave' to be—to rest for a while. Darek hadn't realized it, but his whole body was bone tired, like he had been working nonstop in a quarry for hours. The ground was soft and muddy beneath him, but it wasn't as disgusting or uncomfortable as it sounded.

Yet even as Darek sat there, he found it hard to rest. He did not want to be attacked from the shadows by some strange sea monster. He did not hear, smell, or sense any nearby, but he knew enough about marine life to understand how hard they were to detect even for aquarians; thus, he kept one hand on his glowing magic stone, which was freezing to the touch due to the cold magical energy flowing through it, as a way to remind him to keep his guard up at all times.

He wished he could see Auratus. Despite knowing that she was there, he felt completely alone in the tunnel, at the mercy of whatever sea creature that might come along. He just wanted to have the visual assurance that he was indeed not alone.

Then he heard Auratus's voice in his head again. *Kuroshio ... dead.*

The pain in her voice was as obvious as it was heart-wrenching. Darek had forgotten that Auratus and Kuroshio had likely been friends for years, maybe even decades. No doubt she was hurting even worse than he was, which made him feel silly for thinking she was less affected by it than he was earlier.

So he responded aloud, "Yes, he is. Do you miss him already?"

Yes, was her one word answer.

"He died for a good cause," Darek said, trying to keep the sadness out of his voice. "I don't know how he pulled off that explosion or whether he knew it would work, but he did it anyway, just so we could live. He must have really cared about the Institute a lot."

No answer at first. Darek figured Auratus was probably trying to dissect what he said. She seemed to have an even worse grasp of Divina than Kuroshio, but that was okay. He was just glad that they were able to talk like this. It made him feel less alone and terrified.

Then came her halting, jerky answer. *Did ... a lot. Kuroshio loved school. Yes.*

Darek nodded, even though he knew that Auratus couldn't see him. "Yeah. He told me he was going to East Yudra after he graduated, to study under some mage call Eerk Dah. Guess he'll never get to do that now."

Yes, said Auratus. *Never. Miss him.*

"I know," said Darek. "I know."

He would have said more—although he wasn't really sure how much there was to be said, as he didn't know as much about Kuroshio as he would have liked—but then a small, bright light flashed out of the corner of his eye.

His heart beating fast, Darek whipped his head in that direction, already drawing the magical energy from his magic stone in case the light turned out to belong to a threat. While Darek was rarely the 'shoot first, ask questions later' guy, he thought that that attitude might be prudent in a world where everyone and everything could kill you if you weren't careful.

The light further down the tunnel—which Darek now noticed sloped downwards—was faint and white. It was too far away to see what was generating the light, but it was bright enough to allow him to see Auratus's outline and some of her facial features, which calmed him down somewhat.

"Should we go back?" said Darek, pointing back the way they'd came. "Or should we go see what that light is?"

Auratus shook her head. *Forward. Eel back. Danger.*

Darek understood and agreed. While the eel was probably dead or at least seriously wounded by the explosion, it most likely was safer to investigate the light's source. At least they would be able to see it if it was a threat; going back out into the darkness of the Trenches would simply leave them exposed to whatever creatures lurked out there.

After readjusting his chest strap again, Darek stood up and began swimming toward the light. Auratus swam to his right, but she kept pace with him, even though she could have overtaken him if she wanted. No complaints there; Darek liked having her by his side, as it made him feel safer.

The light grew brighter the closer they drew to it, though it was hardly blinding. They still didn't see what was generating the light, however, until they were about two dozen or so feet away from it.

Lying in the muddy, dirty floor of the tunnel was what appeared to be an aquarian man. A pair of spectacles—with golden frames and shining, though cracked, lenses—lay on the ground next to him, as if they had been knocked off. An aquarian book was on his chest, though the cover had no title or any other information to identify it.

Even odder, however, was the light shining on his fist. Even though the aquarian man appeared unconscious, his body somehow continued to generate luminimancy. That didn't make any sense, seeing as magic was impossible to maintain if you were unconscious, but Darek was starting to think that this man, whoever he was, was hardly a normal mortal.

"Auratus, do you know who this guy is?" said Darek, looking at his friend. "One of the students who originally explored the Trenches? Auratus?"

In the dull light given off by the unconscious aquarian's fist, Auratus's goldfish-like face looked as if she had been sucker-punched without warning. Her eyes kept scanning the unconscious aquarian's body, as if she could not believe what she was looking at.

"Auratus?" Darek repeated. "Hello? What's up?"

Not mortal, Auratus's voice rang in his head like a bell. *A god.*

Darek's eyes widened and he looked back down on the aquarian man lying on the tunnel floor. He almost said that Auratus was wrong, but then he sensed the immense magical power practically gushing forth from the unconscious aquarian's body. And he could sense that the being was not using even half of his power right now, probably due to being unconscious.

"You're right," Darek said in a low voice. "No mortal, not

even a Limitless, can generate that kind of magical energy. Only a god can."

Right, Auratus said. *Why here?*

Darek shook his head. "I have no idea. Do you know who this god is, at least?"

Auratus shook her head. *Not sure.*

"Well, let's try to awaken him, then," said Darek. "If we can wake him up, I'm sure that he will tell us how he got in this position. Maybe he'll even be able to help us find out where all of this unnatural darkness came from."

Auratus grabbed Darek's arm, causing him to look at her in surprise. Her eyes were wide, maybe with warning, maybe with fear, and she said, *Bad news.*

"How is he bad news if you don't even know which god he is?" said Darek. "Worst case scenario, he turns out to be a southern god. Even then, he won't be able to eat us; remember, we're north of the Dividing Line, so none of the southern gods can eat us here even if they wanted to."

Auratus frowned like she hadn't understood a word Darek had said. Which seemed likely, given her lack of understanding of Divina, but Darek didn't think it was necessary to try to explain to her what he just said in simpler terms.

So he wrenched his arm out of her hand and swam down to the unconscious god. Auratus hung back, looking worried and uncertain, but Darek saw no reason for her to be that way. If they had a god on their side, the Trenches would be much easier to explore. Darek would feel safe for the first time since entering this treacherous part of the ocean, so it seemed like a worthwhile risk to him.

He now swam above the unknown god, who still had not moved a muscle since Darek and Auratus's discovery of him. The god's face was oddly human, despite the fish-like skin, especially with his eyes closed. He almost looked like he was taking a long nap.

Awakening him should be easy, Darek thought. *Just shake him until he wakes up. What could possibly go wrong?*

Danger, Auratus's voice in his head said. *Bad danger.*

If you could be a bit more specific than that, I'd really appreciate it, Darek thought back.

Auratus did not respond, probably because she didn't know the best words to use to describe in greater detail what she was trying to tell him. Darek knew she only had his best interests at heart, but he thought she was being too cautious, maybe even a little bit silly.

So Darek reached down toward the unconscious god and prodded his shoulder gently.

As soon as he did so, the god's eyes shot open, revealing not actual eyes, but empty sockets, like someone had gouged out the god's eyes long ago. A strong hand flew up and grabbed Darek by the neck, causing him to choke as the god's slimy, muddy fingers tightened around his neck.

"Trying to kill me while I'm down, are you?" said the god in a paranoid, conspiratorial voice. "Oh no you don't, you servant of the Void or Uron or whoever. I may not be the strongest god in the world, but it still won't take much for me to turn you into dust and scatter you across the sea floor like so much sand."

Chapter Eleven

The darkness of the Void closed up underneath Durima, obscuring the graveyard on the ocean floor. Not sure what else to do, Durima swam toward Aorja and Zeeree, thinking that they would be safer together than apart.

She reached out and grabbed Zeeree's arm as Aorja said, "What do we do now? The Void's gonna kill us!"

Durima shook her head hopelessly, but then Uron said, "Durima, tell Aorja and Zeeree that we will continue swimming to the entrance to the Old Ruins. We are not far from it now, so it shouldn't take us long to get there if we hurry."

"Just keep swimming down, like we did before," said Durima. Her arm still hurt, though she ignored it for now. "If we stay still, that will make it that much easier for the Void to—"

She was interrupted by the sound of something large and thick hurtling through the water toward them. It was impossible to tell where it was coming from, but Zeeree swam downwards as if he had heard and understood everything Durima had just said. The large and thick thing, whatever it was, raced by their heads, Durima feeling the water it left behind them rushing by.

Durima held onto Zeeree as tightly as she could as the half-god swam surprisingly fast considering how much weight he was hauling. Aorja hurled all sorts of human curses at the Void that Durima did not know, but which she understood the meanings of well enough. She didn't hear Uron at all, but she knew that he was probably right by her side, either amused by their fear or angry at the Void for getting in their way.

A hot, sticky tentacle slapped against Durima's arm as they swam, but she managed to swat it away before it could grab her. Then she heard Aorja scream before a loud explosion followed, which was probably Aorja casting some kind of spell on whatever had tried to get her, though it was hard to tell in the darkness.

"We're getting closer," Uron said in Durima's ear as Zeeree swam faster than ever. "Tell Zeeree to go a little to the right, and we should enter the tunnel with no problem."

Durima did not know if she could trust Uron, but she said to Zeeree anyway, "To the right, you big lummox, to the right!"

Zeeree must have heard her because he did in fact move to the right, though that may also have been because Durima had also been poking the side of his face to get him to turn.

Then, without warning, they barreled into something that felt like steel netting. It cut into Durima's skin as Zeeree pushed against it, making her feel like she was being crushed. The netting, if that was what it was, must have been incredibly strong because it held even with Zeeree struggling against it.

You cannot escape me, said the Void. **No one can. Soon, all of Martir will be consumed by the Void, which is the ultimate fate of everything. Fighting against that is foolishness.**

"Watch out!" Aorja called from somewhere above Zeeree. "I got this!"

A glowing red laser shot out of the darkness, probably from Aorja's wand, and cut through the netting holding them back. The netting collapsed as Zeeree surged forward like a bullet, kicking his powerful legs so fast that they sounded almost like a motorboat zooming through the water.

Then a loud, irritating screeching sound assaulted Durima's ears and she felt what might have been a piranha biting at her legs. But it was only for a moment, because Zeeree was now going so fast that they soon left the fish behind.

"Almost there," Uron said, the anticipation in his voice as thick as the darkness of the Void. "Just a little closer ... a little closer ..."

Without warning, Zeeree shuddered and veered to the right sharply. Durima knew they weren't on the right path anymore because Uron was shouting, "No! You idiot! Wrong way, wrong way!"

But Zeeree didn't—couldn't—hear Uron. It was impossible to tell where he was going until they crashed, quite abruptly, into the dirty sea floor.

The sudden crash sent Durima flying off Zeeree's arm. She spun crazily through the water, unable to control her trajectory, the water in her ears making her deaf to everything until she hit the sea floor and rolled to a clumsy stop.

Durima's skull felt like it had been cracked open like an egg. She rubbed the back of her head as she sat up, wincing as she felt the bones of the dead cutting into her behind and thighs. Her sense of direction was completely messed up; she had no idea where she was or where Aorja and Zeeree had landed.

But she did hear Uron, who was saying in her ear, "Get up, get up, you dumb katabans! Don't just sit there like an idiot. Get to Aorja and Zeeree and then to the Old Ruins!"

"But I don't know where they are," said Durima, feeling like a child trying to justify her actions to her mother. "They could be anywhere."

"Just follow my directions," Uron snapped. "By the Alignment, I wish I was actually here because then I would be able to slap that thick skull of yours."

"Am I bleeding?" Durima asked, feeling the back of her head, though underwater it was hard to tell whether that was blood or just warm water. "Can you tell?"

"It doesn't matter if you're bleeding or not, you stupid katabans," Uron shouted. "Now, unless you want the Void to kill you, stop whining and start swimming!"

Scowling, Durima nonetheless obeyed Uron's command. She pushed herself off the sea floor and began swimming forward because she could feel Uron urging her to go in that direction. She assumed that that was the direction that Aorja and Zeeree were in, but she was so tired and weak that she did not know for sure.

"On your right!" Uron shouted.

Durima ducked, feeling something long and spidery pass by overhead, but then Uron shouted, "Left! Your left!"

This time, Durima rolled out of the way. Something sizzling zipped by her, burning so hot that she felt its heat even though it didn't even brush against her. She shuddered at the thought of what that might have done to her if she hadn't avoided it in time.

"Aorja!" Durima shouted. "Zeeree! Where are you?"

The answer she received was what sounded like skin being ripped in half, followed by a pungent scent of blood that filled her nostrils like a toxic fume.

"Yeah, Zeeree!" Aorja's voice vibrated through the water. "Teach those bastards what happens when they mess with a Limitless mage and her servant!"

Aorja's sounded extremely close by, so Durima reached out and grabbed one of her skinny human arms. It was at first reassuring to feel the arm of an ally; at least, until Aorja shrieked in fear and Durima felt Zeeree's strong, thick hands manhandle her.

"Hold it!" Durima shouted, beating her hands and feet against Zeeree's grip. "It's me! Aorja, tell your stupid pet to let me down before he tears me apart!"

"Zeeree, hold!" Aorja shouted. "Let her go. Durima's a friend, remember?"

As soon as Aorja said that, Durima felt Zeeree's hands let go of her. She swam up out of Zeeree's reach and shouted, "Come on, you two! It's not far now. Just a little further, and we'll be safe."

"We're coming," said Aorja, sounding annoyed. "Feeling better, Zeeree?"

Zeeree roared, an echoing sound that was loud even underwater.

"Then let's go," said Durima, turning around as she spoke, "before it's too—"

Once more, she heard something swimming through the water toward her; this time, it was coming at her too fast for her to dodge. A strong fist, like the fist of a trained boxer, slammed into Durima's jaw, sending her spinning head over heels through the water before two powerful hands grabbed her legs and spun her around before throwing her away.

Like before, Durima went hurtling uncontrollably through the water, though with far less understanding of why than before. She slammed into what felt like a rock wall, the impact stunning her and making the back of her head feel like mushed eggs now.

"Excellent," said Uron, who no longer sounded as bothered as he had earlier. "That being who threw you hurled you right next to the entrance to the tunnel that leads to the Old Ruins. How thoughtful of the Void to do that."

Durima didn't think that getting punched in the jaw and thrown into a rock wall was very 'thoughtful,' but she did not say that aloud because she heard something coming at her again—probably whatever had just tossed her—and she moved out of the way just in time. She heard whatever it was crash into the rock wall, giving Durima what she believed was the perfect opportunity to attack it.

Channeling as much of her magical energy as she could, Durima slammed her fist into the rock wall, using her geomancy to find where the being was. When she located it, she forced the rock wall to enclose around it, like a second skin, hoping to crush it beneath the rock.

But just as she felt the rock begin to enclose the being, the sound of rock getting smashed into pebbles followed. A moment later, a slimy, sticky hand grabbed her by the throat and slammed her against the rock wall again. The blow made the back of her head hurt so badly that she could barely think. Even worse, the being was now constricting its fingers around her throat as if attempting to choke her.

Die, you fool, the Void hissed, her voice sounding much closer now than before. **Why do you resist? The Void is the natural state of all things. Return to it. Embrace it. Embrace *me*.**

It was no use. The strong fingers were crushing Durima's neck. She wasn't sure if she could choke underwater, but she realized she would die anyway if the being choking her managed to break her neck.

Then the sound of something large rushing through the water entered her ears, followed by Zeeree's familiar roar. The fingers around her throat vanished, the pressure lifting rapidly, and with it, the pain, too.

Gasping involuntarily, Durima heard Zeeree hurl the

being through the water as Aorja shouted, "Durima, where is the tunnel entrance?"

"Not far," Durima said, her voice weak. "Just to my right, I think. Zeeree can take us."

"All right," said Aorja. "Zeeree? Go into the cave on Durima's right!"

Zeeree's powerful hands grabbed Durima and hauled her to the right. It was still too dark to tell, but Durima felt them enter a much more enclosed space, like a tunnel, although she also heard creatures following right behind them.

"Zeeree, block off the entrance!" Aorja ordered.

Durima felt Zeeree shift her to his right hand, which made him wonder what he was going to do with his left hand until she saw a burst of bright green energy lance out of the darkness and strike the top of the tunnel entrance. The sound of crumbling rubble and the angry roar of some unknown sea monster on the other side told Durima that the entrance had indeed been blocked off.

I should probably praise the gods for that, Durima thought. *But since it was technically a half-god who did it, maybe I shouldn't.*

"You don't need to praise anyone, Durima," said Uron, the glee in his voice evident. "Because now that we're past the hardest part, the rest of the journey should be much easier from here on out."

Durima said nothing in response to that because she was too tired to do even that much. Meanwhile, Zeeree was still rushing through the water as if his life depended on it, even though they were now safe in the tunnel.

"Zeeree!" Aorja shouted again. "Stop! You're going too fast."

Abruptly, they came to a halt in the water. The sudden stop made Durima's stomach churn, which didn't help her aching head. She just pried Zeeree's fingers off her body and floated down onto the tunnel floor, feeling too tired to swim.

"Let's rest here for a bit," said Durima. "I need you to look at my injuries, Aorja, and heal them if possible. How much panamancy do you know?"

From somewhere above Durima, Aorja said, "Only some basic healing spells. Panamancy was never my strong suit, so I can't do anything very complicated."

Durima sighed in frustration. "It doesn't matter. Just do the best you can. I don't think it's safe for me to go any further until you heal me."

"Very well," said Aorja, sounding annoyed. "Just let me get some light on in here. I can't see anything."

A sudden light—as bright as sunshine—erupted near Zeeree's head, causing Durima to look away to protect her vision. She had been in the darkness for so long that even the dimmest light seemed too bright to her, although she was grateful for it just the same.

Aorja swam down next to her. It was the first time Durima had seen Aorja since they had entered the Void's darkness. Aorja was missing her robes, the light from her wand revealing her thin, lithe body. The only pieces of clothing she now wore were a thick strip of red cloth covering her breasts and some shorts; besides that, she was naked.

"What happened to your robes?" said Durima as she held out her wounded arm for Aorja to inspect.

Aorja's scowl looked half-finished thanks to the shadows that her light cast on her face. "Something in the Void ripped them off me while I wasn't looking. Think it was trying to rip my arms off my body, but I let it have the robes instead. Not even all that inconvenient; those robes weren't all that great for swimming in anyway."

"It makes you look like a stick," said Durima.

"Is that any way to treat your partner?" Aorja asked in a mock offended voice. "Maybe I should just let your arm get infected if you're going to say mean things like that."

Durima sighed, bubbles emitting from her mouth, and said, "All right. I'm sorry. Now will you just heal my arm or not?"

"I will, I will, don't worry," said Aorja as she lowered her wand over Durima's wounded arm. "No way am I going any deeper into this tunnel without you in front."

"What, are you scared of the darkness now?" said Durima.

"No," said Aorja, shaking her head as white dust came from her wand and fell on Durima's arm. "I'd just rather risk your own life than mine. If there are any monsters in here, they can have you first."

Durima scowled, but said nothing to that, partly because she wanted Aorja to heal her, partly because the back of her head still hurt like hell.

Thanks to Aorja's light, Durima could now see Uron

again. He stood next to her, rubbing his hands together excitedly as he looked down the dark tunnel.

"I can hardly believe it," said Uron, his voice more gleeful than Durima had ever heard it. "Can hardly believe it. I thought for sure that your bumbling foolishness or maybe Aorja's idiocy would doom this mission, but if we have gotten this far, then maybe we have a chance at success after all."

Durima said nothing to that, mostly because if she did say something, Aorja would hear it and demand to know who Durima was talking to. Nonetheless, she felt uneasy about his happiness.

"There," said Aorja, sitting back. "Your arm should be better now. How does it feel?"

Durima held up her now-healed arm and looked at it from a few different angles. "It feels ... normal. It stings a little, though."

"Like I said, I'm not a panamancer, nor have I ever tried to heal a katabans before," said Aorja. "So don't be surprised if I didn't do all that great a job. It's not my specialty."

Durima rubbed her arm as she said, "Well, it will have to do for now. It's not like there's a hospital just down the street I could go to, right?"

"Right," said Aorja. "Well, do you feel well enough to continue, at least?"

"No," said Durima, rubbing the back of her head. "I feel like a baba raga sat on my head. I just want to sit and rest for a bit before we go any further."

Aorja frowned and sighed in disappointment. "Very well. Zeeree? Please be a dear and keep an eye on the tunnel. If you see anything dangerous, don't hesitate to let us know. Or just kill it and show us the body. Either way works."

Zeeree nodded and grunted to show that he understood. Then he swam beyond them and stopped in the center of the tunnel, looking like a big wall of fat, muscle, and metal more than anything. He folded his arms and did not look back at them, although Durima wondered if Zeeree was indeed capable of handling whatever might be lurking in this tunnel.

Her thoughts were interrupted when Aorja said, "So this darkness is the Void, then."

Durima looked at her. "What?"

Aorja gestured at the shadows being held back by her light, her arms making swirling sounds through the water as she did so. "You heard the voice. It claimed to be the Void, of all things."

"Oh," said Durima with a gulp. "Yes, I heard that. Hard to believe, isn't it?"

"Well, duh," said Aorja. "It's like if the sky started talking to us. Personally, I think that 'the Void' is someone else just pretending to be the Void in order to scare us."

"Maybe," said Durima. "I doubt it, though. I was in the Void once and this darkness ... it feels exactly like how the Void had felt. I believe this is the real thing, as hard to believe as that may be."

"Yeah, but what about that reference to Uron?" said Aorja. "She talked like Uron was actually here. He's not.

Does she think one of us is Uron or something?"

Durima gulped and glanced at Uron. He was still rubbing his hands together excitedly and did not seem to be paying any attention to their conversation, but knowing Uron, he was probably listening to every word.

"I don't know," said Durima with a shrug, in her most innocent voice. "I mean, no one ever said that the Void was sane, right?"

"Right, but she seemed to think he was with us anyway," said Aorja. "I don't even know how she possibly could have confused one of us for him. From what Zeeree has told me, Uron looks kind of like a humanoid snake."

Durima felt Uron looking at them now, as if he had just realized that they were talking about him. She didn't dare look at him, though, again to avoid arousing Aorja's suspicions.

"Wait, Zeeree can speak Divina?" said Durima, hoping to change the topic.

"Barely," said Aorja. "He doesn't have a large vocabulary or anything, but he knows enough to communicate with me. He just doesn't like talking in it is all. That's why you've never heard him speak around me."

"I see," said Durima. "I wonder how he learned that."

"I think he learned it from Uron, personally," said Aorja. "He used to be part of Uron's half-god army, after all. He probably knows more about Uron than any of us."

Beside Durima, Uron laughed, as if Aorja had just told a great joke. Durima didn't see what was so funny about what Aorja had just said, though she knew better than to ask while Aorja was around.

"He might," said Durima. "But even if he does, it's hardly as if that knowledge could help us. Uron, after all, is stuck inside the ethereal. And he's probably going to be stuck in there for a long time, maybe forever."

Uron stopped laughing. Durima would have smirked, but she did not. She did, however, give herself the pleasure of imagining how angry he must have looked.

"I know," said Aorja. "But from what I've heard about him, Uron was dangerously smart. Much smarter than any of us. I find it hard to believe that he is just locked up in the ethereal, unable to get out."

"Then you're paranoid," said Durima. "And paranoia never served anyone very well."

"It's not paranoia if it's based in fact," said Aorja. "Still, I guess you have a point. Maybe the Void was confused or something."

"Yes, probably," said Durima, nodding. "Maybe it mistook Zeeree for Uron. I don't know how anyone could possibly confuse the two, but hey, it's possible."

Of course, Durima wanted to say, *Actually, Uron is here, sort of, and he's having me manipulate you in order to get us to free him from the ethereal.*

But she could not bring herself to say those words. It was probably because of Uron standing beside her; even though there was nothing at all he could do to harm her, she still didn't want to anger him more than she already had. There was no telling what he, living inside her mind, could do to her.

And if I told Aorja I have been lying to and manipulating her all this time, she'd probably kill me in cold blood, Durima thought. *Or maybe have Zeeree break my back and let me slowly die in the ocean. And I would rather not die, at least not here and now.*

Aorja simply shrugged and sat back on the tunnel floor. She winced and looked down at the mud underneath her. "Ugh. Mud. Why can't this tunnel be a *clean* tunnel? Would it really kill the Void to get rid of this mud?"

That seemed like the most inconsequential, trivial thing to complain about to Durima at the moment, and she would have said so, before Zeeree started.

Aorja floated up in the water, holding her wand before her as she said, "Zeeree, what did you see?"

Just then, a loud, ear-ringing screech filled the tunnel, so loud that it forced Durima to cover her ears to protect them. Aorja also covered her ears, while Zeeree simply stood his ground, though based on the grunting noises he was making, he clearly was in some kind of pain as well.

And then the voice of the Void whispered in Durima's ears, like a burning hot wind, **Think you can get away from me, do you? Of course you can't. I am everywhere in this place. When I decide that someone within me must die, they die. And today, I have decided that you four must die.**

Chapter Twelve

The god's grip on Darek's neck was as crushing as a thousand pounds of rock. Darek couldn't even move because of the severe and intense pain that was ripping through his body. It was as though the god had found the exact spot he needed to grab in order to paralyze Darek.

Even worse, Darek could not talk and explain who he was. The god clearly thought that he was some kind of threat, even though he wasn't. Yet he had no way of informing the god of that, and if the god kept strangling his windpipe, he would never be able to tell him that.

"I will crush you like an egg, you little cretin," the god hissed, his eyeless sockets squinting. "Crush you like an egg, yes, I will."

Just as Darek was certain that he was indeed going to be crushed like an egg, the god cried out in pain and let go of him. The pain on his neck suddenly leaving, Darek swam backwards away from the god, rubbing the bruises on his neck where the god had gripped him, watching the god's arm, which was as black as death now.

Then Darek heard someone swimming nearby and he

looked over his shoulder and saw Auratus swimming toward him. She looked over him in concern before returning her attention to the god, who was now sitting up and holding his blackened arm as if it was made of clay.

"Thanks," Darek said to Auratus, his voice hoarse. "I thought I was a goner there. What kind of spell did you cast on him?"

Auratus nodded to show she had understood what Darek said. Then he heard her voice in his mind. *Sickness.*

"Ah," said Darek. "So you gave a god a disease. Amazing."

Auratus smiled sheepishly, but then the god growled in anger and his blackened arm immediately returned to normal. Darek thought the god would now try to attack them, but instead, the god began patting the mud around him, saying as he did so, "Where are my glasses? Damn things keep disappearing. Sometimes it seems like they grow two legs and walk off all on their own, the little bastards."

The god's gold-framed glasses still lay on the sand not far from him. Darek immediately used his telemancy to make the glasses fly from the sand and into his hands.

"Hey, god," said Darek, holding up the glasses. "I've got your glasses right here. And I will give them to you only if you agree not to destroy us."

"Are you blackmailing me?" the god demanded, his sightless sockets looking in their direction. "How dare you! I may not be the most important or well-known god in the world, but I am still a god of Martir. I should crush you where you swim, you little bottom feeder."

"I think there's been some confusion," said Darek, still holding the glasses. "We're not your enemies. I am a Xocionian Monk named Darek Takren. Auratus here is a student at the Undersea Institute; actually, she's the pupil of the Archmage herself. We both worship and honor the gods as best as we can. We do not want to hurt you."

"Then why did you take my glasses?" the god demanded. "No true mage of Martir would take away my glasses. Give them here."

"Only if you promise not to kill us," said Darek, holding the glasses close to his chest.

"Fine," said the god with a sigh. "I will not kill either of you. Just give me my glasses back."

Darek sensed that the god was telling the truth, but even if he wasn't, it was hardly like there was much Darek could do about it. The god probably had enough power to bring this whole tunnel down on them if he wanted. Better to give him what he wants.

So Darek threw the glasses toward the god, using telekinesis to send them back to their original owner. The god caught the glasses when they were within arm reach and put them on his face, adjusting them slightly as he did so.

When the god looked up, Darek no longer saw eyeless sockets through the lenses. Instead, he saw two sharp, blue eyes—almost human-like, which looked odd on the god's aquarian face—peering at him through the lenses, blinking as rapidly as if the god was seeing for the very first time in his life.

"That's better," said the god. "Now I can actually see, and I can see that you two are indeed mortal mages. My apologies for earlier. I thought you two might have been minions of my enemies, trying to finish me off."

Darek's neck still ached, especially the bruises made by the god's hands, but he nodded anyway and said, "Yeah, we understand. I guess you can't see without your glasses?"

"Not very well," said the god, "which is why I wear them. Additionally, they help me read every language in the world. Useful for a god like myself."

"Right," said Darek. "Well, maybe we should all introduce ourselves again, now that we have that figured out. My name is Darek Takren, a North Academy graduate and a Xocionian monk, as I said. And she," he added, pointing at Auratus, "is Auratus, a student at Undersea Institute and the pupil of Archmage Yorak."

"Darek Takren," the god repeated. "I seem to have heard that name somewhere recently. Weren't you the one who helped stop Jakuuth Grinfborn's invasion of North Academy and World's End?"

"I did," said Darek, scratching the back of his head. "Sort of."

"Yes," said the god, nodding. "Now I remember. When my siblings and I were talking about how to deal with Jakuuth, my brother the Ghostly God, suggested using you to infiltrate his Army and take him down from the inside. I admit I was skeptical that a mortal student could do it, but I guess that my brother had more faith in you than I did.

Funny, seeing as I am a northern god and he a southern god."

Then he looked at Auratus. "And I do believe I have heard of you as well. You were cursed by my sister, Amare, years ago, yes?"

Auratus looked away as Darek asked, "Wait, what?"

"You mean she hasn't told you why she's mute?" said the god in surprise. "I thought everyone knew that. But as I can see that she obviously doesn't want to talk about it, let's move onto a more pressing topic."

"But I don't understand," said Darek. "Why did Amare curse her? What did she do to earn that punishment?"

"As I said, why don't we move onto another topic?" the god said, in a sharper voice. "The exact details of an event that happened a while ago is irrelevant to our current situation. Right, Auratus?"

Auratus nodded, but still did not look at the god or Darek. As much as Darek wanted to know more, with both Auratus and the god unwilling to discuss it, he figured that it was probably not something to push at the moment. Maybe later, Auratus would feel more comfortable discussing it.

"All right," said Darek. "But, god, you still haven't told us your name or what your domain is."

The god patted the book on his chest. "I thought that was obvious; then again, I am hardly famous among you mortals, except among those of you who identify as linguists. I am known as Ranama to humans and Iknor to aquarians. In both languages, I am the God of Language, the Master Linguist and Decipherer of Lost Tongues."

"Oh," said Darek. "I see. Forgive me for not recognizing you right away, Lord Ranama. You just don't look like your usual human depictions."

"That's because this is my aquarian form," said Ranama, gesturing at his body. "I took on this form so I may travel underwater more efficiently. I did not expect to run into a human down here, though."

"Neither did we expect to run into a god," said Darek. "Tell us, Lord Ranama, what brings you all the way down here to the Undersea? More specifically, why were you lying unconscious in this tunnel?"

Ranama shuddered and looked around. "Oh, bollocks. I thought I was going to end up in the Old Ruins. The Void must have blocked me from teleporting directly into that chamber. Curse her darkness."

"Excuse me?" said Darek. "The Void? What do you mean by that?"

"I suppose I should start from the beginning," said Ranama with a sigh. "But it is a complicated situation that my siblings and I have found ourselves in, quite unlike any we've faced before. I will do my best to summarize it."

Ranama adjusted his glasses again, though it seemed to be more out of habit than necessity, and said, "You two may or may not be aware, but the evil being from the Prior World, known as Uron, has been banished into the ethereal."

"Of course we know that," said Darek. "Skimif told me about it personally."

"Good," said Ranama. "Yes, I remember Skimif said he was going to tell you. Anyway, weeks ago, Skimif called a meeting of the gods on World's End to discuss what to do with Uron. The meeting itself did not take place until earlier today, however, because we gods were busy taking care of the aftermath of Uron's attack on World's End."

"I remember Skimif mentioning that meeting to me as well," said Darek. "What happened after it? Did you guys come up with a way to deal with Uron once and for all?"

Ranama shook his head sadly. "No, we did not. As always when discussing matters of supreme importance among ourselves, we became divided and got into a huge argument about the best way to dispose of Uron. The argument ended quickly, however, when the Void trapped us in the Temple of the Gods."

Darek blinked and looked at Auratus. Based on her blank expression, she clearly did not understand what Ranama had said any better than Darek did.

"I should explain," said Ranama. "You see, the Void is not merely some strange natural environment that is hostile to mortal life. It has an intelligence of its own, one that the Powers kept at bay to prevent it from destroying Martir. But now the Void has gotten around the Powers's defenses and is steadily encroaching on Martir even as we speak."

"That's not good, is it?" said Darek.

"Of course it's not," said Ranama, pushing his glasses up the bridge of his nose. "And even worse, it has somehow already gotten this far north."

"Wait," said Darek, looking around the tunnel in alarm.

"Are you saying that we are actually inside the Void itself?"

"A portion of it, yes," said Ranama. "Normally, the Void is hostile to mortal life, but I suspect that this part of the Void is weaker than other parts due to its separation from the main source, which is why you two have not yet died."

Darek gulped. He now understood why he had been feeling weaker than usual while in here. He had thought it was because he was getting tired from all of the swimming, but he now wondered if it was because the Void was slowly killing him. It was a terrifying thought, to be sure.

"But can't you gods escape the Void?" said Darek, pointing at Ranama. "I always heard that only the gods could enter and exit the Void at will. And you're here, so obviously you found a way to escape."

"We could only do that when there was a firm boundary line between Martir and the Void," said Ranama. "But that boundary is quickly blurring, making it impossible to tell for sure where one ends and the other begins. As for how I escaped, I got lucky; we gods worked together to open a gap in the Void large enough for one of us to escape and I was chosen to do it. The gap closed after I escaped."

"Why you?" said Darek. "Wouldn't it make more sense to send Skimif instead? Not to disparage your abilities or power, Lord Ranama, but I would think freeing Skimif would be very important."

"Skimif insisted I go in his place," said Ranama. "He wanted to stay behind and work with the other gods on how to deal with the Void. He told me to go because he wanted me to go to the Old Ruins and find the secret to defeating

Uron once and for all."

Darek tilted his head to the side. "But isn't freeing the gods from the Void more important than going to whatever these 'Old Ruins' you speak of are? It's more urgent, at any rate."

"The Void can be dealt with," said Ranama. "As powerful as she is, that I succeeded in escaping at all proves that the other gods will eventually be able to deal with her on their own. But Uron ... he is a long-term threat and is most likely behind the Void's sudden expansion into Martir as well."

"This is all a bit much to take in at once," said Darek. "So Uron weakened the boundary between Martir and the Void, which is apparently an intelligent being, and this weakening of the Void's boundaries has allowed the Void to move in and trap the rest of the gods—except for you."

"Except for me," Ranama agreed. "You understand it all perfectly so far."

"And then Skimif sent you to go to the 'Old Ruins,' whatever those are, and find the secret to defeating Uron," Darek finished. "Just one question: What *are* the Old Ruins?"

"Remnants of Uron's world, from before Martir," said Ranama. "It's a place I know well because I have spent thousands of years attempting to translate the language written on everything in it. I have had little luck in understanding more than a few words, as the language is not Martirian."

"I see," said Darek. "Where are the Old Ruins?"

Ranama gestured down the tunnel behind him. "Down

this tunnel; though in truth, there are actually a series of underwater tunnels leading down to it. This is but one of many, though that does not make it easy or simple."

"Oh," said Darek. "So all we need to do is go to the Old Ruins and find the secret to defeating Uron?"

"It sounds simple, but I fear it will be slightly more complicated than that," said Ranama. "We do not know for sure if the Old Ruins even mention Uron. We assume that they do because the Old Ruins come from Uron's world, but again, that is just a theory. I believe it is a likely theory, but having had little success in translating the writings we have found there, we don't know for sure."

"All right," said Darek. "Then what were you doing lying here like you were attacked?"

Ranama rubbed the side of his face as if he had been punched there. "When I attempted to teleport directly into the Old Ruins, the Void intercepted my teleportation and I ended up here. I doubt I will be able to teleport into there now; the Void has likely made it impossible for us gods to enter that way."

"Why would she do that?" said Darek. "What does the Void care if you find out how to defeat Uron?"

"I believe she is an ally of Uron," said Ranama. "As I said, Uron helped to weaken the boundaries separating the Void from Martir. She probably thinks Uron will help her destroy everything; therefore, she does not want us gods to figure out how to kill him. After all, we gods can drive her back to where she belongs, which would no doubt ruin her plans for destroying Martir."

"I see," said Darek. "So how will we get to the Old Ruins now, if you can't teleport directly into them?"

"We will have to travel through the tunnel system leading down to them, of course," said Ranama. Then he frowned. "But when did *we* become involved in this? You two are mortals. The path to the Old Ruins is dangerous, even for us gods. I think it would be wiser if you two went back to wherever you came from and let me handle this on my own."

"I don't think we can," said Darek. "The Void tried to kill us not long ago by sending some of its minions after us. Going back now would be suicide."

"Then I will grant you my godly protection," said Ranama, holding out one hand. "It should be enough to keep you safe from the worst of it."

That sounded reasonable enough to Darek. Now that they actually knew what the problem was, he felt more comfortable handing it over to Ranama. Sure, he would have liked to have helped solve it, but after his failure to kill Jakuuth a while back, Darek thought it would make more sense to let the gods handle this situation.

He was about to ask Auratus if she agreed, but one look at her face told him what she was already thinking. She was frowning, even scowling, and she didn't look like she wanted to leave.

"What's her problem?" said Ranama.

He went silent for a moment; based on his expression, Darek assumed that Auratus was communicating with him via telepathy. Darek wished he could hear what she was saying to him, but even if he could, he probably wouldn't be able to understand it, seeing as Auratus was most likely speaking in Aqua.

Then Ranama stroked his chin. "I see. So you lost the life of a close friend of yours and you want to honor his death by completing the mission."

Auratus gave a short, cut nod, as if challenging Ranama to tell her to go home; that surprised Darek, as Auratus had never come across as that strong-willed to him.

"Well, I suppose it wouldn't hurt if you came along with me," said Ranama. "I would rather you not, but you might be useful or helpful at some point down the road, and anyway, I have no time to waste trying to make you go away. Darek, do you still wish to leave?"

Both Ranama and Auratus were looking at Darek now. The pressure of their gazes made Darek feel uncomfortable, to put it mildly. He still wanted to go back—after all, the situation would probably be over fairly quickly now that a god was handling it—but then he thought about what lay in the darkness behind him. The eel might have been destroyed by Kuroshio, but that didn't mean there weren't other kinds of dangerous monsters out there, especially if the Void was behind them.

And anyway, Darek realized Auratus had a point. Kuroshio had indeed given his life so that he and Auratus could complete the mission. To turn back now, just because a god was here? That would render Kuroshio's sacrifice useless, a thought Darek could not tolerate.

So Darek said, "No, Lord Ranama, I will come with you

and Auratus into the Old Ruins and help however I can."

"Very well," said Ranama. He waved his shining fist behind him. "Then let's go. We are lucky that the Void has decided, for whatever reason, not to attack us right now. Let's not push our luck any further by wasting time standing —or perhaps I should say *floating*, as that is technically more correct—around doing nothing."

That seemed like a good idea to Darek, but before he could say that aloud, the tunnel began shaking. Cracks appeared in the floor and ceiling, while vibrations floated through the water and made Darek's head ache.

"Oh, great," said Darek, looking around in alarm as a chunk of the ceiling fell off and landed on the tunnel floor below. "What now? Auratus, do the Trenches have natural earthquakes or is this something else?"

Auratus shook her head and two words—*Not natural*—echoed in his mind.

"The Void must be behind it," said Ranama, swimming to the side to avoid getting hit on the head by another chunk of falling debris. "She is trying to bury us alive. Quickly, we must swim as fast as we can unless you want to die an early death."

Neither Darek nor Auratus hesitated to swim after Ranama, who swam surprisingly fast down the tunnel. As they did, Darek heard the loud sound of the rock ceiling giving away, stone crashing into the sandy floor, slightly muffled underwater, but close enough that Darek kicked his legs harder to go faster.

But just as suddenly as it started, the shaking ended and

no more chunks of the ceiling fell. Ranama stopped abruptly, forcing Darek and Auratus to come to an awkward halt to avoid crashing into his back. It was especially awkward for Darek, who had to kick his legs and swing his arms unnaturally to stop himself.

"Why did the shaking stop?" Ranama asked, looking over his shoulder at the two of them in surprise. "I thought she was trying to kill us."

Darek almost said he didn't know, but then he looked back in the direction in which they came. Thanks to the light from Ranama's fist, he could now see that the exit was completely blocked off by chunks of rock. Darkness seemed to be leaking from the cracks in the rocks, as if it was a dam holding back a river of shadow.

"I don't think she was trying to kill us," said Darek, looking back at Auratus and Ranama. "I think she was trying to make sure we couldn't escape."

"But why would she do that?" said Ranama. He gestured at the narrow tunnel all around them. "It would not take her much effort to cave this tunnel in on us, I should think."

"I was going to ask you the same question," said Darek. "The answer, as far as I can tell, is as enigmatic as the Void herself."

Not up to any good, came Auratus's voice in his head in the longest Divina sentence Darek had ever heard her speak. *Herding us.*

Darek sighed. "Undoubtedly. Most likely, she's set some kind of trap up ahead that she wants us to swim into. Or maybe there's something down there already that could kill us and so she doesn't see the point in wasting time and energy doing it herself."

"That makes no sense," said Ranama. "I have been down this tunnel before. There's nothing down here that could kill a god."

"What about a human and an aquarian?" said Darek. "Mortals aren't supposed to be down here at all, right?"

Ranama again stroked his chin, as if he had never considered that before. "You're correct, but it still doesn't make any sense. I suspect the Void has different reasons entirely for keeping us down here, but what those reasons are, I don't know. I can only say that they are probably not benevolent."

"What choice do we have but to keep going forward?" said Darek with a shrug. "I mean, sure, we could use our magic to get out, but considering what is probably waiting for us on the other side, that may not be the wisest decision for us to make."

"I do not like this at all," said Ranama, his blue eyes darting cautiously around the tunnel, "but you are correct. We must go forward regardless. I already know what lies ahead, after all, so we should be able to handle it just fine. Follow me."

With that, Ranama turned and once again went swimming deeper into the tunnel. Auratus followed without hesitation, while Darek cast one last glance over his shoulder at the shadowy rocks and then followed after Auratus.

Ranama might know what was in here before *the Void*

came, but who says he knows what's in here after *she came?* Darek thought. *I just hope that the only thing she did was make this place darker than usual. Because if not ...*

He decided not to think such depressing thoughts. Better to focus on the here and now and take whatever would come as it came.

Still, he adjusted the magic stone strapped to his chest anyway. If there were any servants of the Void in here, then he would at least be prepared to fight them, if nothing else.

Chapter Thirteen

That irritating screeching sound assaulted Durima's ears like a battering ram. She couldn't hear Zeeree's roars, even though she could see him roaring in the light of Aorja's wand. Nor could she hear Aorja's curses or Uron, who was saying something; the loud screeching sound drowned it all out.

But she could hear the Void, laughing all the while, as if seeing them all suffer like that was her idea of high-brow comedy. Durima wanted to grab the Void and strangle it, but that was of course impossible because the Void did not have a physical form that she could strangle.

I will simply have to settle for whichever of her servants is currently trying to make us all deaf, Durima thought, though she barely heard even her own thoughts.

Then about a dozen long, blade-covered tentacles shot out of the darkness and wrapped around Zeeree's body. Zeeree struggled against them, pulling back as hard as he could, but the tentacles continued to drag him deeper into the shadows nonetheless.

That was when Durima realized that those weren't mere tentacles, but the shadows themselves forming physical tendrils in order to grab Zeeree. Looking up, she saw several similar shadow tendrils reaching down for her, causing her to swim away from their reach.

Or try to, anyway. The shadow tendrils shot toward her far faster than she could swim. One of them looped around her left ankle, throwing her off-balance long enough for the other dozen or so to wrap around her arms and legs and hold her still.

Don't think I've forgotten about you, silly katabans, the Void said in a hissing voice. **I know what you are *truly* doing down here, and I will not allow it. If I succeed in nothing else, I will at least kill you and end Uron's plan in the womb.**

Durima extended her claws from her fingers, but there was no way she could bend her wrists far enough to cut through the shadow tendrils. Even if she could, she doubted her claws were capable of cutting through pure shadow; extending her claws was a purely reactionary measure, and nothing else.

Nearby, Aorja was blasting away shadow tendrils that slithered toward her using bursts of lights, but the light bursts seemed weak and ineffectual. There were too many tendrils for Aorja to blast away; one of them got through an opening and slapped her in the face. The blow must have been stronger than it looked because it sent Aorja crashing into the ground, dropping her wand, its glow going out as soon as she let go of it.

Without Aorja's light, the tunnel plunged into the blackest darkness Durima had ever seen in her life. Even worse, the loud screeching sound made it impossible for Durima to tell how Aorja and Zeeree were doing. She had no idea if they were dead or still struggling against the Void's power.

You are all on your own now, little katabans, the Void said. **Yes, I remember you. I almost got you once. If it hadn't been for that skeleton, I would have gotten you for good. But now, there is no one to save you ... no one to save you and Uron from the fate you both deserve.**

All strength had left Durima's muscles now. She began to feel as sleepy as she had when she and Gujak had fallen into the ocean in the Void. The loud screeching sound no longer annoyed her; in fact, it was almost like an unusually screechy lullaby.

Sleep, said the Void. **Sleep and be no more.**

Durima almost closed her eyes—she was tired, after all, and hadn't had a good night's sleep in a long time—but then felt something stir in the back of her mind, something that poked and prodded her like might cattle.

"Don't sleep, Durima," said Uron, his voice somehow now audible even above the screeching noise. "If you sleep, you will never wake again. Those who listen to the soothing words of the Void never listen to anything else again."

Shut up, you pathetic snake, the Void snapped. **I will deal with you later, after I have successfully consumed all of Martir. I no longer need your assistance, now that I am free to consume and absorb as much as I please.**

"Good, because I did not want to renew this alliance anyway," said Uron. "But yes, please continue to believe that you will be able to 'deal with me.' The only reason *I* haven't dealt with *you* yet is because I am stuck in the ethereal."

Excuses, the Void said. **You are nowhere near as strong as I. No one is. Not even the gods can defeat me.**

"The gods are hardly a reliable metric for determining your strength in comparison to mine," said Uron. "The gods can't defeat me either, after all. Try again."

Durima barely paid attention to the argument between the Void and Uron. She didn't like listening to either of them, but in this situation, she understood that listening to Uron was paramount to her survival. That thought sickened her, and she considered going to sleep just to spite him, but her physical body's survival instincts kicked in, forcing herself to stay awake no matter what.

Must ... escape, Durima thought. *Must ... be ... some way ... to do that ...*

Unfortunately, she was too weak to break free on her own, and her mind was sluggish. It didn't help that Uron and the Void were bickering like an old couple (*No, I do* not *want that mental image*) and that irritating screeching sound was still blaring in her ears like the bleating of a goat.

I don't think there is a way out of here, Durima thought. *If only Uron actually had a physical body, maybe we'd have a chance. Too bad he's just in my mind where he can't do anything except annoy me.*

"Durima," said Uron, snapping her out of her thoughts. "Are you listening to me? There is a way out of this."

"What?" said Durima, though she did not look at Uron because it was too dark to tell where he was. "What do you mean? How?"

He lies, the Void said. **Do not listen to his lies. Sleep. Sleep the eternal sleep that all living beings must succumb to sooner or later.**

"Don't listen to her," said Uron, his voice more urgent than ever. "Durima, you can escape by becoming the Demon once more. Unleash your inner rage; unleash the Demon inside you that cannot be stopped by anyone, no matter what."

Durima did not even respond to that, mostly because she was too out of it to think. She didn't see how unleashing that strange rage in her that she had first learned about during the Katabans War would help her. It wasn't like it would do much against the Void, after all.

It doesn't matter what she does, the Void said with a laugh. **She's dead. Even if she became this 'Demon' you speak of, it won't matter. I will drown her in my darkness, as is the fate of all who try to escape the Void.**

"Do it, Durima," said Uron, as if the Void had not spoken. "With my power added to yours, we could beat back the Void long enough for us to reach the Old Ruins. Just trust me."

"This ... isn't the time ... for bad jokes, Uron," Durima said, though her voice was so weak she barely heard herself say it. "We're not strong enough to beat her back."

"If you will not do it, then you *will* die," said Uron. "I've always taken you for an idiot, Durima, but I did not think that you were a suicidal idiot. Is this what Gujak would have wanted if he was still alive?"

Something inside Durima snapped. She turned her head in what she thought was the direction Uron's voice had come from—though she had no idea for sure if it was, thanks to the darkness and the endless screeching—and uttered, "Don't ... mention ... Gujak ..."

"Why not?" said Uron. "Clearly, you must not believe that his sacrifice was worth much, if you're just going to let yourself die like this."

"Gujak ... was murdered ..." Durima spat out.

"True, but my point still stands that I doubt he'd be happy to see his strong and true friend giving into the same darkness even he did not fall into," said Uron. "Dare I say it, he might even think you're being a bit of an idiot."

Rage filled Durima's veins. She felt the Void clinging to her skin and fur like a second skin, but as the rage took over her mind, she became less and less aware of the Void. Her attention was fixated on Uron and his foul, mocking voice.

"How ... dare ... you ... say that," Durima said. Her voice was stronger now; her rational thought was becoming weaker.

"Say what?" said Uron. "State the facts? Plainly, it appears that I know your friend better than you do, if you'd think he'd be happy to see you let yourself die."

Listen not to his words, pathetic katabans, the

Void roared. **He does not care for you. He is only using you for his own ends. I know how persuasive he can be, but deep down, Uron is selfish and manipulative. Embrace sleep. Embrace the Void.**

Despite the volume of the Void's voice, Durima barely even registered that she had said anything. She pulled against the Void's tendrils, which used to seem so hard to fight, but which now seemed more like minor annoyances than anything. All she wanted to do right now was grab Uron and smack him around the tunnel for daring to use Gujak's name like that.

And then one of the tendrils snapped off her right arm and vanished into the darkness. The shrill screeching sound became quieter, as if an audimancer had muted it.

No! Where did this strength come from? came the Void's panicked voice. **Impossible. No mortal can escape my grasp.**

"Yes," said Uron, his voice pleased. "Good job, Durima. Believe in yourself. Be the Demon once again."

Durima no longer really understood what Uron, the Void, or anyone else was saying. She tore off half a dozen other tendrils, only for another dozen to burst out of the darkness and wrap tightly around her body.

You will stay where you are, said the Void. **As I said, no mortal can escape my grasp.**

"By herself, perhaps," said Uron. "But what if she had help?"

At that moment, Durima felt some kind of presence enter her limbs and her whole body. Power—unlike anything she had ever dreamed of or experienced in her life —filled her like a water fountain. It was like the gods had poured all of their power into her bones, as if she could take on the whole world by herself.

This was not the Demon. The shred of rationality still present in her mind recognized this as Uron. That normally would have frightened her, but fear was as foreign a concept to her as human homesickness.

As effortlessly as if they were the thinnest strings, Durima snapped the tendrils off her arms and legs. She heard—no, felt—the Void shrink back in terror, as if the Void had not expected something like this could happen even in her wildest dreams.

The sheer darkness of the Void continued to fill the tunnel, but Durima did not care about it. She glared at the shadows, glared at it with the strength of two beings.

What is this? the Void asked. Then her fear turned into anger. **Never mind. I am not afraid. I am the Void. You are still a being, even if one with two spirits.**

Durima chuckled, which sounded to her more like Uron's voice than her own. "You may be the Void, but I am Uron, the destroyer of Martir and savior of Harnum. I fear *nothing*."

Then Durima spread her arms; actually, it was more like watching someone else move them for her. She was dully horrified by this realization, but unable to act on those horrified feelings, she continued to watch herself act.

"And to you, Void, I say: *Be gone!*"

179

Without warning, the Void vanished. Though the tunnel was still dark, it was a far more natural darkness, unlike the Void's; that much Durima's partially rational mind understood. She could even see the last of the Void's darkness retreating, a sight that made no sense to her whatsoever until she began to understand what happened.

By the time she did, Uron was back by her side. As usual, his deep, wicked smile was plastered across his face as he patted Durima on the head.

"Good job," said Uron, in that all-too-familiar condescending tone other authority figures in Durima's life usually addressed her with. "Very good job. You certainly showed her, didn't you?"

Durima looked up at Uron. The tiredness she had dealt with before had returned in full measure now. Her eyelids felt as heavy as mountains. Just swimming in place there was a challenge in itself.

The Demon was leaving her now, while rationality was returning, causing her to say, "You ... manipulated me ..."

Uron didn't stop smiling. "Of course. If I hadn't, you would have died, Aorja and Zeeree would have died, too, and my entire plan would have ended right there. I'm not an idiot, though I am afraid I can't say the same about you."

Durima glanced at the tunnel floor. Aorja still lay there, looking almost dead, though she twitched every now and then. Zeeree lay sprawled across the tunnel, but like Aorja, he was clearly still alive because his chest heaved up and down to show that he was breathing (underwater ... somehow).

"Don't worry," said Uron, again patting her on the head. "Aorja and Zeeree both lost consciousness before they heard anything, so they still don't know that I'm here. And with luck, by the time they do, it will be too late for them to do anything about it."

Durima would have said something in response to that, but all of the action of the past few hours caught up with her. She closed her eyes and allowed herself to slowly sink to the bottom of the tunnel, landing on it just before she lost consciousness completely.

Chapter Fourteen

Ranama stopped in the water. His abrupt stop made Darek reach for his wand instinctively before remembering it was gone. So he reached for his magic stone instead, even though there was no real reason to.

"What's the problem, Lord Ranama?" said Darek. He kept his voice calm, though tense. "Did you see something?"

Ranama's back was to Darek, but he nodded anyway. "Not see. Felt."

Darek exchanged puzzled looks with Auratus. He then looked at Ranama's back again. "We didn't feel anything."

"It wasn't something mortals like you could feel," said Ranama. "I don't say that to insult you. It's just that we gods are able to feel different—what's the best word to describe it?—energies that you mortals can't. It is in our nature."

Darek believed that. The gods, after all, were quite different from mortals (although, as Darek had learned over the last year, they were quite similar as well). He had always believed that gods had greater senses than mortals, mostly because he had been taught such while training at North Academy.

His only question was, "So, what did you sense?"

"The Void," said Ranama. He touched the arms of his glasses. "It felt like it was … retreating. Yes, that's the word."

"Retreating?" said Darek. He looked around at the shadows all around them. "This tunnel looks as black as ever to me."

"There's a subtle difference in the darkness that you mortals most likely cannot see," said Ranama. "This darkness is not the same darkness as the kind that is the Void. It is natural darkness, the kind that my brother Ooka controls."

To Darek, the darkness around them did seem a little less black, though he had originally dismissed it as his mind playing tricks on him. He decided to believe Ranama, however, because Ranama did not seem like the kind of god to lie to them about that.

"But why would the Void retreat?" Darek asked. "How is that even possible? We didn't do anything to make it leave."

Ranama turned around. The light shining from his fist revealed a deeply troubled frown. "That is what puzzles me as well. I doubt the Void departed of her own free will. Someone or something made her leave."

Considering how powerful the darkness was, Darek felt a chill go down his spine when he thought about the power of whoever had managed to dispel the Void like that.

So he said, "Well, maybe this isn't so bad. The Void was easily the biggest obstacle between us and the Old Ruins, after all. And hey, since the Void was the reason behind the problems that plagued the Undersea Institute, I guess we can say mission accomplished, right?"

Unfortunately, Ranama shook his head in disagreement. "I don't know the full details of what happened, but I doubt the Void will be gone forever. Most likely, she will return, and with a vengeance."

Darek groaned. "So what do we do?"

"Keep going," said Ranama. "And try not to think too deeply about whatever might be strong enough to cause the Void itself to retreat, even though I suspect he or she is not far from our current location."

With that, Ranama turned around again and resumed swimming down the tunnel. Auratus followed as silently as ever, and so did Darek, though slightly behind both of them. He still could not swim as fast as they, but in truth, the real reason for Darek's slowness was his worry over whoever had made the Void retreat.

I would think that only a god or goddess would have that kind of power, Darek thought. *But according to Ranama, all of the gods are currently trapped by the Void. Even Skimif is trapped. That means that there is someone else down here, someone of immense strength and power. But who?*

No answer came to him, nor did he ask Auratus or Ranama, as he didn't want to distract them with his questions. One possible candidate was Uron, but he rejected that idea swiftly because Uron was currently in the ethereal and unable to do anything to anyone. Besides, Ranama said that Uron and the Void were working together; why would Uron make the Void run away?

Or maybe this is all part of some elaborate plan on the Void's part, Darek thought. *Make us* think *she's run away, and then strike when we let our guard down.*

Although Darek didn't know the Void—mostly because he hadn't known it was even possible to know the Void— somehow that didn't seem right to him. Clearly, they were not the only beings in these tunnels attempting to reach the Old Ruins.

But who else could be down here? Darek thought. *Who else would be crazy enough to try to go to the bottom of the sea and try to locate ruins from a world that no longer exists?*

He looked at Auratus as they swam. She didn't seem disturbed or trouble by these thoughts, but Darek had always had a hard time reading aquarian facial expressions and body language. That she was completely mute only added to the language barrier—more like a language border wall—that existed between them.

That reminded him of what Ranama had said earlier, about Amare, the Goddess of Sound, cursing Auratus years ago. Darek was well-versed in the curses that the northern gods were sometimes known to place on mortals, such as the story of the man who blasphemed Kos, the Goddess of Rain. Kos had responded to his blasphemy by making it impossible for rain to fall on his lands. Without any rain water to water his crops—his only reliable source of food, as he was a farmer—the man died, along with his wife and children, who had been just as blasphemous as the man himself.

And of course, Darek remembered well the story of Vashnas, the aquarian woman who had been cursed by Senva, Goddess of Aging and Wool, for stealing from the gods. Vashnas had been cursed with eternal life and lived thousands of years before being killed by Kano, the Goddess of the Sea, Sand, and Poetry, after attempting to kill the gods who had wronged her.

Something similar must have happened to Auratus at some point, Darek thought. *But what did Auratus do to earn that punishment? She's a loyal servant of the gods like everyone else, isn't she? I mean, she's the pupil of the Archmage, after all, a position I highly doubt a heathen could get.*

Auratus's situation was so unusual that it sparked the interest of Darek's inner scholar, but he refrained from asking her about it. Aside from the fact that it was a very personal question, it just wasn't relevant to their current situation.

Not like Amare is anywhere near us right now, Darek thought. *She's trapped by the Void like the other gods, after all.*

After what felt like hours of swimming, during which no one said anything, the temperature in the water gradually began to rise. Darek didn't really pay much attention to it until Ranama said, "Feel the heat?"

Auratus nodded, while Darek said, "Yes. It's not really that hot, though. Where is it coming from?"

"We are near the layer of lava that exists underneath Martir's bedrock, what you mortals call the Mican layer," said Ranama. He gestured at the walls. "Touch them."

Darek, who swam closer to the walls than Auratus, reached out to the wall at his right and brushed the tips of his webbed fingers against the stone wall. He immediately pulled them back, which threw off his balance in the water briefly before he succeeded in righting himself.

"Ow," said Darek, warily eying the wall he had touched. "That's hot."

"Of course," said Ranama. "But don't worry. As long as you don't touch the walls, floor, or ceiling, you should be fine. The Mican layer is just above us; however, we do not have to worry about it collapsing on us. The ceiling is thick and strong, so all we will have to deal with is the uncomfortably hot temperature in the tunnel."

It had never occurred to Darek to be afraid of the ceiling collapsing on them. He glanced up at the ceiling, which seemed to be glowing red from the heat of the lava, though that might only have been his eyes playing tricks on him again. Surely the lava layer was not *that* close .... right?

"Wait," said Darek as he swam a little faster, the hot water uncomfortable but not unbearable. "The Mican layer is supposed to be thousands of feet beneath the sea floor. That's what I was taught in school."

"Of course," said Ranama, while Auratus nodded in agreement. "And?"

"I just didn't realize how deeply we had traveled underneath Martir," said Darek. "I thought for sure it would take us longer to get this deep. As in days, or even months."

"You've already traveled to the ocean floor," Ranama

pointed out. "And the Mican layer isn't that far beneath it. I see nothing to be surprised about."

"Guess you're right," said Darek. "It's just that I've never heard of anyone traveling beneath the Mican layer before. I didn't even know it was possible."

"Few beings have ever gone this deep beneath Martir before," said Ranama. "Even most of the gods haven't gone down this far. The only ones who spend any regular amount of time down here are me, my sister Mica, Goddess of Earth and Ink, and my younger brother, Golar, God of Lava."

The water's temperature was growing warmer, almost too warm for Darek's tastes. It wasn't boiling yet—he would already be dead if it was—but he was reminded of the time, in his teenage years, he had dunked his head in one of the underground springs in the Great Berg. He didn't remember why he did that (most likely due to the fact that he had been an idiot as teenager), but he did remember how decidedly non-relaxing the water had been.

To keep his mind off the heat, Darek said, "So the Old Ruins are below even the Mican layer? I thought there was nothing down here except for bedrock."

"That you mortals have ever been able to access," said Ranama. He nodded at the floor of the tunnel underneath them. "If you could get below the Mican layer, you would find all sorts of strange and interesting things that you can't find on Martir's surface. Such as the resting golems."

"The what?" said Darek. "Forgive me, Lord Ranama, but I don't think I caught that."

Ranama sighed. "Oh, it's nothing you need to know

about. Just be aware that Martir is much bigger than the Surface and the Undersea."

"Wow," said Darek. "I never studied this stuff too thoroughly in school—I'm a pagomancer, as you might guess, not a geomancer—but this is all pretty mind-blowing. I gotta tell someone about this after we get out of here."

"*If* we get out of here," Ranama corrected, in the tone of a teacher correcting a student's wrong answer. "*If.* There is no certainty that the Void will not come back and stop us. Well, I would probably survive, but I can't say the same for you two. Even if I grant you my godly protection, the Void is a tricky enemy, always looking for ways around our protections and defenses."

"Uh, yeah," said Darek. He wished he could sweat in the heat now, but that was impossible to do underwater. "But back to the topic of Martir's lower layers: So if the Old Ruins are beneath the Mican layer, what is beneath the Old Ruins?"

Ranama laughed. It was an abrupt, awkward sound, as if Ranama did not laugh very often. It almost sounded forced, though Darek then realized that it was actually Ranama's real laugh when the god laughed for a little too long.

"Even we gods do not know the answer to *that* particular question, young mortal," said Ranama, shaking his head. "There might be another mortal civilization unknown to humans and aquarians alike, perhaps clinging to the underside of Martir like mud, or maybe there is another Sleeping Beast that the Powers forgot to tell us about. Who knows?"

Auratus's eyes widened at Ranama's answer. She then furrowed her brow, which Darek understood was her way of showing that she was mentally asking Ranama a question.

"How can we gods not know what lies underneath the Old Ruins, young Auratus?" said Ranama. He shrugged, an awkward motion, as he was still swimming. "Simply put, we've been too caught up in our own internal squabbles and problems on Martir to do much exploration. Perhaps the Mysterious One would know, but no one knows where he is, so it is irrelevant to think about it."

Auratus seemed absolutely floored by the idea that the gods did not know everything there was to know about Martir. That didn't take Darek by surprise quite so much, as he had had enough personal experience with the gods to know that, though they may have been all-powerful, they were hardly all-knowing.

"Darek, Skimif tells me that you were the last one to see the Mysterious One before he vanished again," said Ranama, looking over his shoulder briefly. "Did he say anything about where he was going?"

Darek shook his head. "No. He just said that North Academy was even more important to him than it was to me, which is why he intervened the way he did."

"Odd," said Ranama. "Why would he say that?"

"I have no idea," said Darek. "But that's not too surprising; after all, he is the *Mysterious* One, isn't he?"

"True," said Ranama with a sigh. "Perhaps someday, after all of this is over, I will get a chance to talk with him. I'm not the God of Knowledge, but even I could see learning much from him."

"Yeah," said Darek. "If he would ever speak plainly, anyway."

That was when he noticed how confused Auratus looked. He said to Ranama, "Lord Ranama, what's the Mysterious One's aquarian name? Doesn't he have one?"

"Not to my knowledge," said Ranama. "The southern gods in general don't have aquarian names, as they have had very little contact with aquarians in general. The closest translation I can think of is *Kaah-ak-kun*, an Old Aqua term essentially translating to 'Mysterious One.' Even you humans technically don't have a name for him; the 'Mysterious One' is not much of a name."

Language had always been one of Darek's least favorite subjects, but he listened to Ranama anyway. Auratus perked up a little at the mention of *Kaah-ak-kun*, like she understood that. As a matter of fact, Darek wondered how much Auratus understood of their conversation. He and Ranama had been speaking in Divina the whole time; on the other hand, as the God of Language, Ranama was most likely capable of speaking in two languages at once.

Remember your lessons about the Northern Pantheon, Darek, Darek told himself. *What did Noharf say were Ranama's powers?*

Of course, he recalled few mentions of Ranama, which wasn't much of a surprise. The only mages Darek knew who considered themselves followers of Ranama were linguists and historians, a definite minority among mages, and not a loud minority, either. It thus felt a little awkward to swim with this god, as he did not know as much about him as he did about the other gods.

His thoughts were interrupted by a definite *crack*ing noise above his head. He looked up abruptly. A thin crack had appeared in the rock overhead; it widened, and a jet of steam shot out of it and struck him in the face.

It was burning hot water, the pain feeling like getting shot with a bullet. He cried out in pain and swam out of the way instinctively, while simultaneously rubbing his hand against his cheek. He tried channeling some of his ice energy through his hands over the burning spot, but it hardly made much of a difference to the hot pain coursing through his face.

"Darek, what happened?" said Ranama as he and Auratus came to a stop and looked at him.

Darek, still rubbing his cheek, nodded at the jet of steam issuing from the crack. It was incredibly loud in the confined space of the tunnel, making Darek's ears hurt as well.

Ranama's eyes darted up to the crack in the ceiling. "Uh oh."

Those were not the two words Darek ever wanted to hear come from the mouth of a god.

"Uh oh?" said Darek, still swimming away from the jet of steam. "What do you mean by that?"

Ranama looked back down at Darek, his blue eyes glowing with fear.

"The ceiling is cracking. And once it does, this entire tunnel system will be flooded with lava, and you two will die."

Chapter Fifteen

Durima awoke when her head bumped against the ceiling of the tunnel. Blinking rapidly, she looked around, tasting seawater in her mouth, which almost made her panic before she remembered that she could breathe underwater now.

Then an absolutely rancid smell filled her nostrils, like swamp water mixed with pus. Not only that, but the water around her was warmer than usual, which made the stink even worse.

In addition, she soon realized that she wasn't swimming on her own. Something or someone was carrying her on its shoulder. She saw a large, thick green back, with a behind barely covered by a dirty brown loincloth, and metallic legs that looked familiar to her.

"Good," said Uron's voice to her right. "I didn't think the sleeping Demon would ever awake."

Durima rubbed her eyes and looked to her right. Uron floated lazily through the water, apparently without any propulsion, like he was resting on a raft going down a gentle river. He looked far too content for Durima's tastes.

"You look confused," said Uron. "Let me guess, you

barely remember our earlier union, correct?"

Durima blinked. She found she could not speak. Her voice seemed to have left her, maybe as a result of their union or something, so she decided to communicate as much as she could through her facial expressions instead.

"Don't you remember what I said back on World's End?" said Uron. "I know you katabans have short attention spans and memory like goldfish, but you do remember what I said about taking control of your body, if necessary?"

She did recall him threatening to do something along those lines to her if she refused to go along with his insane plan. So she nodded.

"That is all I did back there," said Uron. "I could have done it without provoking you the way that I did, but I wanted to make sure you weren't thinking rationally enough to realize what I was doing."

Bastard, Durima thought, scowling at him with all of her sharp teeth showing.

Uron rolled his eyes. "Is that all the thanks I get for saving you, Aorja, and good old Zeeree here from meeting a sleepy end? Now I understand exactly why the Ghostly God was always berating you and Gujak. How ungrateful."

What's going on? Durima thought. *Where are we now?*

"Zeeree and Aorja awoke before you did," said Uron. "Aorja decided it made sense to keep going until we got to the Old Ruins instead of waiting for you to wake up. Zeeree has been carrying you the entire time."

Durima tilted her head to the side.

"How long have you been out?" said Uron. "A few hours,

I think."

She shook her head.

"Oh," said Uron. "You want to know what Aorja and Zeeree thought caused the Void's retreat?"

Durima nodded.

"Zeeree thought nothing of it, as you probably guessed," said Uron. "Like most half-gods, he only has half a brain … and it is not the intelligent, questioning half, either. As for Aorja, she seemed to think that the gods themselves must have saved us, which was the only rational response she could come up with to explain what happened."

Durima scratched her chin, but stopped because that movement hurt her fingers. It felt like she had smashed her fingers against the ground, though she could not recall doing something like that before.

"Neither of them know you are awake, obviously," said Uron. "Aorja is leading the way. She seems to think that now that the Void is gone—temporarily, anyway—we're home-free until the Old Ruins."

Durima raised an eyebrow.

"But of course we are not," said Uron. "The tunnel system leading down to the Old Ruins has its own tricks and problems that are challenging enough on their own. I believe we'll be able to handle them, though it all depends on how dumb you are."

Durima didn't even scowl at that. She was so used to Uron's constant snide remarks about her, Aorja, and Zeeree that she almost always expected him to demean her in some way every time they talked. He reminded her of how the

Ghostly God—and the gods she had served in general—used to treat her during her service to him.

Maybe it would be better to let Uron kill those bastards, Durima thought. *All they ever do is just boss us katabans around anyway. They didn't save Gujak, after all, or even try to. They only ever abused the kid, even though he was one of their most devoted servants.*

Uron nodded, as if she had said that aloud. "Excellent. I see you are starting to see the light. I was wondering when you would start to realize that the gods aren't as perfect or pure or wise as they appear."

Normally, Durima would have disagreed with Uron or at least rolled her eyes to show she did not approve.

But now, Durima found herself thinking about how tired she was of defending the gods, the gods who never defended her or any of the other katabans she had known. It was tiring and fruitless.

I need to stop thinking like this, Durima thought. *Too depressing. I should let Aorja and Zeeree know I am awake and can swim on my own.*

So Durima patted Zeeree's back and said, in a voice weaker than normal, "Let go of me. I can swim just fine on my own."

She felt Zeeree's hand let go of her body, much to her surprise. Swimming off his shoulder, Durima then swam around his body, where she saw Aorja, who had stopped, perhaps upon hearing Durima's voice, and turned around to see her.

In the light of her wand, Aorja looked a little different

from how Durima had last seen her. She was still missing her robes, still almost naked, though her arms, legs, and body were now marred with ugly, narrow scars. Her face, where she had been slapped by one of the Void's tendrils, had a long scar running across her forehead. Based on the bumpy, uneven surfaces of the scars, Durima guessed that Aorja had healed herself at some point, though not very expertly, which explained her ugly body.

"Durima!" said Aorja, sounding almost genuinely pleased to see her awake. "I thought you would never awake. You were out like a light."

"I was hit pretty hard by the Void," Durima admitted. "Has anything else happened while I was out?"

"Nope," said Aorja as she turned around and began swimming again. "The Void is gone and we haven't run into anything else so far."

Durima swam after her, with Zeeree following close behind. She could feel the half-god's eyes on her, as if he was worried for her condition. Part of her briefly wondered if Zeeree remembered her when he was a part of Uron's army before rejecting that idea. If Zeeree had remembered her from the Void, he probably would have done something to indicate that by now.

"The water is a lot warmer now," Durima observed. "Why is that?"

"I don't know," said Aorja. She nodded at the ceiling. "If I had to guess, I'd say we're below the Mican layer, but I don't know because I didn't pay attention to that in school. Just watch out for the ceiling, floor, and walls. They're burning hot."

Based on Aorja's tone, it was pretty clear how she knew that, especially when Durima noticed the way Aorja delicately held her wand.

"Aorja is correct," said Uron, now swimming by Durima's side. "The tunnel system to the Old Ruins extends well underneath the Mican layer. It should be survivable— the bedrock above us is thick—but it will probably be very uncomfortable until we reach the next level."

Durima nodded, though she said nothing. She remembered the story of the Mican layer, how it had been discovered by human geomancers about a century ago, who had named it after Mica under the mistaken belief that the Goddess of Earth also controlled lava. Mica had never bothered to correct that notion, even after her brother, Golar, the God of Lava, had demanded that she do so.

She remembered it because she had once served Golar in her early years and he had ranted about that story to her. His version had been much longer, filled with the kind of curses only a wrathful god could come up with to describe his sister, but that was the gist of it. Her first mission under Golar, actually, had been to thwart a human celebration of Mica just to anger her.

The gods can be pretty petty sometimes, can't they? Durima thought. *Just like little children. No wonder the Powers made Skimif their leader. They needed* someone *to keep them in line, after all, though how much success Skimif has seen in that area, I don't know.*

"As for any other threats, I believe this path to the Old

Ruins is largely free of most danger," Uron continued. "That is why I told you to use this one, of course. I wanted us to take the path of least resistance, quite literally in this case, in order for us to reach the Old Ruins faster."

Durima nodded and thought, *So the Mican layer won't fall on us?*

"Of course not," said Uron. He pointed at the ceiling, which did not affect his ability to swim whatsoever. "There are miles and miles of bedrock between us and the layer. We are in as much danger of the ceiling collapsing on us and killing us as Martir is of the gods putting aside their differences and working together like they're supposed to."

Durima sighed a sigh of relief, though quietly, as she did not want Aorja to hear her.

"But don't let your guard down for even a second," Uron continued. "The Void may be gone for now, but I imagine she has left more than a few of her servants down here to keep us from advancing. I don't know which ones, exactly, but I am sure we will find them nonetheless."

I did not expect anything else, Durima thought.

That was when her thoughts were interrupted by Aorja crying out, "What?"

Durima looked ahead. Through Aorja's light, she saw a stone wall standing blocking off their path. It wasn't just partially blocking their path, either. It completely blocked it, giving them no way to go around, over, or under it. Not only that, but the wall looked like it had always been there, as if it was a natural formation in the earth.

"Oh, come on," said Aorja in a frustrated voice. "A dead

end? Really? Durima, did you know about this?"

Durima shook her head as she swam up beside Aorja. "No. Do you think we can break it down?"

"You can't," said Uron, while Aorja said, "I'm sure Zeeree could. Zeeree? Tear down that wall."

Durima looked at Uron, who was shaking his head as if he had seen this before, as Zeeree swam toward the wall. The half-god cracked his knuckles before swinging both fists at the stone wall.

That did not work out well for Zeeree. As soon as his fists made contact with the wall, he howled in pain and staggered backward through the water, forcing Durima and Aorja to separate to avoid getting sat on by him. He then stuffed his fists into his mouth, like a little child, and began sucking on them in an apparent attempt to soothe them.

"Poor Zeeree," said Aorja, frowning at him. "Do your fists hurt?"

Zeeree nodded, his deformed face looking like he was about to cry.

"Idiot," said Uron, rolling his eyes. "The wall is as hot as the rest of the tunnel due to its proximity to the Mican layer. You might as well bash your head against it for all the good that will do."

Durima looked at the wall again and thought, *Then what do you suggest we do? Turn around and go home?*

Much to her surprise, Durima found herself disappointed by that thought. Granted, she had always been the kind of katabans to complete any job she was given, no matter how difficult it was, but she was surprised that she was disappointed at the idea of failing to reach the Old Ruins, even though that would guarantee that Uron would never escape from the ethereal.

"Of course not," said Uron. "Go up to the wall and tell me what you see on it."

Durima obeyed, swimming up to it as Aorja soothed Zeeree like a mother comforting a distressed child. At first, the wall did not look unusual, but the closer she got to it, the more details she noticed.

There were hundreds of scratches and marks on the wall, and to her surprise, she could read most of it. It appeared to be written in Godly Divina, the language of the gods and katabans, and the only language Durima knew how to read.

She peered at the writing more closely. Her eyes were drawn to the line at the top, faded slightly, but still quite readable in its large, jagged font:

BEYOND THIS POINT LIES THE GRAVE OF A WORLD THAT ONCE WAS. IN ORDER TO PASS THROUGH, AN OFFERING OF BLOOD MUST BE GIVEN.

The rest of the writing was much smaller and therefore harder to read. Not only that, but it was in a different font, as if someone else had come by and written on it. Multiple someones, actually, as if Durima, Aorja, and Zeeree had not been the first ones to come this way.

"Before you ask, this was placed here by the Powers around the dawn of Martir," said Uron, gesturing at the writing. "They did not want mortals coming this way very easily, so they put this wall here that, as the warning so subtly suggests, can be passed only if you make a blood offering."

Durima grimaced.

"Gruesome, I know," said Uron. "But no one ever said the Powers were kind or gentle. Considering how they tried to destroy their own creations a mere three decades ago, I would say this is only fitting of them."

Seems too easy, Durima thought. *There has to be something more.*

"It *is* that easy, though," said Uron. "As I said, I chose this path out of all of the other possible paths because it is the easiest to get past."

What kind of blood offering does it want? Durima thought.

"Any will do," said Uron. "Godly blood, katabans blood, human blood, aquarian blood ... Martirian blood, in other words. I imagine the only difficulty you will face is getting the blood on the wall. The water might dilute it too much to make it work."

So if I refuse to cut myself, we can't go any farther, Durima thought. *And I doubt Aorja will want to do it. She doesn't strike me as the kind of human to make even the most minor of sacrifices. Would Zeeree work?*

"I have no idea," said Uron. "The half-gods were created by the Powers just like the regular gods, but they were never intended to live in Martir. I wouldn't bet on it, myself."

Durima looked back toward Aorja and Zeeree. Zeeree was still sucking on his burning fists, while Aorja continued to pat him on the shoulder and mutter soothing words to him. It was an oddly comforting sight in the darkness of the tunnel, as if it was a sign that not everything was as bad as it seemed.

Couldn't Aorja use her magic to destroy the wall? Durima thought. *She's a Limitless. Surely it wouldn't take much for her to knock it down, even though she's not a geomancer.*

"Won't work," said Uron. "The Powers specifically designed this wall to be impossible to destroy with magic. Even if you and Aorja worked together, you would not come close to scratching it."

That made Durima scowl. If she went and told Aorja and Zeeree that the wall was impassable, then they would most likely have to go back. If they went back, then it was unlikely that Uron would ever escape the Void.

Of course, Uron could take control of Durima again, but she suspected it was not an easy thing for him to do, considering how he had to first manipulate her into becoming the Demon before he could do it. If she resisted strongly enough, then Uron might not be able to control her at all.

It was tempting to decide that the sacrifice was not worth it, that she should just abandon it and head home. The gods were still trapped by the Void; however, they would probably be able to escape on their own sooner or later, and then deal with Uron once and for all.

The thought of the gods escaping made her stomach twist. As much as she hated to admit it, she was starting to think that the gods were better off in the Void, where they couldn't do anything, than out in Martir, where they squabbled among themselves and abused their servants.

She was again drawn to the question of why she felt any loyalty to the gods whatsoever. Some of the gods were good —Nimiko, the God of Light, had treated her kindly, and Skimif was fairer than most of the gods—but overall, the gods had a well-known history of discarding and mistreating the katabans like tools. If Uron killed them all, would Martir really be worse off?

And if Martir itself was destroyed, would that really be a terrible strategy? What if she made a deal with Uron to spare the katabans in exchange for the destruction of the gods and Martir?

She shook her head. *What am I thinking? This isn't right. Helping Uron is wrong. It would be better to kill myself than help him.*

Yet that thought didn't seem quite as compelling as her negative thoughts about the gods. She wondered if the katabans in general, not just herself, would be better off without the gods bossing them around.

The gods certainly didn't intervene when Gujak and I were tried by the Council and banished beyond the Void, Durima thought. *Only Skimif acknowledged the injustice of that. And as far as I know, none of the Council members were punished for their crimes against us, not even by Grinf.*

Uron was quiet the whole time she thought this. She found it strange how he could read her thoughts but she couldn't really hear his.

Not as disturbing as the constant abuse I took from the gods I have served all my life, Durima thought. *The same gods who did nothing as my kind slaughtered each other during the Katabans War.*

"Just so you know," said Uron, in a low voice, "I am not reading your thoughts at the moment because I trust you will do the right thing, without me telling you what it is."

That sounded like bull to her, but deep down, she didn't care. She had already made her decision now, a decision she knew she wouldn't be able to go back on once she did it.

She raised her right arm, bringing it as close to the wall as she could. With her left arm, she cut a tiny sliver of a cut in her right forearm; deep enough to feel a tiny prick of pain, but not deep enough to cause any serious or permanent damage.

Red blood leaked out of her arm and into the water around her. With her arm so close to the wall, the blood had no chance to dilute too much. In a second, a tiny portion of her blood touched the wall, not much larger than a fleck of paint.

As soon as it did, the wall rumbled and shook. Durima pushed back through the water as the wall slowly descended into the tunnel floor, revealing the rest of the tunnel that stretched far into the darkness well beyond Aorja's light.

Durima then turned around, ignoring Uron's serpentine smile, to face Aorja and Zeeree, who were looking at her in surprise. Zeeree's fists were still in his mouth, though he didn't even seem to be aware of them.

"The way is open," said Durima, jerking a thumb over

her shoulder. "No telling when the Void will return, so let's not waste time floating around looking like idiots."

She turned and began swimming into the deep shadows without waiting to see if Aorja or Zeeree would follow. She soon heard them swimming after her, but she still did not look back. She just looked forward, thinking only of what a world without the gods would be like ... and how much better it would be than the world she lived in now.

Chapter Sixteen

Auratus's magic stone flashed with a brown light and she pointed at the jet of steam shooting into the water, boiling it like a cauldron. The ceiling above immediately closed itself, though awkwardly, likely because Auratus was no geomancer; still, it looked like it would hold for now.

"Lord Ranama," said Darek, looking at the spot that Auratus had sealed with her magic, "you must be mistaken. That's just one crack. And look, it's all sealed up now, so we're probably going to be safe."

"Don't be so foolish," said Ranama, shaking his head. "Look at the ceiling and tell me what you see. Look *closely* at the ceiling, I should say."

Darek did as Ranama ordered. He swam up a little closer to the ceiling to get a better look.

Then he noticed minute cracks in the ceiling. He noticed them because of the bubbling water around them, a sign that this part of the tunnel was significantly hotter than the rest.

He then backed away from it quickly, his face still burning from where the steam jet had hit him. He looked back at Ranama and Auratus as he rubbed the burning spot on his face.

"There are cracks in the ceiling," said Darek. "But they're really small. Barely noticeable."

"The biggest threats usually start out 'barely noticeable,' Darek," said Ranama. "I'm not the God of Earth, but even I can tell that they are only widening. After all, one of them already broke open, as you very well know."

The pain in his face burned harder, or so it seemed to Darek. He decided to try some burn healing spells instead of ice spells later. He had been taught how to heal basic burns, so it shouldn't be a difficult thing for him to do.

"But why is the ceiling cracking?" said Darek. "I thought it was reinforced and too thick to crack."

"I have no idea," said Ranama, shaking his head. "As I said, I am not the God of Earth. I suspect it may be because Mica is trapped in the Void, which has no doubt weakened her connection to the earth."

"We can fix these cracks," said Darek, gesturing at himself and Auratus. "We both know geomancy. It won't be very difficult for us to fix them, I bet."

Darek was about to tap the magic stone on his chest when Ranama snapped, "Hold it."

The tips of his fingers hovering above the magic stone, Darek looked up at Ranama. The God of Language's blue eyes were full of warning, a look so powerful that Darek momentarily forgot about his original plan.

"Neither of you specialize in geomancy," said Ranama, pointing at both of them. "I don't doubt you two are good mages, but neither of you understand the geology of Martir as well as an actual geomancer. One false move, and you could send tons of lava falling down on all of us."

Darek gulped and looked up at the ceiling again. The bubbling, boiling water seemed to have gotten a little bigger now and the cracks were more visible, though he didn't know if he could trust his vision or not. He decided to believe that the cracks weren't any bigger than when he first saw them; it made him feel less panicky.

"Then what should we do?" said Darek, keeping his tone as steady as he could. "Leave it as is?"

"We will have to," said Ranama. "Right now, the ceiling seems to be holding, but I don't doubt it will get worse. The best we can do is keep going forward until we reach the next level."

"What if the ceiling collapses while we're swimming?" said Darek. "Will you protect us?"

"I will try, assuming that happens," said Ranama. "But I can't guarantee anything. If it's too sudden, I might not be able to act quickly enough to save either of you."

"Then what are we waiting for?" said Darek. "Let's get going while we still have a—"

Loud hissing sounds erupted as several more steam jets fired out of cracks in the water. The sounds made Darek jump in shock, while Ranama said, "Swim for your lives!"

Ranama and Auratus took off like fish in a river. Darek followed as fast as he could, but the temperature in the water was rising fast and the burn on his face almost blinded him with pain. It slowed him down before he reminded himself what would happen if he swam too slowly, forcing him to increase his speed, to push his body to go as fast as possible.

More jets of steam shot through the cracks in the ceiling like bullets from a gun. One even shot down in his path, temporarily blocking his view of Ranama and Auratus and forcing him to veer out of the way to avoid swimming into it. He caught another glimpse of Ranama and Auratus before yet another steam jet burst through the rock above and obscured his view of them.

Once again, he was forced to dodge it to avoid getting hit, only for another steam jet to cut his path off. He now found himself separated from Ranama and Auratus, who might not even realize that he was no longer following them. By the time they did ...

Darek didn't want to think about it. He forced himself to keep calm, even with the water temperature near boiling now. He was a Limitless, after all. He couldn't allow himself to get worried and panic.

So Darek tapped his magic stone and pointed his hand at the steam jets in front of him. A rock pillar rose out of the ground, pushing the steam up, but the steam must have been stronger than it appeared because it rapidly tore through the rock wall as if it was paper.

But there was just the tiniest opening afforded by the collapse of the rock wall that gave Darek a glimpse of the other side. He closed his eyes and felt the hot water around him vanish before it returned.

Opening his eyes, Darek saw that his teleportation had

been successful; he was now on the other side of the steam jets. He also saw Ranama and Auratus, dodging steam jets shooting down from the ceiling, and he took off after them, kicking his legs with all of the strength he could muster.

Yet he still couldn't catch up with them. Both of them were far better swimmers than he was. Not to mention neither of them suffered from his burning face, which was still a very real distraction that he was forced to ignore if he was going to survive.

He would have teleported after them, but every time he thought about doing so, a steam jet would fire out of the ceiling and block his vision. He didn't dare teleport without being able to see where he was going; even as a Limitless, that was too risky a move to even think about doing.

Need some way to increase my speed, Darek thought, jerking to the left to avoid an unusually large steam jet that would have probably killed him if he hadn't dodged it. *How?*

A loud, ominous cracking sound above told him that he had better figure it out quickly, because the ceiling was not going to hold the Mican layer forever. He did not know how much time they had left, but it probably wasn't very much.

Then, like lightning, he realized something.

If I'm underwater, then I could use hydromancy to make me go faster, Darek thought. *How come I didn't realize that before?*

Of course, Darek was no hydromancer, but he knew it well enough that he was confident he could do it. He was a Limitless, after all. No magic was too great for him.

So he tapped his magic stone again and focused on creating a water jet behind him that would increase his speed. And he did it quickly, too, because the steam jets were getting bigger and more numerous and the water was getting so hot that he was sure that it was boiling now.

Then what felt like the hand of a giant slapping him sent him flying through the water, but he cast the spell awkwardly and found himself stumbling head over heel, unable to control his trajectory. He slammed into the floor, which burned as hot as an oven, and bounced off it, still unable to do anything more except hope that he didn't hit into any steam jets.

The tunnel spun around him as he stumbled through the water so fast that he could no longer tell the difference between the ceiling and the floor. He was so disoriented that even the steam jets did not help him in that area.

Finally, a new steam jet burst through the ceiling and glanced off his arm. It burned through his jumpsuit, causing him to cry out in pain. The steam jet did, however, stop his constant spinning, but it unfortunately also sent him smacking straight into the floor again.

This time, however, Darek didn't bounce off it. The floor still burned as hotly as an oven, prompting him to push off it instantly. His chest, face, and legs burned, but he barely paid any attention to them because he kept forcing himself to swim faster and faster.

This unfortunate turn of events, however, had left him so exhausted that he could barely do it. His arms and legs felt like lead, not helped by the hot water. He began to doubt that he could keep going; indeed, he slowed down, feeling the pain in his body more acutely than anything else.

This is it, Darek thought. *My life is done. No way I can get out of this. I just hope Ranama and Auratus at least reach the Old Ruins and figure out how to stop Uron and the Void.*

But before he could give up completely, Ranama appeared at his side, grabbed Darek by the arm, and then pulled.

Everything around Darek went black for a moment before he found himself back in the tunnel, except this time Ranama was on his right and Auratus on his left. Not only that, but the water here was much cooler than the water back there, though it was still uncomfortably hot.

Darek would have thanked Ranama for saving him, but he was so busy swimming that he couldn't find the strength to utter even one word of thanks. He would do it later, if they survived.

It was at that moment that the loud sound of rock cracking and breaking rang like a gun shot in his ears. Looking over his shoulder, Darek saw that a chunk of the ceiling had finally given away, allowing volcanic lava to pour through the gap into the tunnel. It wasn't near them, but it was rapidly falling out of the gap, causing the water to steam and hiss wherever it touched.

"We're almost there!" Ranama shouted, his voice barely audible above the sound of the white hot lava mixing with the water. "Not much longer!"

Darek did not know where 'there' was until he noticed a

hole in the floor at the very end of the tunnel, now visible thanks to Ranama's light. It wasn't very large at all, but it looked like they could swim through it if they were fast.

Seeing that hole sent courage coursing through Darek's soul. His tiredness vanished as easily as if he had taken a good nap. They just had to keep going … keep going … keep —

A loud crashing sound above Darek's head caused him to look up abruptly. His eyes were burned by a shining hot light: lava, which was falling down toward him like a waterfall.

This is it, Darek thought. *We're dead.*

Then Ranama slammed into him and Auratus and again, Darek's world went black. But only for the briefest of moments; in the next, they were floating above the hole.

Ranama then grabbed the surprised Darek and Auratus and dragged them down the hole. Darek caught a glimpse of the lava flowing through the ceiling before they went down through the hole and ended up in another tunnel, this one shockingly dark to Darek after the brightness of the lava's glow.

"Seal the hole now!" Ranama shouted at them. "Do it, before the lava leaks through and follows us!"

Darek and Auratus did not even hesitate. As one, they turned and pointed at the hole. Thick rock grew over the hole; in addition, Darek conjured a layer of the coldest ice he could generate to cover it better, while Auratus made a pillar of earth rise up and pin the ice to the hole.

They did that in less than a second, or so it felt to Darek.

214

Even so, he heard the lava above, trying to melt through, but as far as he could tell, the lava was not in danger of getting past the barrier that he and Auratus had created, at least for now.

Sighing with relief, Darek allowed his shoulders to slump as he sank to the tunnel floor. The water down here was as cold as the rest of the sea; yet after being in the hot water from the upper tunnel before, it irritated his burns and made him want to itch and scratch his body.

"That was close," said Ranama, shaking his head as he floated above Darek and Auratus. "Too close."

"At least ..." Darek had to stop for a moment to rub his face. "At least we're past the most dangerous part, right?"

"How you wish that was true, young mage," said a light, almost frilly, voice behind Darek that made him freeze. "Because now you've entered my domain ... and I do not treat intruders upon my domain very lightly."

Chapter Seventeen

So far, the Void had not yet returned, but when she inevitably did, she probably wouldn't even let them know ahead of time. Whether the Void would or wouldn't, Durima did know that they would have to keep their guard up at all times. If the Void had been angry before, she was likely murderous now.

And of course, if the Void decided to kill them, it was hardly as if they had an easy escape route. After passing beyond the wall with the warning of the grave of Uron's world, Durima, Aorja, Zeeree, and Uron had ended up in yet another tunnel, this one even narrower and smaller than the previous two. Uron had told her, in an excited voice, that they were extremely close to the Old Ruins now and that soon he would be free once again.

That thought normally would have distressed Durima greatly, and she had to admit, she wasn't jumping in joy at it.

Nonetheless, she did not make any snide remarks to Uron or anything like that; if anything, she found she actually enjoyed Uron's excitement—she didn't really know why, seeing as Uron was nothing more than a psychotic god-killer who only cared about his old world and was willing to destroy hers to get it back.

The thought that she actually enjoyed Uron's excitement did indeed bother a small part of her, but she ignored that small part of her mind. She had a job to do, after all, and she could not let her doubts get in the way of that job.

Aorja led the way now, swimming at a leisurely pace. This tunnel was still dark, but when Durima had told Aorja that they were close to the Old Ruins, Aorja seemed to believe that that meant they were basically home-free. She had even said that she didn't think that there was any threat down here.

That had caused Durima to glance at Uron, to see if he agreed. Uron had said nothing, like he thought Aorja was correct, but he could just as easily have been keeping any threats a secret from them. Maybe he wanted Aorja to get killed by whatever was lying in wait for them, or maybe he had other reasons for saying nothing.

In any event, Durima decided to keep her guard up. Though Aorja's light revealed nothing dangerous or out of the ordinary, Durima knew better than to relax in this place.

Of course, their progress was slowed by Zeeree. Due to the narrowness and shortness of the tunnel, Zeeree could not swim as fast as Durima or Aorja. He had to do a strange combination of kicking his feet in the water and walking on the tunnel floor in order to move. He moved infuriatingly slow as a result, but as there was no way to safely widen the tunnel and give him more room to swim, Durima and Aorja had to match their speed with his so they wouldn't leave him behind accidentally.

As they swam, Durima noticed strange marks on the walls, barely visible in the shadows. They looked like writing to her, like the warning on the wall before, but she did not sit around to look at them too closely because they had to keep moving.

"See the writing?" said Uron, speaking for the first time since they had descended into this tunnel.

What? Durima thought.

Uron gestured at the markings on the walls. "This writing. It's writing from my world and my language. Of course, it is faded from the constant exposure to water over the millennia, but even so, I recognize it."

But I thought we wouldn't see anything from your world until we got to the Old Ruins, Durima thought.

"Technically, we are directly *above* the Old Ruins," said Uron, "which is to say that this is what you might call the 'attic' of the Old Ruins. It looks like a natural tunnel, but it was created long ago by my people, just like the rest of the Ruins awaiting us below."

What does the writing say? Durima thought. *Did you write it?*

Uron glanced at the walls with a frown on his face. "I can no longer read it due to the water fading most of it, so I don't know what it says. And of course I didn't write it; just because it is from my world, doesn't mean I wrote it."

Who did? Durima thought.

"Oh, I doubt you'd recognize any name I gave you," said Uron. "All I can say is that the writer of these words was the wisest person I ever knew ... unfortunately, not wise enough to see the apocalypse which swallowed our world like a snake."

Durima bit her lower lip. She had never been intensely curious about the cause of the destruction of Uron's world. It had always seemed like an abstract problem, as it had happened ages ago, before Martir, and thus irrelevant to their current situation.

Nonetheless, she did note Uron's sad tone of voice. He sounded genuinely depressed at his wise friend's apparent lack of understanding of the forces that destroyed his world. It made her wonder if Uron had tried to convince his friend to believe him, only to face skepticism and rejection for his theory.

Just like how no one believed that Gujak and I had only killed the Spider Goddess accidentally, Durima thought.

Then Aorja stopped and said, "Zeeree, Durima. Stop."

Durima, snapped out of her thoughts, looked up to see Aorja floating before them. Behind her, she heard Zeeree come to a stop as well, his wide shoulders scraping against the walls of the tunnel. She could smell his stink, but ignored it in order to focus on what Aorja's light revealed.

Standing in their way was what appeared to be thick, black netting, like the kind used by katabans fishermen back on World's End. Every now and then, a purple glow would course through it. It completely blocked off their path; there was no way to swim around or under it.

"What is that?" said Durima, though something about it felt vaguely familiar to her, like she had heard about this from someone a long time ago.

She was really addressing Uron, but it was Aorja who answered, "No idea. But I doubt it's friendly."

Uron nodded. "I agree. But I have no idea what it is, either."

Durima glance at Uron in annoyance. *I thought you said you knew every threat down here.*

Uron held his hands in a pacifying way. "This is new to me. Perhaps the Void put it here in order to block our progress, or maybe it is a natural Martirian phenomena that made its home here."

"I don't like it," said Aorja. She pointed her wand at it. "Looks like it's alive. Let's kill it and find out what it is later."

Before Aorja could shoot it with her wand, the netting shuddered in the water. Then it launched itself at Aorja and latched onto her, wrapping its stringy body around her like a blanket.

Aorja screamed in shock, while Durima swam back into Zeeree's legs. Zeeree gave a moan of surprise, but Durima did not pay much attention to him. She was looking at Aorja, who now lay on the floor of the tunnel struggling against whatever that thing clinging to her skin was.

"Get it off me!" Aorja shouted. "Durima, Zeeree, don't just stand there looking like idiots! Help me!"

Durima shook her head and swam toward Aorja. Floating above the thrashing, captured mage, Durima tried to figure out how to get that thing off her without harming Aorja, but it clung to her skin like some kind of parasite.

Not only that, but Aorja did not stay still enough for Durima to feel confident she could remove it without accidentally injuring Aorja as well.

"If I may, I think you should probably leave her behind," Uron suggested. "We only needed her to get this far, although I am starting to think we could have done it just as well without her and her miserable half-god pet. The Old Ruins are just around the corner, after all. No reason to wait."

Durima ignored him. She was not overly-fond of Aorja; however, she did not want to leave an ally behind to die. It was probably her old soldier instincts kicking in, but Durima didn't care. She would find a way to help Aorja, no matter what Uron said.

The strange black netting that held Aorja like a trapped shark glowed purple every now and then. It didn't look very thick or strong, so Durima figured that her claws ought to be able to cut through it. That would be the easiest solution; though if Aorja continued to thrash about, there was a good chance Durima could accidentally cut her, perhaps badly if she didn't do it right.

"Aorja, you're going to have to stop thrashing like a wild baba raga if you want me to help you," said Durima, pulling her legs up for a moment to avoid Aorja's swinging arms. "Can't you do that?"

"But it hurts!" Aorja shouted. "And I can feel … can feel my control slipping away."

Durima had no idea what that meant, but before she could ask, she heard Zeeree's shoulders scraping against the tunnel walls. Looking over her shoulder, she saw Zeeree approaching just as he swatted her out of the way.

His blow sent Durima stumbling through the water. She landed hard on her behind on the tunnel floor, her head spinning from the blow. Uron floated above her, shaking his head in disapproval.

"See? This is why I said we should just abandon her," said Uron. "Because now Zeeree thinks you did something to her."

Rubbing the back of her head, Durima stood up and turned to see Zeeree cradling Aorja in his arms, who still screamed and flailed against the netting, though none of her blows seemed to hurt Zeeree much. It was just the sort of clumsy helpfulness Durima had come to expect from Zeeree.

Except in this case, there was a good chance that his 'helpfulness' would result in Aorja's death if Durima did not act quickly.

So Durima raised her voice above Aorja's screams, saying, "Zeeree, put her down. I can't rescue her if you keep holding her like that."

To her surprise—and frustration—Zeeree pulled Aorja closer to him, like a child that did not want to share its toy with anyone else. She had hoped he wouldn't, but if he was going to do that, then she had no choice but to make him drop her.

Durima placed her hand against the floor of the tunnel. The stone beneath her fingers, wet and sandy, felt older than any stone she had ever felt in her life, though she channeled her geomancy through it just fine.

A pillar of rock shot out of the left wall, striking Zeeree in the face. The blow had been swift and hard; Durima was aiming to knock Zeeree out cold, even if that meant spending time later to wake him up. Right now, saving Aorja's life was her top priority.

"Actually," said Uron, "your top priority *should* be leaving Aorja and Zeeree behind in order to get to the Old Ruins. You're wasting time by trying to help her."

Again, Durima ignored him. Ever since she and Uron had merged back there, she had found it easier to ignore him than she had before. She did not know why. Perhaps it was because she had received a glimpse of his true nature. She now knew him well enough that he did not scare her at all.

She could not say the same for Zeeree, though. When the rock pillar slammed into the side of his face—slamming into his jaw with a sickening *crack*—the half-god roared in pain. He dropped Aorja, which was what Durima wanted, and swam toward Durima with murderous intent in his gray eyes, which was not what Durima wanted.

There was no room in the narrow tunnel for Durima to dodge the barreling half-god. A low growl escaped from his lips, causing Durima to swim back slightly.

Yet she did not allow her fear to overwhelm her. As Zeeree drew closer to her, Durima brought her fists down onto the floor again. Twin rock spikes shot out of the ceiling and stabbed straight through Zeeree as he passed underneath them. They pinned him directly to the floor, causing a strange greenish blood to squirt out of the now-squirming half-god and color the water with its strange hue.

"Oh," said Uron, sounding genuinely impressed. "That won't hold him for long, you know. He's a half-god."

"I know," said Durima.

She then swam above Zeeree—whose constant struggle had caused more of his strange half-god blood to squirt from his body—and slammed both of her fists down on his head as hard as she could. Zeeree's head felt like a metal box, but he immediately stopped struggling, which told Durima that she had indeed knocked him out.

Then, making sure to swim over the greenish blood (which, while small, was probably dangerous if its acidic smell meant anything), Durima swam between the two stalactites over to Aorja. Aorja now lay on the tunnel floor as still as a corpse, though the strange netting on her body continued to glow purple every now and then. Aorja's violet eyes were still wide open, but Durima saw no life in them.

"Looks like you're too late," said Uron, shaking his head, though he didn't sound at all unhappy about that. "You took down a half-god only to fail to save your ally who you didn't even like. I hope that teaches you a lesson about the foolhardiness you confuse with heroism."

Just then, Aorja stirred, causing Durima to start. Aorja slowly sat up, but unnaturally, almost like a puppet. Her violet eyes now glowed the same shade of purple as the netting around her.

It was then, rather abruptly, that Durima remembered exactly what that creature was: A deceitful webbing. She remembered it because she recalled, years ago during the Katabans War, having been told a ghost story about them by a fellow soldier of hers around a campfire once.

If what that soldier had told her was true, deceitful webbings were dangerous. They could take control of other living creatures, humans included, and force their hosts to do their bidding. The story Durima had been told had ended with the host being killed, as it was the only way for his friends to save him from the deceitful webbing once and for all.

And judging by Aorja's jerky, unnatural movements, and her glowing purple eyes, Durima was sure now that Aorja was indeed under the control of the deceitful webbing. And Durima was not sure there was anything she could do about it.

Chapter Eighteen

Darek really did not want to end up in some strange, dangerous creature's lair. After managing to avoid getting melted into goo by lava, he was in no mood at all to run into yet another obstacle. All he wanted was for the rest of the trip through the tunnel to be easy. That might have been a bit whiny, perhaps even self-pitying, especially for a Limitless like himself; even so, Darek was just tired and beginning to regret ever agreeing to come with Ranama and Auratus to the Old Ruins.

Still, he turned around to face the owner of that voice anyway. He figured that whoever it was should probably not be very hard to defeat, seeing as Darek and Auratus had a god on their side, after all. Yes, Ranama was no God of War, but he was still a god, which automatically put him on a level above almost everything else in Martir.

Thus, he was surprised when he saw a strange little fish-like creature floating directly in their path. It was orange, a shade similar to Auratus's, though it had eyes like a human's, gray and playful. It looked like nothing more than a simple fish, though as Darek had learned long ago, appearances could be very deceiving.

The little fish floated there with what might have been a smile on its face, like it was amused at Darek and Auratus's shocked expressions. Ranama, on the other hand, sighed and adjusted his glasses, which had gone slightly askew in their attempt to escape the lava.

"Not you," said Ranama, addressing the fish as if it was the last person in the world that he wanted to see. "Why are you even here? I thought you were in the eastern tunnel."

"You must have forgotten, Lord of Language," said the fish. "Because I have always been here. It's where the Kraken Goddess placed me after I was created, after all."

"Sir," said Darek as he rubbed his burning face. "Just what *is* that thing?"

"Her name is Oranz," said Ranama in a displeased voice. "She's technically a chimera—I'm sure you know what that is—but an unusual one, as she was created by the Kraken Goddess and placed down here to keep intruders from reaching the Old Ruins, which, if I am not mistaken, should be directly below us now."

Darek looked at Oranz a bit more closely. She looked nothing like the chimera that Darek had killed last year, though he supposed her being a chimera explained her human-like eyes and intelligence.

"Seems like a pretty small guard," said Darek. He held up his fist. "She's no bigger than my fist."

"She may be small, but that does not mean that she isn't a threat," said Ranama. "But we will not need to fight her. My sister gave her specific orders to allow any and all gods who came this way to go past her."

"Yeah," said Oranz. Her smile became more threatening. "About that. I am aware that my goddess—and the rest of the gods—are currently trapped by the Void."

"Yes," said Ranama, nodding. "That is why it is imperative that you let us pass. By standing in our way, you only prolong the inevitable consumption of Martir by the Void's foul darkness, which doesn't even account for the threat Uron continues to pose to our world even while trapped in the ethereal."

Oranz didn't look disturbed by Ranama's words. "I'm aware of that, too. That's why I no longer follow the gods."

Darek and Auratus gasped, while Ranama said, "What kind of sick joke is this? Oranz, it was the gods who gave you life and purpose. How could you reject us?"

There seemed to be a darkness in Oranz's eyes, a darkness that was all too familiar to Darek now. "The Void offered me a better deal. She said that if I served her and kept anyone from going down this way, I would be free to go where I please. I get bored down here, because very few people come this way, and those few who do are rarely a challenge. I would like to explore the rest of the Undersea and see the wider world."

"Blasphemy," said Ranama. He held up a hand. "My sister will probably hate me for this, but if you are indeed working for the Void now, then I will have to end your rebellious life, which wasn't even supposed to exist in the first place."

"You may try," said Oranz. "But here's the thing: I'm not just the Void's servant. I was given a power boost to go with my new job ... a power boost I will show you now."

Without warning, darkness as thick as the Ghostly God's mist poured out of Oranz's eyes and mouth. It looked almost like sludge, as if Oranz was expelling all forms of toxic waste from her body, but there was too much coming out of it to have fit inside that little body of hers.

The darkness, which was the same shade of black as the Void, soon coalesced around her body like a storm cloud. A thick, black sphere now floated in the water before them, so dark that it was impossible to see the fish-like chimera within.

Soon, two legs—strong and agile-looking—sprouted from the black sphere, followed by a pair of arms that looked as equally strong and agile.

Then the black sphere expanded until it was about the size of Auratus's torso. Like an island rising out of the ocean, Oranz slowly rose from the shadow sphere; only, Darek realized, Oranz's original tiny fish body had turned into the head of a new, humanoid body.

The black sphere dissipated from around Oranz's new torso, revealing a feminine yet muscular body that looked like the body of a goddess. She floated in the water, blocking off their pathway completely, resembling a perversion of an actual aquarian.

"This is the new form that the Void gave me," said Oranz, gesturing at her impressive physique. "Faster, taller, stronger, better in every way than that weak form that the Kraken Goddess originally gave me."

Ranama shook his head. "Even if it's stronger, I am still

a god. I should be able to defeat you with little problem."

Oranz smiled and held up one of her hands. She gestured for Ranama to attack, saying as she did so, "Then fight me, old god. Let's see what kind of fighting skills a linguist like you has."

"Fine," said Ranama as he adjusted his glasses again. "Darek, Auratus, stand back. I will not require your assistance here. With luck, this fight should be over in as little as five minutes."

Darek would have objected, but he knew better than to argue with a god of any sort. Still, as he watched Ranama swim toward Oranz, he could not help but feel a deep sense of unease about the chimera's confidence. The only reason Oranz would look this way was if she thought she could beat Ranama.

She must just be ridiculously arrogant, Darek thought. *Even with the Void's power, I doubt she'll be able to so much as scratch Ranama's pinkie finger. Maybe she's just acting this way to intimidate us.*

As Ranama swam toward Oranz, he reared back his fist, like he was going to punch her hard. Oranz didn't even bother to move. She just floated there, as calmly as ever, watching as Ranama drew closer and closer every second.

Just as Ranama threw his fist at Oranz, the chimera vanished. Thrown forward by the momentum of his own punch, Ranama could not stop himself from going forward, punching nothing except empty water, which was as effective as it sounded.

Then Oranz reappeared behind Ranama and grabbed

him by the shoulders. She whirled in the water a few times, swinging Ranama around like a broken toy, and then slammed Ranama, *hard*, against the left stone wall.

The blow left a small crater in the wall where Ranama's face had been smashed in. Oranz pulled Ranama out of it and dropped him to the tunnel floor, which he fell down to without another word.

Ranama's glasses—the lenses cracked—fell off the crater onto the unconscious God of Language, who did not so much as stir where he lay on the floor.

Oranz looked over toward Darek and Auratus, a wicked smile on her fishy lips. "Looks like Ranama was correct. This fight really did last less than five minutes."

Darek expected Ranama to jump right back up to his feet. But the longer Ranama lay there, as unmoving as a fallen tree, Darek realized that Oranz really *had* knocked him out cold.

That thought made him back up quickly. Auratus must have come to the same conclusion, because she also backed up with him, though when they both hit the stone pillar keeping the lava out, Darek realized that there was nowhere they could run to.

Oranz began swimming toward them slowly. "Afraid of me? Good. You should be. The Void gave me so much more power than I even know what to do with. I intend to use it to fully explore Martir ... after I finish you two off, of course."

Darek's first instinct was to fight Oranz. He had already fought and killed a chimera once, after all, and that was well-before he became the Limitless that he was today. If

Oranz was just a chimera, he could take her down no problem.

But there was the problem: Oranz *wasn't* a 'mere' chimera. She was strong enough to knock out a god as easily as if he was nothing more than a minor annoyance. Granted, once Ranama woke up, he would probably be able to defeat her with ease, now that he knew what he was up against.

That's the catch, though, Darek thought. *By the time Ranama wakes up, Auratus and I will be fish food.*

It didn't help that it was quite dark down here, even with Auratus's tiny light. It wasn't Void darkness—the Void still seemed to be gone, for which Darek was quite thankful—but it only added to Oranz's menace, for her eyes glowed gray in the darkness, making Darek want to run.

Nonetheless, he tapped his magic stone, intending to freeze Oranz in a solid block of ice, when Auratus grabbed his arm. Surprised, he looked at her, wondering what she was doing.

Wait, Auratus's voice said in his mind. *Have plan.*

Plan? What plan? Darek asked.

Auratus did not answer. She just tightened her grip on Darek's arm, as if she wanted to make sure that he was not going to do anything without her permission.

He almost resisted—what did she know about plans? She wasn't a Limitless like him. She was just an ordinary mage. Whatever plan she had, he doubted it would work better than Ranama's.

Still, Darek had learned to trust Auratus. She may have

had a poor grasp of Divina, but that did not mean she was unintelligent. Somehow, Auratus had come up with a plan to take down Oranz ... or at least give them an opportunity to escape her alive, anyway.

"Not going to run after all?" said Oranz. "That's good. I mean, there's nowhere for you *to* run, of course, but I'm glad to see you are just going to let me kill you. Soon, freedom will be mine, just as the Void promised."

Oranz was so close now that Darek could smell her death-like scent on the water. He was tempted to shrug off Auratus's hand and begin blasting away at Oranz, but a voice in his head told him to trust Auratus and her plan, whatever it was.

Oranz had claws on her hands, claws with red tips, like blood. It made him wonder for a moment just what kind of powers she had possessed in her original form if she had been designed to protect the Old Ruins.

Maybe she could shoot lasers from her eyes or make intruders lose their minds, Darek thought. *I guess we're about to find out for ourselves, aren't we?*

Without so much as a hint as to what she was about to do, Auratus raised her arm and unleashed a blast of sand from her palm. Oranz ducked to avoid the sand, giving Darek and Auratus a clearer view of the rest of the tunnel.

Then Auratus tugged on Darek's arm and they teleported. Darek had no idea where they were teleporting to, however, until they reappeared at the other end of the tunnel, because they now floated above a fairly wide hole that was as dark as night.

It took him a moment to realize that Auratus had teleported them both to the very end of the tunnel, past Oranz. It took him another moment to realize that Auratus had been able to see the end of the tunnel thanks to her night vision, and yet another moment to be incredibly thankful for her ingenuity.

At least, he was thankful until Oranz shrieked behind them. Whirling around through the water, Darek saw Oranz's angrily glowing eyes rushing through the darkness toward them, like some strange disembodied spirit of destruction. He would have attacked her, but then Auratus grabbed his arm and jerked him down through the hole.

As they passed through it, Auratus waved her hand behind them. Thick rock and earth immediately covered the hole, cutting off Oranz's unnatural shriek. He heard her clawing at it on the other side, but based on the thickness of the rock, he doubted she would succeed anytime soon.

Shaking his head, Darek looked at Auratus, who floated next to him, still holding his arm like she was afraid he might float away.

"Fast-thinking back there," said Darek, glancing up at the sealed hole again. "It would never have occurred to me to try something like that."

Auratus shrugged, as if it was no big deal.

"But ..." Darek frowned. "What about Ranama? We left him behind back there. Don't you think we should go back for him?"

Auratus shook her head. *He ... fine.*

Darek nodded, though somewhat reluctantly. "I guess

you're right. Oranz can't even kill him, after all. Once Ranama wakes up, he'll probably take her down easily and then catch up with us later."

Auratus smiled, then looked around at the incredibly dark area into which they had descended.

So did Darek, who sensed that they had ended up in a much larger, more wide-open area than the tunnels had been. It felt almost as wide-open as the Undersea had been, though it smelled different, like an underwater cave that had not been exposed to open air for years.

Curious to see where they had ended up, Darek tapped his magic stone and channeled a little bit of luminimancy through his right hand. Combined with the brightness of Auratus's light, this gave them both a good look at what lay below them. And it was unlike anything Darek had expected to find.

Rolling out into the darkness beyond their collective light was an entire underwater city of stone ... one which looked like nothing from Martir.

Chapter Nineteen

"And here I was seriously considering sparing Aorja's life once I got out of the ethereal," Uron complained. "But now, it looks like you will have no choice but to kill her, doesn't it?"

Durima gritted her teeth, even though she knew Uron was probably correct. The deceitful webbing appeared to be attached too tightly to Aorja's body for Durima to remove it without killing Aorja herself. It didn't help that Durima had no experience removing deceitful webbings before.

I'll just have to kill it somehow, Durima thought, without *also killing Aorja.*

"Good luck with that," said Uron. "Because you have made it pretty clear you don't want to hear a word I say, I am not even going to help. I am just going to stand here and let Aorja beat you senseless until you finally decide to kill her yourself."

"What, you aren't going to take over my body again and force me to abandon her?" said Durima, her eyes focused firmly on Aorja, who was now swimming jerkily.

"I firmly believe that experience is the best teacher," said Uron. "And I hope that this experience teaches you what happens when you refuse to listen to your betters."

Durima rolled her eyes, but did not get a chance to respond to that because Aorja lunged at her without warning. Durima ducked, allowing Aorja to go flying over her. As the mage did so, Durima grabbed her legs and then threw her back the way they'd come.

Aorja went spinning out of control through the water, disappearing into the darkness before Durima heard her regain control of her trajectory. Then Aorja surged out of the shadows again, her glowing violet eyes even more violent than they normally were.

Then Aorja pointed her wand at Durima.

Durima's immediate thought was, *It just* had *to be smart enough to figure out how to use her magic,* before electricity lanced from the wand's tip. Durima had to duck to avoid getting hit by what would surely have been a lethal blow if she had not been smart enough to dodge it.

Seeing an opening, Durima swam forward and struck with her fist as hard as she could. The blow connected with Aorja's body, sending her tumbling back through the water, though the punch wasn't as strong as it could have been because Durima was still unused to fighting underwater.

But Aorja, under the control of the deceitful webbing, apparently had no trouble at all fighting underwater. She recovered from the punch quickly and then aimed her wand at Durima's face. Durima instinctively reached for the wand, even though it was out of her reach.

A loud *bang* emitted from the wand and Durima went flying. She slammed into the two stalactites she had brought down on Zeeree; actually, she was sent flying so hard that she actually broke through them. She crashed onto the hard, sandy stone floor, but recovered and swam up quickly as Aorja swam over the unconscious Zeeree, her wand glowing with power.

With a growl deep in her throat, Durima shot toward Aorja like a bullet. Aorja pointed her wand at Durima again, but the katabans was ready for this.

Swimming close to the floor, Durima slammed her fists against it. Two pillars of rock shot out of the floor, both striking Aorja, one in the gut, the other in her wand hand. Aorja gasped, though she did not let go of her wand, while the deceitful webbing around her body glowed purple, maybe a sign that the webbing had felt that.

Good, Durima thought. *It better.*

Taking advantage of Aorja's momentary shock, Durima swam up to her and slashed at her with her claws, hoping not to harm Aorja herself. She cut through the deceitful webbing that clung to Aorja's skin, causing Aorja to scream out in pain before she collapsed unconscious, likely from the shock.

Her scream had been loud; in fact, it had been so loud that Zeeree stirred behind her and looked up. His dumb gray eyes were uncomprehending before they fixed on Aorja and then darted over to Durima. He must have put two and two together, because soon he stood up, with more of that green blood spilling out of his wounds, and growled deeply in anger, his dislocated jaw still preventing him from speaking.

Durima expected Zeeree to charge her, but oddly enough, Zeeree remained where he was. He then began pounding his chest, each pound sending out more and more of his greenish blood. Soon, Zeeree was lost in a diluted cloud of green blood, a foul, toxic smell that made Durima's stomach churn and her head feel light.

She wondered exactly what he was doing before Uron said, in a rather casual voice, "Oh. I think I know what kind of half-god he is now."

Though she would have preferred to ignore him, Durima was in no mood to find out what Zeeree's powers were firsthand. Whatever that green blood was, it probably wasn't any good.

So she glanced at Uron and asked, "Oh? And what kind of half-god *is* he, exactly?"

"The Half-God of Poison," said Uron. He gestured at the green cloud covering Zeeree's body. "That green liquid? That isn't his blood. It's poison, though not being an expert on Martirian poisons, I cannot say what kind of poison it is or if it's even one you can find on Martir."

"Poison?" said Durima. She grabbed her throat. "Did I already swallow some of his poison earlier?"

"Probably not enough to cause you any serious damage," said Uron, "which is why Zeeree is pounding out as much of that stuff as he can. He is planning to fill the whole tunnel with his poison so you will be forced to breathe it in and die a quick—though probably not painless—death."

Durima grimaced. She grabbed Aorja, who still floated in the water unconscious, and ripped off the remaining deceitful webbing, which had ceased glowing by now. Tossing the dead parasite to the sea floor, Durima hauled Aorja over her shoulder as she backed up from Zeeree's ever-growing green poison cloud.

"When will he stop?" said Durima, looking at Uron while trying to keep her eyes on Zeeree as well. "He can't keep producing that stuff forever, can he?"

"No," said Uron in agreement. "He cannot. However, Zeeree is obviously a determined little pet and he will probably not stop until he has squeezed out every last droplet of poison flowing through his veins. Considering how he is the Half-God of Poison, I imagine he must have enough of that toxic stuff inside him to turn the entire Crystal Sea into a wasteland if he wanted."

Still backing away, Durima said, "So what do you suggest I do, O Great Uron? Fight?"

"Run," said Uron simply. He jerked a thumb over his shoulder. "The entrance to the Old Ruins is right there, after all. We don't even *need* Zeeree, anyway, now that we've made it this far. Abandon him."

Durima did not need to be told that twice. She turned and swam in the direction that Uron had indicated, the only direction she could go in, while hauling Aorja over her shoulder like a sack of rocks. Of course, Aorja was more like a bundle of sticks than a sack of rocks; either way, swimming with her was a lot harder for Durima than swimming on her own had been.

But it did seem like she was going to outrun the poison cloud, at least, because it was moving very slowly after her.

Indeed, Durima began to believe that she would escape after all. Zeeree would waste all of his poison for nothing, a thought which left her more satisfied than she had been in a long time.

That was when she heard something massive swimming in the water towards her. Wishing she didn't have to, Durima once again looked over her shoulder.

Zeeree was now barreling toward her through the water like a massive battleship. There was no mistaking the hate and anger in his ugly eyes. Nor was there any mistaking the green liquid trailing from the open wounds on his body like a cloud as anything other than his weapon of choice for killing her.

"So he was smart enough to realize that hoping you are dumb enough to stand around and inhale the poison was not a very smart plan," said Uron. "You know, Durima, I think he's starting to learn."

He said that like it was a *good* thing, though there was no time for disagreement. Durima slammed her fist against the nearest wall, the one to her left, and a thick stone barrier shot out of the wall, cutting her off from Zeeree.

But not for long. A loud *crunch* indicated that Zeeree had run straight into the barrier, followed by a couple of *whomp*s from his fists beating against it. One of his fists even broke through the wall entirely before he pulled it back through and stuck his head through the hole, a murderous scowl on his misshapen teeth.

"He will keep coming until you are nothing more than paste under his feet," said Uron. "Tell me, Durima, what is your plan for stopping him for good? I'm all out of ideas."

Of course Uron had 'ideas,' but he obviously didn't want to share them with Durima. She found it childish how obstinate he was being, but she had no time to think about his childishness. She had to act.

So she stopped in the water for a moment, her short legs kicking hard to keep her and Aorja afloat, and aimed her free hand at Zeeree. The half-god was almost through the barrier now; his shoulders were visible and the rock barrier was cracking and breaking apart.

Then he smashed through completely. Behind him, there was nothing more than a thick green cloud of poison, completely impossible to see through now. Zeeree swam at her, a malicious grin on his face, as if he was anticipating breaking Durima's skull open like a rock.

Durima, however, didn't even hesitate. She sent a charged ball of electricity—like what Aorja had tried to hit her with earlier—spinning through the water at Zeeree. Durima was no electromancer, but she knew this would work. It *had* to work, otherwise they were both dead.

Zeeree didn't seem to sense the danger of the electric ball; however, right before it hit him in the face, Durima thought she saw a look of fear dawn in his eyes.

Then the ball hit and completely exploded, the sound of lightning striking mixed with Zeeree's roars of shock and pain. Zeeree shook and jerked, his skin darkening from the heat of the electric ball, while the poison gas from his body continued to expel at a fantastic rate. There were even some small explosions, like the heat from the electricity was burning the poison coming from his body.

But Durima did not stay to see if Zeeree was going to stay down. She turned around and shot toward the opening at the end, which she knew had to be the entrance to the Old Ruins. Aorja flopped uselessly over her shoulder, but she didn't care to stop and see if Aorja was all right, not when that poison cloud—and Zeeree—was still a threat.

And when Durima descended through the opening into a wide-open, dark chamber, Uron yelled out, in the happiest voice she had ever heard him speak in: "We did it, Durima. I am ... home."

She would have responded to that, but Durima noticed the light in the distance ... and based on the glow, it was definitely *not* a natural light.

Chapter Twenty

Darek could not take his eyes off the Old Ruins below, not even when the burn on his face flared. When Ranama had first told him about the Old Ruins, Darek had assumed that it was nothing more than a handful of old buildings, maybe a temple or two, with some mysterious statues and markings here and there to add to the mystery of its true nature.

Instead, he saw a city of stone, hundreds upon hundreds of buildings, all arranged in neat metric squares like someone had taken the time to plan out their arrangement. At one point, they might have been skyscrapers, extending out towards the heavens above, but now they were trapped down here, with the roof above them, completely separated from the outside world.

Many of these buildings were like arrows in their straight and narrowness, but he also saw one that looked like a box being supported by two logs. Though Darek was no architect, he could tell that most of these buildings were not Martirian in design.

Even stranger was how well-preserved these buildings were. Sure, some of them looked damaged, such as one building whose pointed roof had apparently been ripped off at some point, but aside from that, they appeared as they might have looked prior to the destruction of Uron's world.

He figured he wasn't looking at even half of the buildings in the Old Ruins. Though Darek and Auratus managed to generate a bright light together, there was still much darkness obscuring their view of the rest of it. Darek suspected that the Old Ruins had to be larger than any city on Martir, although he didn't know if that was true because he had not visited many cities in his life.

"Wow," said Darek; that word seeming even tinier down here than it did normally. "This isn't just a bunch of ruins. This is an entire *city*."

Auratus nodded, her head rotating as she tried to look in every direction at once. Darek didn't blame her.

"But the only question is, where do we start?" said Darek. "It's huge."

Auratus shrugged. *Search.*

Darek grimaced when he looked down at the city below again. "Well ... I guess you're right. We can just go down into the streets below and start looking that way. Think we should wait for Ranama first, though?"

Yes, Auratus said.

"That's a good idea," said Darek, glancing up at the sealed hole above them. "Yeah, Ranama will probably be back any minute now, once he wakes up and deals with Oranz back there."

As soon as he said that, his legs began to feel tired. Of course, they had been tired for a long time now; however, with nothing to distract him, he was now beginning to notice how weak his legs felt.

"Why don't we go wait down in the Old Ruins?" Darek suggested, pointing at one of the few flat-roofed buildings in the city. "This way, we can rest while still remaining easy for Ranama to find after he deals with Oranz."

He did not know whether Auratus would agree or disagree with him; thus, he was pleasantly surprised when she nodded and began swimming toward the building he had indicated. He soon followed.

Landing on the building, Darek sat down on his behind. The roof under him felt beyond ancient, though it seemed strong enough to support his and Auratus's weight, at least. It felt good to be able to rest; he didn't even worry about how much time they had to do this.

He just closed his eyes to rest for a minute before hearing Auratus's voice in his mind say, *Kuroshio.*

Darek's eyes snapped right back open and he looked at Auratus again. She still floated in the water, as if she wasn't tired at all. She was looking up at the ceiling above, like she expected Kuroshio to come swimming down at any moment to show that he was all right.

Darek didn't want to think or talk about Kuroshio right now. Just thinking about the aquarian student's sacrifice made his throat swell with depression.

And so soon after the Magical Superior's death as well, Darek thought, which only made his throat swell even more. *But hey, maybe no one else will have to die anymore. Once Ranama gets here and we help him find the secret to* destroying Uron once and for all, then maybe life will finally go back to normal.

His eyes wandered over to the buildings that stood all around them. He was surprised at how well-preserved most of them were; indeed, he could even see markings on them, though faded, likely by the constant exposure to water over the years. He was surprised at how clear the markings were, though even then, he could not read them because they were written in a language he didn't understand.

Another thing he noticed about the Old Ruins was how quiet it was. As far as he could tell, there was not a single other living creature in the entire city aside from Auratus and himself. That made sense, of course, seeing as the Old Ruins had been kept off-limits from mortals and other non-godly creatures for centuries, but it still felt strange to see rows upon rows of buildings, at least some of which had to have been the living quarters of the city's former inhabitants, and yet hear nothing, not even the sound of the tiniest fish swimming by.

Auratus finally landed near him, but she didn't seem like she wanted to relax. She paced back and forth across the roof of the building in an agitated way, most likely worried about Ranama. Darek didn't know what to say to her, largely because he was not worried about Ranama or anyone else right now.

Then again, I suppose the Void does *have all of the gods captive,* Darek thought. *That's definitely something to be concerned about; even then, Ranama said the gods would probably escape on their own sooner or later, so they're safe for now.*

Still, Auratus's constant pacing made Darek antsy, so he said, "Auratus, could you please just take it easy for a moment? We've been swimming for hours. Ranama will get here when he gets here."

Auratus looked at Darek with uncomprehending eyes. Most likely she had understood only a portion of what Darek had just said, which was why she resumed pacing back and forth.

Darek frowned. Watching Auratus pace like this reminded him of what Ranama had said earlier about Auratus being 'cursed' by Amare. He was tempted to ask her about that now, since they had time in which to talk about it, but considering how agitated Auratus appeared to be, he wondered if it would be wise to do so.

Rubbing his cheek—which still hurt from the steam earlier, though it was thankfully cooling off—he decided that it might be worth asking her about it. Worst she could do was refuse to answer his questions, after all.

So Darek, steeling himself for whatever Auratus's reaction might be, said, "So, Auratus, can I ask you something?"

She stopped pacing again and looked down at Darek. *Yes?*

"Earlier," he said, speaking each word carefully so Auratus could understand him more easily, "when we first met Ranama, he said that you were cursed by Amare. You know, the Goddess of Sound?"

Auratus blinked, but nodded anyway. *Yes?*

She didn't seem angry; however, Darek detected a hint of reluctance in her voice. No doubt the subject was painful to her; still, she had not refused to look at him, so he figured that was a good sign to keep asking.

"I was wondering why that happened," said Darek, his voice as careful as ever. "I mean, you're a mage just like anyone and you can't be a mage if you hate the gods. Why would Amare curse you like that?"

Auratus looked down at her feet before returning her gaze to Darek. He thought she wasn't going to answer him before she said, in halting, uncertain Divina, *Long time go, used to be Heathen. Hated Amare. Desecrated temple. Cursed with no tongue. Lasts forever.*

Darek put a hand up to his mouth. "Oh. So the curse Amare put on you is muteness?"

Auratus nodded. *I no speak. Impossible to heal. Only Amare can lift curse.*

"Why hasn't she lifted the curse yet?" said Darek. "After all, you're a loyal mage now, in line to become the next Archmage. It doesn't seem just to leave you like this."

Auratus shrugged. *Goddesses do what want. Respect goddesses.*

"I wish there was something I could do to help you," said Darek. He ceased rubbing his face. "It's just not fair that you should spend the rest of your life like this."

Auratus shook her head. *Not your problem. Don't worry.*

Darek supposed she had a point. It was said that it was never wise to interfere with the punishments or curses that the gods brought down on the people who blasphemed them. Still, the thought left Darek unsettled. After all, Auratus was clearly no longer a blasphemer, so why did she have to suffer from one of her mistakes for as long as she lived?

Maybe one of these days, I'll talk to Skimif and ask him to lift her curse, Darek thought. *She's a good person and doesn't deserve to live this kind of life forever.*

But that would be later, after Uron and the Void were no longer threats to Martir. Right now, their most immediate problem was waiting for Ranama so they could begin their exploration of the Old Ruins.

Then Auratus started. She started so abruptly that Darek almost fell over onto his back before putting out his arms to catch himself. She was looking to the east, her eyes focused on something far in the distance.

"What do you see?" Darek asked. "Auratus, did you see something move?"

Auratus pointed in the direction she was looking. *Light.*

Curious, Darek followed her pointing finger to see just what she was pointing at.

Far away—though not out of sight—was a glowing, bright light ... a light that neither of them had made.

Chapter Twenty-One

"**L**ooks like we're not the only ones here," said Uron, following behind Durima as she looked at the light that shimmered far away. "I wonder who that could be."

Durima wanted to rage against the heavens. Here, she had managed to get past all of that crap standing between them and the Old Ruins, only to learn that someone else had already beat her to it. Not only that, but she had a sneaking suspicion that this person, whoever he was, was not here to help her.

Whoever that bastard is, I am going to tear his spine from his body and shove it down Zeeree's throat when I get a chance, Durima thought.

"An interesting threat, but I would advise against engaging with whoever is creating that light," Uron said. He gestured down toward the darkness below. "You must first free me. I will show you where to go in order to do that. After we accomplish that task, then we can deal with whoever those fools are."

Durima wanted to tell Uron to go and free himself, but her rational side realized that Uron had a point. After narrowly escaping Zeeree, Durima was in no condition to fight anyone. Especially with the unconscious Aorja over her shoulder; getting into a fight with anyone now would be suicide.

Still, Durima had to ask, "But doesn't this mess up your plans?"

"How?" said Uron. "I doubt the people who made that light are very strong or powerful. They are definitely not gods, either, so we don't have to worry much. Now stop worrying and start swimming. I will give you directions as we go."

Durima bit her lower lip and looked at the light in the distance again. It was indeed a small light, tiny against the darkness of the Old Ruins, but as it didn't seem to be drawing closer to them, she decided to heed Uron's advice.

Thus, Durima descended slowly into the darkness. Her night vision allowed her to see tall, sharp-looking buildings, much narrower and more numerous than the skyscrapers of World's End. All of them were that same stone-brown color, which made them all look the same to her.

"What a boring-looking city," said Durima the closer they got to it. "This is your 'home'?"

Uron huffed. "This city was once the most beautiful city in all of Hanum."

"Hanum?"

"What you might know as the Prior World," said Uron. "Yes, Hanum was its name. As for why this city is no longer as beautiful as it once was, that is because the water exposure to the buildings has stripped them of their beautiful coats of paint. They used to be as white as the stars."

He sounded extremely nostalgic as he said that. No doubt he was remembering all of the good times he had experienced in this city in his past life, though Durima was not really curious to hear about them.

Nonetheless, as they descended between two one of the spire-shaped buildings, Uron pointed and said, "These streets used to be full of children playing games like nock-nick and silver hop. You could walk these streets completely unarmed and not feel even slightly afraid. And over there, yes, I remember a vendor setting up a shop to sell the finest, freshest bread in all of Hanum."

All Durima saw, as the darkness of the Old Ruins slowly gave way, was an empty, barren stone street that was cracked, with seaweed rising out of the cracks in clumps. She did not even see the shop Uron had pointed out, though she did notice what appeared to be a storefront whose door had been smashed off its hinges long ago.

"So many memories are coming back to me," said Uron. "Memories I have not thought of in a long time due to my anger and hatred against my people and the Powers— bittersweet memories, many of them, but memories nonetheless."

"All right," said Durima, not sure what to say about that. "Well, we're in the city now. Tell me which way to go and I will follow."

"Keep swimming," said Uron, pointing directly ahead of them. "We're going to the Superioratorium."

"The what?"

"You'll see," said Uron. "It's not far from here. You will know it when you see it."

Durima obeyed Uron's orders. She swam directly ahead, keeping her eyes and ears open for any potential threats hiding in wait, but she did not see or hear anything except her legs kicking against the water, propelling her further and further into the unknown.

As they swam, Durima got a better look at the Old Ruins. The street was cracked in several places—in one section, cracked in half like an earthquake had come through. Many of the buildings had old, abandoned looks to them. One building was missing its roof plus several upper floors; another had a chunk of rock sticking out of the open door. What looked like a ball attached to a stick by a rope lay in the street, which Uron pointed out as a children's toy, though he did not explain what had happened to the child who had once played with it (though given the history of Harnum, Durima had a feeling she already knew).

The Old Ruins reminded Durima somewhat of World's End, but it was only a vague resemblance in that they were both large cities. In other ways, they could not be more different. World's End was dominated by huge, gorgeous skyscrapers dedicated to the gods; the Old Ruins were the remnant of a world that had existed before and would not likely exist again (unless Uron had his way, anyway).

So she could not see what Uron saw in it, but whenever she looked at Uron, she thought that he probably wasn't actually seeing the Old Ruins as they currently were. His nostalgia was making him see the Old Ruins as they once were; a beautiful world, full of life, where he had grown up and lived until it ended.

She wondered what it would be like to look at the world from Uron's point of view. He was the last surviving member of his species, of his whole world. She found herself feeling a little sorry for him, considering how he had spent thousands upon thousands of years alone deep beneath Martir.

But then she shook her head. *Uron doesn't need my sympathy. Can't forget how he ripped off Gujak's arm last year, now can I?*

Now she really did not want to think about Gujak, but she had little choice, because the Old Ruins were quiet and uneventful at the moment. Thinking about Gujak made her angry because she remembered how Erich had killed him and how the Katabans Council had unjustly banished her and Gujak beyond the Void for a crime they did not commit.

Maybe letting Uron succeed is the right thing to do, Durima thought. *Maybe if I serve him, I will get a chance to kill those Council bastards. Maybe we katabans won't have to blindly serve the gods anymore. Maybe I was wrong to hate him all this time.*

These thoughts occupied her mind as she swam, though occasionally she was forced to readjust Aorja to keep her from falling off her shoulder. Aorja still had not awoken, hadn't even stirred, but Durima figured that sooner or later she would. And if she didn't ... well, Aorja's death wouldn't be a huge loss to the world, she supposed.

"We're almost there," said Uron as they rounded the corner of a building. "Getting closer and closer."

Durima looked at him. "What is the Superioratorium?"

"My work space," said Uron. "Prior to the end of Harnum, I lived and worked in a place known as the Superioratorium. It was the most famous laboratory in all of Harnum, where significant advances in science and technology were made every day."

"So you think there is something in there that will help you escape the ethereal?" said Durima.

"If memory serves, yes," said Uron, nodding. "Of course, there is always the possibility that the tech I am thinking of exists no longer, either destroyed by the passage of time or taken by the gods. I doubt it, however, because the gods have more or less left this city alone, except for Ranama, of course."

"The God of Language?" said Durima.

"The same," said Uron. "He's been known to come down here and try to decipher the various writings on the buildings. He's had little success, seeing as none of it is written in any Martirian language. He's shown no interest in any of the tech lying around, though I suppose that is also because he doesn't seem to be aware it even exists."

"What kind of tech do you think will help you escape?" said Durima.

"You will see once we get there," said Uron. "I don't want to raise your spirits only to be disappointed when we get there and find out that it is either missing or destroyed."

Durima doubted she would be terribly disappointed if

the tech that Uron spoke of was missing or destroyed, as she had no emotional investment in it. Still, she nodded anyway as she continued to swim.

After a few more turns down various side streets and alleys, Uron pointed and said, "We're here."

Durima looked at the large building rising before them. The Superioratorium was much larger than the other buildings around it, shaped like a dome, although there was a huge hole in the metal roof, like a giant had punched it in. A statue lay on the ground in front of it, though it had been shattered into dozens of pieces, which made it impossible to identify.

"Let's go in," said Uron, rubbing his hands together in anticipation. "We have no time to lose."

So Durima swam closer to the Superioratorium. The closer she got to it, the more details she noticed, such as the mold growing on the walls and the cracks on its exterior. Again, she noticed some markings on it, but as with all of the other markings in the Old Ruins, they were too faded and illegible to read.

A set of steps—finely carved and made of what appeared to be marble, though it could just as easily have been some other type of stone—led up from the street to its front doors, which stood open as if someone was throwing a party and everyone was invited. Durima swam up the steps, though not very fast, as Aorja slowed her progress considerably.

Then Uron said, "Did you hear that?"

Durima stopped about halfway up the steps and looked at Uron. He was now facing the direction in which they had came, his eyes focused on the dark city behind them.

"Hear what?" said Durima.

Uron stared into the darkness for a couple of moments before shaking his head and turning around. "Never mind. I thought I had heard someone following us, but I suppose it was just my imagination at work."

Durima tried listening, but she didn't hear anything in the silence of the Old Ruins. She was reminded of that light they had seen earlier, though she did not know for sure if the creators of that light had tried to follow her or not.

Unlikely, Durima decided. *They probably didn't even notice me. Maybe there is some kind of fish down here or something.*

"Then again," said Uron, stroking his chin, "I wonder if the Void has put any of her minions down here. I doubt it, myself, as we would have already been attacked if that was the case, but she can be awfully crafty when she needs to be. Better to keep our guard up."

"If there's no point in worrying about that, then why are we floating here like idiots?" said Durima. "Let's just go into the Superioratorium, find what you're looking for, and get out."

Uron nodded. "For once, you speak sense. Let us not waste anymore time letting our imaginations frighten us."

Uron then resumed floating toward the open doors of the Superioratorium. Durima followed as quickly as she could, though she found herself wanting to look over her shoulder anyway just to be sure they weren't being followed.

She refrained from doing so, however, because she

doubted that there was anyone else down here except for themselves.

There was that light, though, she thought. *That light that clearly was not natural.*

It was a fish, Durima argued. *Some kind of fish that can emit light. I've heard of those kinds of fish before. It's nothing to get scared of or worried about.*

And anyway, even if there was someone down here, pretty soon, Uron would be freed, and once he was, no one would be able to stand in his way, no matter how strong they might have been.

Chapter Twenty-Two

Darek followed the light, with Auratus trailing behind him uncertainly. The light was still too far ahead of them for Darek to make out who was using it, but he still swam after it anyway, curious to know what it was.

Go back, Auratus's voice in his head said. *Light dangerous.*

Darek ignored her. He understood Auratus's worries, of course. It probably would have been wiser for them to stay back on that building back there, directly below the sealed tunnel exit, where Ranama could find them without trouble. Besides, without Ranama, how were they supposed to decipher the words written on the buildings?

Nonetheless, Darek had a bad feeling about that light. It didn't look like the kind of light that was created by some harmless sea creature. It resembled the Light of Nimiko, a soft white shade of light that most luminimancers could summon. It could only be created by light magic, which meant either Nimiko himself was somehow here or there was a luminimancer down here.

Even if it turned out to be as dangerous as Auratus

thought it was, Darek was confident he could protect them from it. Sure, he was tired from the events of the last few hours, but he was still a Limitless through and through. A simple ice spell and he could turn even the greatest sea creature into a glorified icicle.

The light weaved in and out of the buildings, forcing Darek to huff to keep up. The light seemed to know that they were following it; of course, that could just as easily have been Darek's imagination making him attribute things to the light that weren't there.

Yet why else would the light be taking such a circuitous, crazy route if it wasn't trying to lose them?

Not like it even can *lose us down here,* Darek thought. *Even the dimmest light stands out like a sore thumb in this darkness.*

He paid little attention to the buildings they passed as they followed the light, because he didn't want to take his eyes off it for even a second. Nonetheless, he had the distinct feeling that he did not belong here, as if this was a forbidden area that he was trespassing on.

He disregarded that feeling as nothing more than his own unease at the thick darkness and empty buildings everywhere. Whose permission was he supposed to get, anyway, considering how there didn't seem to be anyone down here except for them?

Of course, there was the simple fact that he was in a place that technically wasn't even a part of Martir. It dawned on him that this was the very first time he had seen or visited some place that had not been created by the

Powers, a thought that he was unsure how to deal with.

Forget about it, Darek, he told himself, watching the light as it wound in and around the buildings of the Old Ruins. *Focus on the light. Don't let it get away.*

He ducked underneath a crumbling bridge between two buildings. Thanks to the glow of the light that he was following, he could see that the light was heading toward what appeared to be a large, metal-roofed domed structure nestled among several smaller buildings. The dome had a large hole in the roof, though he could not guess how it had gotten there or what might be lurking within. He was almost afraid that that giant eel from earlier was going to jump out of the hole and attack before he reminded himself that the eel was probably dead, thanks to Kuroshio's explosive sacrifice earlier.

Still, he slowed down as he and Auratus approached the domed building. He doubted there was anything inside the building. Maybe a few harmless sea creatures that had made their homes in it, as it was clearly abandoned. Or maybe there was some seaweed and other aquatic plant life; he had seen some seaweed growing in the cracks of the streets, after all, so it wasn't an unlikely possibility.

The light, however, picked up speed and soon vanished within its open front doors. Auratus held up her hand, which shone with light, but all it did was show the steps leading up to the doors. What lay beyond those steps, inside the building itself, was still unknown.

Darek looked at Auratus. "Do you want to go in?"

Auratus shook her head. *No. Wait for Iknor.*

Darek frowned. "Why? Ranama himself said there shouldn't be anything down here."

Don't trust light, were the only words she said.

"I don't *trust* the light," said Darek. "I'm just *curious* about it. I want to find out what it is. Why is that such a bad thing all of a sudden?"

Though Darek was no expert in aquarian facial expressions, the expression on Auratus's face right now succeeded in making him feel like he had just said the stupidest thing in the world.

And he didn't know why, either, until he thought about what he'd just said and added, "Oh, right—the fact that the tunnels have tried to kill us several times. So you don't think we should be letting our guard down in here, even if we're seemingly alone."

Yes, was Auratus's one word reply. *Understand.*

She sounded as if she was relieved that Darek understood her.

That didn't mean he agreed with her, though. He didn't like leaving any sort of mystery unsolved, especially one as mysterious as this one. He was going to find out what that light was one way or another, even if it meant leaving Auratus behind.

But he didn't want to leave her behind because she was his only ally at the moment. True, Ranama was still back there in the tunnels, but there was no telling when he would wake up or how long it would take for him to get past the seal that Darek and Auratus had put over the tunnel exit and reunite with them.

Darek just liked having backup, and Auratus was the only backup he could possibly have here. Therefore, he had to figure out how to convince her to come with him.

"Come on, Auratus," said Darek, gesturing at the entrance to the domed building. "Don't you want to find out what that light is, too?"

Auratus folded her arms and looked away. *No.*

Darek looked at her in disbelief. "No? But it's so mysterious."

She looked at him and repeated that one word: *No.*

Auratus seemed pretty stubborn about this issue, so he knew that simply asking her to help wasn't going to work. He needed to appeal to her more dutiful side, which she had to have if she was willing to travel below the bottom of the sea like this just to save her school.

"But what if following that light will show us how to get rid of the Void once and for all," said Darek, "which would help the Undersea Institute? You know, the whole reason we went down here in the first place?"

He could tell she was starting to give. She still didn't seem happy about it, but the way her gaze became softer gave him the encouragement he needed to push further.

"So if you agree, then I say we go in after it right away," said Darek. "We don't want to lose it, after all."

Auratus glanced toward the massive stone ceiling over the Old Ruins, like she hoped to see Ranama coming down toward them. The God of Language, however, was nowhere to be seen, causing her to sigh and look at Darek again.

Fine, Auratus said. *But be careful. Very careful.*

"Of course," said Darek. "I'm so careful, you could call me a careful-mancer."

She just stared at him blankly, which reminded him that Auratus still did not have a very good grasp on Divina, despite the understanding she showed whenever he talked to her.

So he said, "Never mind. It's just a silly joke. Now why don't we go in there and find out just what that light is?"

Chapter Twenty-Three

Entering the Superioratorium was similar to stepping into the Temple of the Gods back on World's End, though dimmer and wetter. The ceiling was tall and wide, so high above her head that if she had not known it was there, she would have assumed that it simply opened out onto the water above like some kind of sports coliseum.

Uron, on the other hand, acted as if he had spent his whole life in this place (though when Durima thought about it, she realized that there was some truth to that thought). He pointed at the rows upon rows of desks below and said, in an excited voice, "Do you see what that is, Durima?"

Durima looked at the desks. They were stone, like almost everything else in the Old Ruins, with what appeared to be piles of stone tablets on their surfaces. Some of the desks had fallen apart; one even looked like it had been smashed in half.

"Those are the desks my colleagues and I used to work at before Harnum's destruction," said Uron. "And look, our research notes are still here. Oh, how I remember the days we used to spend poring over the data and information we

266

had gathered, how we would argue endlessly over the right interpretation of our data, and that memorable time I punched out Xisak for daring to suggest that my Elda Rivers hypothesis was nothing more than bull-hockey."

"Xisak?" said Durima. "What is the Elda Rivers hypothesis?"

"Xisak was a dear old friend of mine," said Uron with a sigh. "He died before Harnum ended. As for the Elda Rivers hypothesis, well, that was just an old theory of mine that actually was disproved at a later date by another scientist, though I was pleased to learn that I got the basics right, anyway."

It all sounded like gibberish to Durima, which was how she felt every time she overheard her fellow katabans discussing the intricacies of magic (a boring subject to her). But she didn't say that to Uron, as she doubted he would take kindly to any dismissive words from her, even though he was in a good mood right now.

Then Uron pointed at the dome above them. "That dome used to have a map of the whole of Harnum on it. Sadly, I can see that time and the sea has washed it away; nonetheless, it is but a map, not the actual Harnum. Therefore, I have little reason to be sad about it, even though it was known as the most beautiful map in the world at the time."

Durima looked up at the dome's ceiling, but it was too dark for her to make out anything, even with her night vision. She decided to take Uron's word for it.

Uron rubbed his cheeks, like he was caught up in his

memories again. "Oh, I could spend months, even years, reminiscing about all of the good times I spent here. I could tell you stories you would never even believe, but which are nonetheless true."

"If you say so," said Durima.

"But I won't," said Uron, shaking his head and lowering his hands. "I don't see the tech I came here for; however, it shouldn't be hard to find. It was put inside a vault, a vault I believe has not been opened since the day Harnum ended. Unfortunately, my memory isn't quite as good as it once was, so I don't remember it's exact location. Therefore, we will have to search for it."

"Okay," said Durima. She looked at Aorja, who still hung over her shoulder unconscious. "But what about Aorja? Shouldn't I try to heal her first? That deceitful webbing left a lot of sores on her body, after all, and I am getting tired of hauling her around like a sack of rocks."

"We don't even need the useless human anymore," said Uron. "We are only yards away from finding the tool needed to free me. If we waste anymore time healing someone we don't even need, I will explode."

"Sure," said Durima as she deposited Aorja on the floor. "But I am getting tired of lugging Aorja around everywhere. I'll heal her enough so she can swim on her own; after that, we can go and find your favorite toy."

Uron scowled, but he did not explode, as he had threatened. He just crossed his arms over his chest as Durima looked at the sores on Aorja's body, which were as red and ugly as sword wounds.

Nonetheless, Durima guessed that they were not as deep as they appeared. She cast a quick healing spell over every sore she could find, which she did not know if it would work or not at first because she didn't understand human biology as well as katabans biology. She just decided to hope for the best.

And if she dies as a result, it's not a great loss, Durima thought.

Even so, she was relieved when she saw her healing spell work. The sores closed up or vanished, leaving Aorja's skin as smooth as ever, though it was also covered in red spots where the sores had been.

At the same time, Aorja groaned and opened her eyes. Her eyes were glassy and unfocused for a few moments before she shook her head and looked around in confusion.

"What ..." Aorja sounded weak. "Where are we? What happened?"

"A deceitful webbing happened," said Durima, standing up to her full height. "It attacked you and took over your mind. You are very lucky to have survived. Most people who fall prey to the deceitful webbing usually die horrible deaths."

Aorja grabbed her chest, feeling some of the red spots where the sores had been. "Oh gods. I remember. It was horrible. Like someone was taking away my free will. I wouldn't wish that fate on *anyone*, not even on Darek." She paused. "Well, maybe I wouldn't object to that happening to Darek, but it's still awful and horrible."

"No doubt about that," said Durima. "Now, do you feel

well enough to swim on your own or do I have to carry you the rest of the way?"

"Zeeree," said Aorja, apparently without hearing Durima's question. She looked up into Durima's eyes. "Where is he?"

"Back in the tunnel where the deceitful webbing was," said Durima. "He thought I was trying to harm you because I was trying to cut the webbing off you. I had to take him down and leave him behind because he was trying to poison me."

"He's still alive, though?" said Aorja.

Durima did not know the answer to that question. Last she had seen, Zeeree had been shocked by electricity underwater. She didn't see how anyone could survive that, but knowing Zeeree was a half-god, she thought it likely that he had.

So she said, "Probably. I'm sure he'll come and rejoin us later, once he recovers."

"Thank the gods," said Aorja with a sigh. "I thought I was going to be stuck with *you* for the rest of the trip."

She said 'you' like it was the worst insult she could come up with. Durima just wanted to take Aorja and bash her head in, but she refrained from doing so, knowing how fruitless and time-wasting that would be.

"If you want to know where we are, we're in the Old Ruins," said Durima. "Specifically, we're in the one building in the whole city where the power I promised you lies."

That seemed to energize Aorja more than anything Durima had ever said to her. She pushed herself off the stone floor and swam up, eagerly looking around the Superioratorium like she thought the power was hiding from her.

"Where is it?" said Aorja, swimming in circles above Durima's head. "Where is it? You said it was here."

Durima looked at Uron—who made a noise of impatience—and then looked at Aorja again. "It's currently locked in a vault. So if you want that power, we'll—"

"On it!" Aorja was already swimming off into the darkness in a random direction, even though Durima hadn't told her where to start looking.

"I admire her eagerness," said Uron reluctantly. "She is the kind of woman who will do anything for power, who won't even let a deceitful webbing attack keep her down very long."

"Still thinking of sparing her?" said Durima.

"Assuming she doesn't want to kill me once she finds out we've been manipulating her this whole time," said Uron. "But anyway, you should go join her. The Superioratorium is a big place, so you will both need to work together to—"

"Found it!" came Aorja's singsong voice from within the darkness of the interior. "Durima, come on, it's over here! Help me figure out how to open the damn thing."

Durima exchanged shocked looks with Uron and whispered, "She couldn't have possibly—"

"Durima!" came Aorja's voice again, except this time more annoyed. "Are you waiting for the sun to set? Come over and help me, you useless piece of trash."

Being called a 'useless piece of trash' did not encourage

Durima to go help Aorja, though she swam through the darkness in the direction that the mage's voice had come from anyway. Beside her, Uron looked like he was once again blown away by Aorja's determination.

It took Durima only a few seconds to find Aorja. She was in the corner of the Superioratorium, standing in front of a huge metal door that appeared to be sealed shut. The metal door was plain and unremarkable, aside from its size. There were no keyholes or locks attached to it; it didn't even have a door handle.

"That's it," said Uron as he and Durima approached the door. "The door to the vault."

Durima heard tight anticipation in Uron's voice. No wonder; he was so close to freedom now that Durima was surprised at how reserved he was acting.

"So how do you open it?" Aorja asked, looking over her shoulder at Durima. "Blow it open with a spell? I could do that. I have some experience with explosions."

"Of course not," said Uron, though he addressed Durima rather than Aorja. "An explosion, even a small and tightly controlled one, could potentially destroy or damage the tech within. A large and uncontrolled one could completely demolish the entire Superioratorium."

"No," said Durima to Aorja, shaking her head. "Explosions are not the answer, in this case. We have to open it a different way."

Aorja folded her arms across her chest and pouted. "But I *like* explosions."

"I hope you like ultimate power more," said Durima,

"because any explosion you create could potentially harm the power within."

Aorja rolled her eyes. "Okay. Fine. Then what do you suggest we do? It's not like we have the vault's key or anything."

"Because it doesn't have a key at all," said Uron. "That's not how we did things back in my day. We knew that locks could be picked, so we came up with a different way of opening it."

"I'm thinking," said Durima, though in reality she was listening to Uron. "Just give me a moment."

"You can open the vault by inputting the pass code on the panel," said Uron. He pointed at a control panel to the door's right.

"We need to enter the pass code to open it," said Durima to Aorja, nodding at the control panel.

"Okay," said Aorja. "What's the pass code?"

"The pass code is 'freedom,'" said Uron.

"'Freedom,'" said Durima. "That's what the pass code is."

Aorja swam up to the control panel and looked down at it, a frown on her face. "The panel isn't written in Divina. I can't tell which letters I'm supposed to input."

Durima swam up to her and looked down at the control panel before them. It was old and rusted, with most of the buttons faded so much it was difficult to make out the symbols on them. From what she could see, Durima noticed that Aorja was correct: The symbols were not Divinan letters.

"Don't worry about that," said Uron. "I will tell you

which buttons to press. I remember, so don't waste time."

"I can do it," said Durima to Aorja. "Just give me a moment. I know a thing or two about cracking codes, so just give me a moment and I will get on it."

Aorja swam back a little to give Durima some room. Nonetheless, Durima could still feel Aorja's eyes on her back, watching her every movement as intently as if Durima was about to reveal the secrets of the universe.

Listening to Uron, Durima pressed every button that he told her to, though she pretended to miss a few every now and then so Aorja wouldn't get suspicious about Durima's code-breaking abilities. She was careful not to skip over or miss any, though she was forced to press a couple of buttons two or three times because they did not go down when she pressed them the first time. The keys felt withered and rusted under her fingers, making her worry that they might pop off, but none of them did, and in a second she had finished inputting the code.

"Now press the big button at the bottom," said Uron, gesturing at a long key below the others.

As soon as Durima pushed the big button down, she heard the loud sound of gears clicking, clacking, and groaning behind the vault door. She swam away from the vault door, as did Aorja, because the door was opening outwards, though slowly and jerkily, probably due to the age of the gears inside it.

When she thought about it, Durima found herself surprised at the fact that the vault door could open at all. She was sure that years of neglect and exposure to the water would have damaged its internal mechanisms. Despite that, it did open, albeit slowly and awkwardly.

"That's because my colleagues and I designed it ourselves using only the finest metals and most advanced door-opening technology," said Uron, floating next to her. "We even invented the locking mechanism because none of the locks available at the time met our own personal safety requirements."

Durima did not have anything to say to that. She could have said that Uron was being arrogant, but she doubted he would care. She just watched as the vault door slowly opened, inch by inch, until soon it stood open entirely, though the interior was too dark to see.

Without warning, a couple of glowing blue lights flickered on inside the vault. Durima was not sure what she had expected to see; however, she was still surprised by what the lights revealed to her.

Long shelves ran along the walls of the vault's interior, full of what appeared to be stone boxes of varying sizes and shapes. Some were tall and thin, others short and big, but all of them were clearly made out of the same materials, maybe even made by the same people or company. Each box had a label on it, though they were written in the same language as the keypad had been, making it impossible for anyone but Uron to read them.

"Boxes?" said Aorja in a disappointed voice. "How will boxes give me the ultimate power that you promised me?"

"The tech is located inside one of the boxes," said Uron. "Go inside and I will tell you which box it is. My memory is coming back to me, so I should be able to identify it."

"It's inside one of the boxes," Durima told Aorja. "So we'll have to go in there and find it."

Aorja groaned, but she nonetheless followed Durima into the vault, though she muttered all the while about how stupid you had to be to put ultimate power inside a box.

The vault did not seem to have been entered by anyone in millennia, from what Durima could tell. None of the boxes appeared to have been disturbed by either people or sea creatures; indeed, every box was closed shut, and a few even had locks on them, though what they were hiding, Durima didn't know. The vault was extremely narrow, which made it hard for Durima to maneuver without rubbing her wide shoulders against the shelves on either side.

Amazing how this stuff managed to survive the end of Harnum, Durima thought. *This vault must be made of stern stuff.*

"If I remember correctly, the tech should be near the back," said Uron. He looked around at the shelves with nostalgia and relief. "I am just glad that no one has gotten in here and taken anything. For a while there, I truly worried that the gods might have tried to open it and take whatever wasn't nailed down, but I see my fears and worries were groundless."

He went silent for the next few seconds before pointing and saying, "There. That box."

Durima followed his pointing finger. On one of the bottom shelves, just barely in view, was a small, square box that was unmarked. Durima probably would have missed it if Uron hadn't pointed it out to her, as it was small and almost hidden between two larger boxes.

Bending over, Durima grasped the small square box and held it close to her eyes to see it better. She saw nothing remarkable about it, except for what appeared to be a symbol of a flame scratched into its lid.

"There it is," said Uron, clapping his hands together in excitement. "I never thought I'd live to see it again, but I did. Oh joy of joy! I could sing a song happier than the Song of Krio, oh yes I could."

"What did you find?" Aorja asked, peering over Durima's shoulder. "A box?"

"The ultimate power I promised to you," said Durima as she stood up. "But I don't want to open it in here. Let's go outside and—"

She froze as the tip of Aorja's wand dug into the back of her neck. Beside her, Uron went silent, a shocked silence.

"Give me the box," said Aorja, her voice as low as an ominous song. "Or I will blow your head off and leave your body here to rot."

"Why don't we get out of the vault first?" said Durima, trying not to show any fear. "There's no telling what might happen if we open it right here in this crowded space. Better to do it in a more open area, right?"

"I don't care," said Aorja. "I have been through hell and back just because you promised me I would be strong enough to get revenge on Darek. Now give it over to me."

"I would do as she says, Durima, if I were you," said

277

Uron. "She's already proven herself to lack any sort of reason whatsoever. Do it."

Durima did not like being threatened like this, but she doubted she could fight, much less defeat, Aorja in this narrow vault. So she lifted the box over her shoulder and felt Aorja grab it from her fingers.

Then she felt the pressure of Aorja's wand lift from the back of her neck and heard the mage swimming away. Durima then turned around and swam after her, although it was no use because Aorja was already well ahead of her; in fact, she swam so fast that she was almost out of Durima's sight.

"Why did you want me to agree to her demands?" Durima asked as she swam after Aorja. "How am I going to free you now if I don't have the tech?"

"Aorja will do it for me," said Uron simply. "She will open the box and use the tech which, if I designed it correctly, should unlock the ethereal. And she won't even realize it until I'm right in front of her."

Durima would have asked how Harnumian tech was supposed to open something from Martir when she heard Aorja shout, "You!" followed by a familiar mortal voice replying, in an incredulous tone, "Aorja? What happened to your robes?"

Curious, Durima picked up speed until she exited the vault. She then saw Aorja's back floating before her not far from the vault entrance, though the traitorous mage was not alone.

Floating before Aorja were two mortals. One was a

human male, but modified, with webbed hands and feet and gills on his neck. He had a glowing whitish blue stone strapped to his chest, and his face and brown hair looked familiar to Durima, though where she had seen him before, she could not immediately recall.

At his side was an aquarian with a goldfish-like head, wearing a green-and-silver jumpsuit similar to his. Now Durima knew she had never seen this particular mortal before. She noted the stone anklet around her ankle, which was almost as black as the Void.

Uron floated up next to her, a look of pure disbelief on his face. "It can't be ... Darek Takren?"

Now Durima remembered where she had last seen that human male's face. It had been a year ago, shortly after Uron's resurrection, when he had made a deal with the Ghostly God to boost his own magical power in order to fight Uron. She had never thought she'd see him again, but here he was.

"What are *you* doing down here?" said Aorja, her voice trembling with anger. She pointed her wand at Darek and his aquarian friend. "I should kill you where you float, you bastard, for completely ruining my life!"

"I was about to ask you the same question," said Darek. "How did you even get down here? And why is Durima, of all beings, behind you? And just what the heck is that box you're clutching to your chest like it's your firstborn?"

He remembered my name, Durima thought. *Strange. We haven't even spoken in a year, and yet he knew who I was immediately. He must have good memory.*

"We're gaining ultimate power, that's what we're doing," said Aorja. "Or rather, *I* am gaining ultimate power. Power even greater than the power of Limitlessness. Power I will use to crush you like an ant."

As soon as those words left Aorja's mouth, the Superioratorium became a deep, inky, eerily familiar black. It completely drowned out Durima's vision of Aorja, Darek, and the aquarian until Aorja conjured a ball of light on the tip of her wand, which only succeeded in weakly illuminating the area around them.

"What's going on?" said Aorja. "Is this a trick of yours, Darek? It must be. You're trying to blind me so you can take me down while I can't see."

"Of course not," Darek snapped. He shivered. "Neither I nor Auratus made this darkness."

"Then who did?" Aorja demanded. "Tell me that, you stupid traitor."

I did.

Everyone in the area froze at the sound of that voice. Even Uron had gone still, as if all of his worst fears had just come true in unison.

"No," said Aorja. "It can't be."

But it is, the voice of the Void continued. **Look up and tell me what you see.**

Durima looked up, despite not wanting to, and saw nothing but the thick black darkness of the Void.

Then she made out a vaguely humanoid outline in the water and shadows above, floating there like Uron. But as her eyes adjusted to the low-light, she noticed that this figure had the head of a manta ray and wore a jumpsuit similar to the kind worn by Darek and Auratus, except it was torn and burned in several places. Not only that, but the aquarian's skin was a deep black, almost the same shade as the Void, while its eyes glowed red.

"Impossible," said Darek, his eyes locked on the figure above, fear etched in his voice. "It can't be ... Kuroshio?"

The eyes of the figure half-closed, as if it was smiling. **This vessel is no longer the aquarian you knew as Kuroshio. This is the host form I have chosen to take on in order to crush you five once and for all.**

She held up a hand, causing the darkness to part and show them the rest of the Superioratorium's interior.

The Void was not the only one here. Everywhere Durima looked, she saw more of its servants floating. Some resembled giant grasshoppers, though modified with fins to swim in the water; others were more like fish, though with missing eyes or split faces or other physical deformities. There was even some kind of mermaid-like giant with a trident, possibly a half-god, though with its missing lips and bony fingers, it could have been anything.

And what was worse was that these creatures surrounded them on every side. No matter what direction Durima looked in, she saw no way for them to escape, no gap they could take advantage of to ensure their survival. They were trapped.

Behold, said the Void, gesturing at the monsters all around them, **and tremble, because this is the last thing any of you will ever see.**

Chapter Twenty-Four

Though Darek did not know why the Void said she was going to crush 'you five' when there was clearly only four (himself, Auratus, Aorja, and Durima), he pushed that thought out of his mind for now. He needed to focus on the current situation, though that was hardly easy, as he was too distracted by the Void's chosen physical appearance to think as clearly as he normally did. She looked just like Kuroshio, except darker and with red eyes. He looked at Auratus, who seemed just as shocked by the Void's body as he was.

"How did you get Kuroshio's body?" Darek demanded, though he found it hard to keep a confident tone with so many monsters surrounding them on every side. "He blew himself up. There shouldn't be anything from his body left."

His explosion wasn't as destructive as you seem to imply, the Void said. **I took control of his body when he passed, as I knew it would come in use very soon. I wanted a physical form with which to confront you five, who have somehow managed to get this far despite everything I've thrown at you. This is the perfect body for this situation.**

Darek grit his teeth. He immediately understood her point. Of course Kuroshio's body was perfect for the Void's purposes. She had most likely been betting on Darek and Auratus being too shocked by Kuroshio's reappearance to fight back. Darek would still fight, of course, but it was an effective psychological attack nonetheless. He glanced at Auratus, who stood on the floor looking up at the Void in shock, like she had been punched out.

And do you remember that light that you followed here, Darek, Auratus? said the Void. She pointed at one of the fish, which glowed the same color as the light from before. **That was also my doing. I lured you two into here so all of my enemies would be in one place, and therefore easier to kill.**

"I don't know who Kuroshio is or why he blew himself up," said Aorja, her voice as shrill and angry as ever. "And you know what? I don't even care to know that. I am going to open this box, get ultimate power, and then destroy everyone here, including you, Void."

Without hesitation, Aorja lifted up the small stone box she held in her hands and ripped open its lid. Tossing the box itself aside, she held in her hand some kind of ancient-looking metal bracelet, which looked like no other bracelet Darek had ever seen in his life. Behind Aorja, Durima stepped back, as if she was afraid it would explode.

Holding up the bracelet before her, Aorja frowned. "What is this? Fancy jewelry? Durima, you said that this box would give me ultimate power. I don't consider jewelry, especially old crappy jewelry like this, 'ultimate power.'"

"Put it on," said Durima, though when she spoke, she sounded like two people were speaking from her mouth: One clearly her voice, the other serpentine and vaguely familiar to Darek, though he could not place it immediately. "By doing so, you will gain the ultimate power I promised you. Trust me."

Aorja continued to frown, but she shrugged and said, "All right. I'll put it on and see what happens, then. If it works like you say, I—"

Without warning, one of the Void's minions—a tiny frog-like creature—shot through the water toward Aorja. It moved too fast for Darek's eyes to follow, but he saw the results. Aorja cried out in pain, sending the bracelet flying through the water toward Darek.

The frog-like minion that had attacked Aorja's hand went for the bracelet, but Darek didn't trust the Void with whatever that bracelet was supposed to do. He tapped his magic stone and fired an ice beam at the frog-like creature, instantly encasing it in a thick block of ice that floated up.

As for the bracelet, he used his telekinesis to pull it toward him. He caught it with one hand and looked down at the bracelet a bit more closely to see if he could figure out exactly what it was.

Unfortunately, while it did indeed have writing on it, it was incomprehensible, written in some language he did not recognize and was unable to read. It felt fragile in his hands, like glass, even though it appeared to be made out of some kind of metal he did not know. It looked big enough to fit around his wrist, though he did not plan to wear it.

"Darek, you bastard!" Aorja screamed, while at the same time the Void growled, **Drop that bracelet, mortal, or I will have my minions tear you and your friends apart piece by piece.**

Darek held the bracelet close to his chest. Auratus moved closer to him, like she had finally gotten over her shock of the Void using Kuroshio's body and was ready to protect Darek from whoever might attack him. He appreciated that, as he did not trust anyone else in the building at the moment, not even Durima, despite remembering what Skimif had told him last month about Durima's help in trapping Uron in the ethereal. If she was working with Aorja, then he wasn't sure he could trust her even slightly.

"First, tell me what this is," said Darek. He addressed both the Void and Aorja as he said that, though he had a feeling that only Durima really knew what it was. "Then I'll think about giving it up."

"It's the key to ultimate power, you idiot," said Aorja. She pointed her wand at him again. "I've already said that."

No, it's not, the Void snarled. She gestured at Durima. **The katabans is trying to trick you. It is a tool that, if used, will free Uron from the ethereal, something I *know* you mortals do not want.**

Though he did not actually trust the Void, Darek nonetheless tensed when he heard her mention Uron's name. "How will it free Uron?"

"It won't," said Aorja. "The Void is just lying to make you scared of giving it to me. Don't listen to a word that bitch says."

I could say the same about *you*, mortal, the Void responded in a sharp tone. **You think you are so intelligent, but you have in fact been manipulated by Uron and the katabans this whole time. By refusing to acknowledge that fact, you are playing directly into his hands.**

"No one manipulates me," said Aorja, jerking her thumb at her chest. "Not anymore. Not after the Ghostly God and Jakuuth."

Then open your eyes and see the truth, said the Void. **But I suppose it doesn't matter. I am the one with an army here, not you. I will have my army slaughter you all like the pigs you are. Then there will be no one to stop me from spreading over Martir, just as I am destined to do.**

"Put the bracelet on, Darek!" Durima shouted. Her voice didn't sound as distorted as before; indeed, it was almost natural, save for a slight hiss. "That bracelet is the only thing that will save us from the Void! Aorja is right; it *will* grant you ultimate power, the power you need to defeat the Void and save Martir, even the power to defeat Uron."

Darek hesitated. He didn't know Durima well, but for some reason he had always thought of her as being more honest, reliable, and trustworthy than Aorja. Especially since she had been the one to trap Uron in the ethereal. He probably should have just trusted her and put on the bracelet.

Yet he found it strange how she was clearly speaking

perfect Divina. The last time he had met her, Durima had been unable to speak in anything other than the katabans language. Granted, that had been a year ago, which was plenty of time for someone to learn a new language, but she spoke it too fluently even for someone who had taken the time to learn it.

Something in this picture isn't right, Darek thought. *But what?*

If you will not listen to the truth, then suffer the fate of all who defy the Void, said the Void. She pointed at them like the commander of an army. **My army, attack!**

Despite his doubts and confusion about everything that was happening, Darek decided that he trusted Durima far more than he trusted the Void.

Thus, as the Void's army closed in on them, its members roaring and hissing and blubbering like the wild beasts they were, Darek slid the bracelet over his right wrist. As soon as he did so, the bracelet tightened around his wrist, so tight that he couldn't budge it even if he tried.

He had no idea what was supposed to happen next. He expected to feel something similar to how he had felt upon becoming a Limitless; an awakening of sorts, in which he transcended his normal limitations and reached a new level of power and awareness.

But that wasn't what he felt at all. Instead, it felt like quite the opposite. His limbs became heavy and weak, causing him to sink toward the floor of the dome building; the magic stone strapped to his chest felt too tight, like it constricted his breathing; and his skin, unless his eyes were mistaken, seemed to be graying.

He sunk down to the floor, too weak to as much as stand, while Auratus swam over him with an alarmed look on her face. The Void's army had stopped charging on them, as if they had been waiting to see what would happen to Darek before slaughtering him and the others. The Void's red eyes widened with horror, while Aorja just looked at Darek with pure and utter rage at what he had done.

The only one who seemed even slightly happy about this was Durima. A small smile crossed her lips, a smile Darek didn't understand, as he did not see what there was to be happy about.

No! the Void cried out. She punched the water. **You fool! You ignorant, idiotic fool. Do you know what you've done? Can you even comprehend the sheer stupidity of what you just did?**

Darek did not respond. He was weaker than he had ever felt in his life; indeed, he didn't even feel his magical energy anymore. A quick glance at his chest showed that his magic stone no longer glowed. It was just an ordinary rock now, uselessly strapped to his chest.

"You took my power," said Aorja, her voice shaking with anger. "I should have expected as much from you, Darek Takren. You've messed up my life a dozen times already; of course you would ruin it one last time, taking away my last chance at getting the revenge I deserve."

He took away nothing from you, stupid mortal, the Void snapped. **He is the one who suffers. He has completely lost his ability to use magic. In**

exchange, the lock Skimif put on the ethereal has been broken and Uron is free once again.

Uron? Free again? That made no sense to Darek. He tried to stand up and tell her that she was wrong, but he was still too weak to do even that much. He could only look at the disbelieving expressions on the faces of Auratus and Aorja as they listened to the Void's words.

"How do you know that?" said Aorja. "You're lying. I know you are. Uron has nothing to do with any of this. He's not even relevant to this discussion."

Ask the katabans, the Void said, pointing an accusing finger at Durima. ***She* knows. Uron has been using her this entire time just to get that bracelet in order to get his freedom. And his plan worked because you mortals are fools who refuse to listen to your superiors.**

"She can't be telling the truth," said Aorja, turning around in the water to face Durima. "Right, Durima? Uron's not using or manipulating you. You've barely even mentioned him to me."

To Darek's horror, Durima did not answer right away. She looked like she was thinking about how she could get out of here alive. Then she shook her head.

"I'm sorry, Aorja, but the Void is correct," said Durima. She nodded at Darek. "Thanks to Darek's naivety, Uron is free once more. He's not down here with us—the ethereal doesn't extend below ground—but he is now in Martir itself, probably laughing at you mortals for being dumb enough to fall for his plan."

"But ..." Aorja sounded lost. "How—"

"He guided me the entire time, despite being inside the Void," said Durima. "He told me exactly what to do, how to act, and where to go. I didn't always listen to or agree with him, but most of the time, I did, which is how we made it as far as we did."

"So there was never really any ultimate power at all?" said Aorja. "Not even just a little?"

"Yes," said Durima. "I duped you the whole time. Uron knew how much you hated Darek and so he taught me how to use that hatred of him to our advantage. Don't worry, though; when Uron destroys Martir, he will probably spare you, as he liked you a lot."

Darek noticed how Durima said '*when* Uron destroys Martir,' not *if.* It was a subtle distinction, perhaps, but it seemed like an important distinction as well.

"I don't care if Uron *likes* me," said Aorja. She raised her wand and pointed it at Durima. "What I *do* care about is that you tricked me, you liar. Just when I thought you and I might have some sort of connection, it turned out that you were just playing me the whole time, like every other person in my whole life!"

"It's not my fault you're a bad judge of character, Aorja," said Durima, not flinching in the slightest at Aorja's raised wand. "If you don't want to be duped and manipulated by people who are smarter than you, then you should probably start using that mortal brain of yours to actually think about the possible motives of other people who claim to be your friend. Though I will grant you that you mortals tend to be even dumber than the gods, so maybe I'm asking too much of you."

"But why would you do it?" said Aorja. "Why would you work for Uron? He's going to destroy Martir, isn't he? He'll kill the gods, which even I know is a bad thing."

Much to Darek's horror, Durima simply shrugged. "What do I care? The gods have more or less treated us katabans as disposable tools, to be discarded at will. Even Skimif hasn't done much to improve the lives of us katabans. Siding with Uron will give us katabans a world where the gods do not exist and so therefore cannot treat us like broken tools when we are no longer useful to them."

"Traitor," Aorja spat, like the word was poison in her mouth. "Traitor!"

"That may be so, but so what?" said Durima. "Are you going to try to kill me? It won't do you any good. Aside from the fact that Uron is now free to do what he likes, the Void is still here, if you hadn't noticed, and she is probably going to kill you as soon as you are done with me."

Aorja involuntarily looked up at the Void for only the briefest moment, but it was enough time for Durima. She shot through the water like a bullet and punched Aorja in the face. The blow sent Aorja flying through the water uncontrollably. She crashed at Darek and Auratus's feet and did not rise again.

Shaking her fist, Durima said, "I've wanted to do that ever since I first met her. Feels good."

Darek looked down at the unconscious Aorja lying before them. The outline of Durima's fist was obvious in

Aorja's cheek and she was so still that if her chest had not been rising and falling, he would have thought she was dead.

"Aorja ..." he said, reaching for her, though she lay just outside of his reach.

Enough, said the Void above, her voice as cold and harsh as the darkness around them. **I have seen enough. While I have no love for the gods or Martir myself, I know that Uron is as much a threat to me as he is to them. I cannot kill Uron right now, so instead, I will kill the katabans who freed him, as well as you foolish mortals. Then I will go and find Uron and finish him off, just as I should have done a long time ago.**

Durima simply smiled. "You sound a lot braver than you did before, when Uron and I scared you off. Is it because Uron is no longer here? I always find it a lot easier to be brave when the thing I am most afraid of isn't anywhere near me, too."

Shut up! the Void snapped, though Darek caught a hint of fear in her voice. **I am the Void. I fear *nothing*, for I am *nothing*.**

"Keep saying nonsense like that," said Durima. "I got over my fear of the dark years ago, when I was young."

The Void roared in anger. As she did so, her army resumed their charge on Darek and the others. Auratus crouched low near Darek, looking ready to fight the army to the death. Darek appreciated the gesture, but he didn't see how Auratus could defeat this army on her own. He was too weak to fight, Aorja was out cold, and Durima seemed unlikely to help. Once the army reached them, Darek had no doubt in his mind that they would die quickly, even if he and Auratus fought as best as they could.

And we will die as failures, Darek thought. *Because I was dumb enough to listen to Durima and put on that stupid bracelet.*

All of a sudden, another roar pierced the waters, a roar so loud that it actually caused the Void's army to halt their attack once again. Even the Void looked around in astonishment and confusion, like she had no idea what was going on.

The roar sounded metallic and unnatural to Darek, almost unfinished. Yet despite that, he could tell one obvious thing about this roar: It was very, very angry.

At that moment, two beings shot through the hole in the domed ceiling above. Darek looked up to try to get a good look at them. To his relief, one of them appeared to be Ranama, who now carried what appeared to be a spear shaped like a giant pen, of all things; the other, some strange half-ogre, half-automaton monstrosity that was the source of the roar.

As he watched, the two beings tore through the part of the Void's army nearest them. Ranama slashed and stabbed with his spear, each blow taking out at least a dozen of the Void's minions while sending the survivors scattering in fear. The strange monstrosity at his side was even more ferocious; it grabbed an eel-like creature and ate it whole, like a pasta noodle, and then crushed an angler-like fish into paste between its fists.

The attention of the rest of the Void's army had turned to Ranama and his strange ally now. The Void herself was also looking at them, her fists shaking with anger and even fear at their sight.

No! the Void shrieked. **How dare you two intervene this way! By fighting against me, you are messing with a force of nature even greater than the gods.**

"Force of nature, eh?" said Ranama as he kicked away a serpentine/aquiline monstrosity that had been biting at him. "That's funny, because we gods control forces of nature. Try another threat."

His ally just roared again, but this time, Darek thought he caught one recognizable word in the ally's roar: "Aorja!"

Why is that thing shouting Aorja's name? Darek thought, looking at Aorja in bewilderment. *For that matter, just what* is *that thing, anyway?*

Then Darek heard movement in the water and he looked up to see Durima swimming away as fast as she could. She seemed to be trying to escape. He tried to stand up to go after her, but the bracelet had sapped him of more than just his magical strength. Additionally, the burn spot on his face flared up, forcing him to rub his face as Durima swam away.

"Auratus," said Darek, his voice so weak he was sure he was dying. "Durima is escaping. Stop her."

To his surprise, Auratus shook her head. She put a hand on Darek's shoulder and said, *No. Stay with you. Keep you safe until Void gone and Kuroshio memory honored.*

Her loyalty touched him, even though rationally he knew

it would have been better for her to go after Durima. Still, he didn't have the strength to argue the point, so he just nodded as Durima swam out of his view.

His attention then was taken up by Ranama and his monstrous ally above, who by now had taken out almost a quarter of the Void's army. They didn't even need to destroy all of it; the monstrous soldiers were now fleeing, some into the various exits on the perimeter of the building, others through the hole in the ceiling, and a few into the darkness, vanishing like ghosts in the mist.

The Void, however, did not look like she was going anywhere. She swam to attack Ranama and his ally, and considering how angry she looked, Darek found himself fearing for Ranama's life.

But even as she moved to attack them, Ranama and his ally met her halfway without fear. Thick shadowy tendrils shot out of her body at them, but Ranama smacked them out of the way with his spear, leaving an opening for his ally, who charged at the Void and body-slammed her.

The blow sent the Void sprawling through the water uncontrollably. She crashed into a pod of stone desks on the other side of the building, sending dust and debris up into the water. But then she recovered quickly and swam back toward them with more tendrils growing from her body, making her look like a grotesque spider.

Darek wished he could help, but all he could do was watch as Ranama and his ally separated as if it was all part of a plan they had already discussed between themselves. The Void halted in the water, looking in both directions, either trying to figure out who to attack or what they were up to.

"Now, Zeeree!" Ranama shouted. "For Martir and Aorja!"

His ally—whose name must have been Zeeree—swam toward the Void faster than a being of his size should have been able to in the water. She whirled to face him, but then he banked to the left at the very last moment, just as the Void's tendrils shot toward him like the heads of a trinity cobra.

As soon as she was distracted, Ranama teleported and reappeared behind her. He shoved his spear directly into her back, the tip piercing through her chest, as he yelled incomprehensibly in the water.

The Void actually screamed in pain. That seemed to have been enough to completely crush the morale of her remaining minions, because they immediately fled without so much as looking at Darek, Auratus, or Aorja.

Then Ranama pulled his spear out of the Void's back and kicked her. She went tumbling through the water again, an inky black liquid pouring out of the hole of her chest, directly into Zeeree's arms.

He didn't even pretend to be merciful. Zeeree ripped her arms off, which dissolved into darkness, and tore off the top of her head with his front teeth like some kind of vicious wolf. The Void kept screaming, though she was cut off when he actually tore her head off completely and swallowed it.

While Darek liked seeing the Void getting her comeuppance, he also found it disturbing, as the Void still looked like Kuroshio. A glance at Auratus, who had covered her eyes, told him that she found it even harder to look at; no mystery there, seeing as she had known Kuroshio better than he had.

In less than ten seconds, the Void's body was completely torn apart. Zeeree actually stuffed the last of it into his mouth, chewed on it like it was candy, and swallowed. The finishing touch: A loud belch that made Darek cringe.

As soon as Zeeree belched, the darkness of the Void retreated, like sludge running down into a hole; indeed, the Void's darkness retreated through the hole in the ceiling. The building, however, was still dark, though it was thankfully normal Martirian darkness, the good kind of darkness or at least the natural kind, anyway.

Darek did not know where the Void had vanished to, but he hoped it had gone back to where it belonged: Beyond the edge of Martir, where it could harm no one, though he figured that that was about as likely as Uron deciding not to destroy Martir.

A moment later, Ranama was at his side, bending down over Darek. His glasses were still cracked; Darek could see the empty eye sockets through the cracks, as well as the blue eyes in the lenses themselves.

"Lord Ranama," said Darek. "Uron is—"

"I know," Ranama cut him off. "I felt the ethereal open again. That means that Uron is on World's End, where he will kill my brothers and sisters, or try to, anyway."

Zeeree landed nearby, but he seemed oblivious to Darek and Auratus. He walked over to Aorja and scooped her up in his arms, cradling her like a baby. He made a bunch of strange, concerned whining noises, which would have been almost touching if he hadn't smelled like death.

"His name is Zeeree," said Ranama, in response to Darek and Auratus's questioning looks. "A derivative of the Itrijan slang *zeere*, which means 'baby' or 'cute pet,' depending on if the speaker is a mother or pet owner of the *zeere* in question."

"What ... is he?" said Darek, still staring at Zeeree. "And why is he cradling Aorja?"

"He's a half-god," said Ranama. "And he is that young mortal woman's pet."

Darek looked at Ranama in astonishment. "How did Aorja tame a half-god?"

"I have no idea," said Ranama, shaking his head. "When I first saw him, I thought he might be working for Uron, since he's a half-god and all, but then I heard him saying Aorja's name. So I offered to help him find Aorja and he accepted, probably because he's too stupid to realize what I am. You know the rest."

Not a threat? Auratus's voice said in Darek's head, though Ranama must have heard it as well because he said, "As far as I can tell, yes. Well, obviously, he was a threat to the Void, but I don't think he will kill us, not unless Aorja tells him to, anyway."

It was still odd to see Zeeree holding Aorja like that, but Darek decided to forget about it for now, because they had more urgent things to discuss.

"We need to go after Durima," said Darek. He said her

298

name with as much hate as he could. "As a traitor, she deserves nothing less than the harshest punishment we can inflict on her."

"I understand your anger, Darek, but she is a single letter in comparison to the book that is Uron," said Ranama. "After we deal with Uron and the Void, then we will go after her."

"Speaking of the Void, is she gone?" Darek asked. "For good?"

"She has retreated," said Ranama. "For now. I think she is unused to fighting physically like that and wants to take some time to regroup. She will probably return—it's in her nature to devour everything—but not right away. I imagine she'll fight against us and Uron, considering how much she hates him."

Darek groaned. "So we have to fight the Void *and* Uron. Great."

"It is a grim turn of events, I agree," said Ranama. "That is why we need to leave the Old Ruins right away. Lord Skimif must be informed of—"

Ranama stopped abruptly. Darek didn't understand why at first, nor did he understand the look of sheer, utter terror crossing Ranama's aquarian features.

Then he felt it. A dark, growing despair—deeper and more real than anything Darek had ever felt in his whole life, even deeper than the despair he had felt at the Magical Superior's passing—permeated his every being. The water in the Old Ruins tasted as bitter as poison; the rock floor beneath seemed to become mud under his hands and knees.

Next to him, Auratus fell to her hands and knees. Her wide eyes, wide with terror, told him all he needed to know about how she felt. For once, he had no trouble reading the facial expression on her features.

Even Zeeree shifted uncomfortably where he stood, while Aorja stirred but did not awake. She clutched Zeeree's arms, as if she was having a terrible nightmare, but this feeling was no nightmare. It was real.

There was no need for anyone to say anything. Even without using telepathy, Darek knew that every person in this room—no, every person in the world, whether human, aquarian, katabans, god, or half-god—knew just what this immense, unrelenting, undeniable sense of despair meant.

Nonetheless, Ranama, who was clutching his chest, said it aloud, maybe out of the mistaken belief that doing so would make it easier to take:

"Uron killed Skimif."

Concluded in:

The Mages of Martir, Book #4:

The Mage's Ghost

With the gods scattered and afraid and Uron now closer than ever to fulfilling his sinister plans, Darek Takren and his ragtag band of allies are now the only obstacle standing between Uron and the complete destruction of their world.

Yet defeating Uron appears utterly impossible until one of Darek's allies suggests a plan so dangerous, so deadly, that no sane human would even dream of trying it: Travel to the afterlife and convince the gatekeeper of the afterlife to summon Uron's soul back to where it belongs.

With no choice but to go with this plan, Darek races to the afterlife to defeat Uron once and for all, although he may not be ready for what he discovers beyond the grave.

The Mage's Ghost is now available in ebook and trade paperback wherever books are sold!

About the Author

Timothy L. Cerepaka writes fantasy and science-fiction stories as an indie author. He is the author of the Prince Malock World fantasy novels, the Mages of Martir fantasy novels, and the science-fantasy standalone novel *The Last Legend: Glitch Apocalypse*. He lives in Texas.

Visit his website at www.timothylcerepaka.com to find out more and to read about his other books.

Other books in the Mages of Martir series

Mages of Martir Book #1: *The Mage's Grave*

Thirty-five-year-old Darek Takren always did his best to keep up with the demands of the prestigious North Academy, a magical school where only those with the drive to succeed are allowed to learn. Having lived in the school for his whole life, Darek Takren sees North Academy as his home, a sanctuary safe from the troubles that plague the outside world.

But when his best friend is injured in an unexpected attack on the school, Darek Takren struggle to uncover the attacker's identity leads him into a much deeper scheme that, if successful, will spell the end not only for the school, but for the whole world and the gods themselves.

And he may not have what it takes to stop it.

Buy *The Mage's Grave* in ebook and trade paperback wherever books are sold!

Mages of Martir Book #2: *The Mage's Limits*

A year after the disappearance of the dangerous god-killer called Uron, Darek Takren is torn between his desire to follow the teachings of his headmaster and his desire to achieve the limitless yet forbidden power he needs to help the gods protect the world.

To make matters worse, a powerful and charismatic mage claiming to be the son of a god has escaped from prison, seeking revenge for wrongs committed against him long ago. His targets: North Academy, the school that Darek calls home, and World's End, the island of the gods.

To save his home and his friends, Darek must infiltrate the deranged demigod's army of former criminals and kill him before it is too late. Yet when this mage offers Darek the unlimited power he desires, killing the mage no longer seems quite as simple the task as it once appeared.

Buy *The Mage's Limits* in ebook and trade paperback wherever books are sold!